They Called Me Margaret

Florence Osmund

Acknowledgments

I continue to rely on others to assist me in the process of writing books—*They Called Me Margaret* is no exception.

The cover design for this book is the creative genius of Deborah Bradseth of Tugboat Design. For all those people who turn the book over to read the back cover because they were intrigued by what they saw on the front, I have Deborah to thank. I also thank Deborah for her meticulous formatting skills for both the paperback and e-book versions of this book.

I thank my editor Carrie Cantor who once again helped me keep the narrative clean, succinct, and flowing. I greatly appreciate her continuing to challenge me to be a better writer.

A big thank you goes to Marge Bousson for Beta reading this book, providing valuable feedback, and finding flaws in the manuscript that I had overlooked even after having read it a million times.

Chapter 1

I didn't take it seriously that Carl threatened to leave me—he was feeling neglected and just trying to get my attention. For several months, I'd been spending my days planning the opening of my bookstore—The Indie Book Nook—and evenings working on my latest novel, leaving little time for him. It wasn't the first time he'd done that—telling me he thought I loved books more than him. I brushed him off, like I'd done before, reminding him of the days when he worked as many hours bucking for his CFO position at The Garfield Group. I worked out of our home, as did he, and back then I would periodically drop in on him in the middle of the day to let him know in person that I still cared—more reassurance than I currently got from him.

I poured myself a glass of wine, retreated to the spare bedroom that I had claimed as my writing sanctuary, and stretched out on my favorite chair, a green and gray paisley chaise lounge I had picked up at an estate sale. It was May, the week before Memorial Day, the same week we always drove up for the summer from our primary home in Chicago. We had purchased the Lake Beulah house six years earlier—in 2009 when foreclosures were at an all-time high—for half of its value in today's market. At the time, I was against it but had let Carl talk me into it, like I had with most things in our marriage. Now, I rather enjoyed having the second home.

Earlier in the day, I had nearly lost it when I couldn't find the pocket watch—one of the few things I'd had of my mother's—engraved with the words TIME IS A GIFT. It appeared to be old, like maybe it had belonged to someone else before my mother.

The previous summer, when my silver bracelet went missing, I thought I must have been careless with it. And then when I couldn't find the Eiffel Tower Limoges box containing one pearl earring, I figured my memory wasn't what it used to be. But the third missing item—the pocket watch—caused me to think differently, that either I was losing my mind, or someone wanted me to think I was.

After careful reflection, I refused to believe there was any possibility that I was going insane. My father's aunt Rosie had been insane. Verifiably insane, from what I'd been told. I wasn't like Aunt Rosie. Nowhere near. But when I failed to locate the pocket watch, my doubts heightened.

The peculiar thing was that something similar had happened to the main character in my debut novel *Break-In at Buttons and Bows,* a book I had written nine years earlier. I was a writer of cozy mysteries and had nine books published. In *Break-In,* my fictional husband brainwashed the wife into thinking she was losing her mind, so he would have just cause to leave her. I started to wonder if Carl was doing the same. Having once been abandoned, I dreaded the thought of going through that again, yet I couldn't ignore the possibility.

When I first confronted Carl, we were relaxing at home, listening to music.

"I hope you don't take this the wrong way, Mags, but I never even read that book," he admitted.

My name is Margaret, but most people have called me everything but Margaret my whole life—Mags, Maggie, Marge, Madge, Margie. Margaret has more nicknames that any other name I know, and I don't much like any of them. The only person I can remember calling me Margaret was my father—the parent who didn't desert me. Carl knew I didn't like any of the nicknames.

"What are you talking about? You said you'd read *all* my books."

"Sorry. They're just not my thing."

"Not your thing?"

"Not my kind of read."

"So, you haven't read *any* of them?"

"I tried. I really did, hon. I think I got the farthest in the one about the music teacher."

"You didn't finish it?"

"Sorry."

"So, you've lied to me all this time?"

"I didn't want to hurt your feelings."

Feeling stung, I left the room. He couldn't have shown his support by forcing himself to read my books even if they "weren't his thing"? Going out on our neighbor's boat every weekend of the summer wasn't exactly my thing either, but I did it.

I couldn't get over it—Carl hadn't read even one of my books all the way through. I wanted him—the most important person in my life—more than anyone else to like my books. I wanted him to be proud of me.

I continued sipping my wine, stewing over his hurtful admission, when Carl entered the room.

"I see you've started happy hour without me," he said.

"It's five o'clock somewhere," I said dryly.

"May I join you, or is this a private party?" he asked.

"Sure. I just felt like stretching out on this chair for a while."

He left and returned with a beer.

I watched him get comfortable in the chair across from me. Without even one wrinkle or gray hair, he appeared younger than his fifty-six years, which I found rather annoying since at forty-eight I had plenty of both.

"You're mad at me, aren't you?" he asked.

"For what?"

"For not reading your books."

I didn't want to have this discussion right then. I wasn't prepared for it. Plus, I had a headache. "Kind of," I said.

"Tell me about the missing butterfly pin."

"What?"

"Your first book. It had to do with things stolen from a jewelry store. That's why you accused me of doing something with your bracelet."

"It was a boutique, not a jewelry store, and how did you know about the butterfly pin if you never read the book?"

"You probably told me. I don't know."

"I wrote that book nine years ago." *I* didn't even remember one of the stolen pieces was a butterfly pin until he'd just mentioned it.

"Maybe it says that on the back cover." He paused. "Look, let's not ruin this day with a petty argument." He laughed and smiled that you-can't-possibly-stay-mad-at-me smile he did so well. "If we're going to argue, let's make it about something worthwhile."

We didn't share the same sense of humor. I ignored him.

He stood up. "Like what time we're going to eat dinner so we can make it to the Richardsons' dock by seven-thirty."

We had met Darlene and Lance Richardson on the very day we'd moved into our lake home—not surprising given Darlene's propensity for making everyone else's business her own. If it weren't for Carl, I probably wouldn't have become such close friends with them. I was more of an over-the-fence "Hi, how are you?" type of neighbor.

"Jesus, Carl, we just got here."

"Look, if you have a problem with—"

"No problem." I got up from the chaise lounge and headed toward the bathroom. "I just need to start taking my Dramamine then."

"Will you tell me about the book when you come back?"

"It's on the bookshelf. Just read the back cover."

After I said it, I wished I hadn't, at least not in that tone. Still, I remained bothered by the missing items, his lack of interest in my work, and the fact that I had to spend the first evening of the summer on the Richardsons' stupid boat.

The sound of the car engine and garage door closing told me he was probably headed to the liquor store, so we wouldn't arrive empty-handed.

When we arrived at the Richardsons' dock, Lance and Darlene were nowhere to be seen, so we boarded their forty-foot cabin cruiser, *Little Thaisa* (named after a Shakespearean character that Lance liked) and sat on the deck to wait. Lance and Carl shared an affinity for Shakespeare—one of many things they shared that meant nada to me.

Within five minutes, Darlene came bouncing down the steps that led away from their house. She wore an animal-print jacket, black tights, ballet slippers, and dangly earrings—a typical outfit for her—and carried a shopping bag holding what I suspected held twice as much food as the four of us would eat during the evening cruise. Waffles, their three-year-old schnoodle, followed close behind her. Why we always ate dinner before going out on their boat, I didn't know.

Darlene—upbeat and always perky, with graceful eyes and a full mouth—rarely wore makeup or did anything special with her hair. I had spent an hour getting myself ready, and even though I was taller, slimmer, and five years younger, I didn't look half as good as she did. Playful, and sometimes overly affectionate, Darlene had spunk—one of those carefree types who was willing to bend the rules if it meant having a good time.

She greeted Carl with a hug. "Jeez, I missed you, handsome! When are you guys going to move up here permanently?" She kissed him on the cheek, clasped her arm around his, and led him to one of the bench seats. "C'mon, Mags. Let's get this party rollin'," she called out to me.

"Where's Lance?" I asked.

"He's not here?" she said.

Carl got up to check the cabin.

"He's not in there," he said when he returned.

"He left the house at least fifteen minutes before me," Darlene told us. "I was packing up the food and stuff." She pulled her cell phone out of her pocket to call him. "That's odd. It went to voice mail."

"Maybe he went on an errand or something or is talking to another neighbor," I told her. Seeing the worried look on her face, I turned to Carl. "Maybe you could take a walk down a few houses…see if you can find him."

Darlene fished a set of keys from her pocket and handed them to Carl. "Sweetheart, be a love and check the garage to see if both cars are in there."

If any other female non-relative had used such terms of endearment with my husband, I might have gotten upset. But not Darlene. She rarely called men by their first names. It was always love, dear, honey, handsome. I didn't take her flirtations seriously—they were just part of her nature. She did it in front of Lance and me all the time.

"When is that man going to loosen up and wear something more casual?" Darlene asked me after Carl had left.

"What's wrong with what he's wearing?" Carl's weekend outfits didn't vary much—sharply creased cotton slacks and a dress shirt with the sleeves rolled up.

"He's so buttoned-up. Does he even own a pair of sweats or a t-shirt?"

"I don't think so. Gee, I hope Lance is okay."

Her face scrunched up before the tears came. I guided her to the seat in the aft of the boat and put my arm around her. Waffles jumped up on her lap as if to comfort her as well.

"Don't think the worst. I'm sure he's fine."

"It's not that," she blubbered.

"What is it?"

Not lacking when it came to theatrics, Darlene threw her arms up in the air and wailed, "I'm going to be a grandma."

"So, these are happy tears?"

"Well, yes and no. I'm not old enough to be a grandmother."

After ten minutes of listening to Darlene talk about her impending grandmotherhood, one would have thought her daughter-in-law was destined to spew royalty from her loins. I cut her some slack since it would be her first, and to keep her mind off her missing husband, I let her drone on about the baby.

"Can I get you something to drink?" I asked her.

"Would you? A glass of my Jewish champagne would be lovely. There's some in the fridge."

Darlene drank Dr. Brown's Cel-Ray soda. Only one store in the area carried it, a Jewish delicatessen in the next town, and even then, Darlene had to call beforehand to make sure they had it in stock before she made the trip. Concocted from celery seeds and I don't know what else, she claimed it calmed her stomach. Its manufacturers were calling it a "healing tonic" until the FDA told them they couldn't call it a tonic anymore. I'd tried it once—a bilious drink that tasted like cod liver oil, only peppery. One sip had been enough for me.

Half an hour passed before Carl returned. "Did he show up?" he asked. We both shook our heads.

"Well, I walked to several houses in each direction and didn't find him."

"What about his car?" Darlene asked.

"Both your cars are in the garage." He handed the keys back to her. "I'm going to grab a beer."

"Bring Mags a glass of wine while you're at it, hon."

"I'm sure he's okay," I said to Darlene.

"Of course he is."

"There will be a very simple explanation for his absence, you'll see."

"We'll probably all laugh at this later," she said when Carl returned with the drinks. But judging by the looks on their faces, I sensed they didn't believe that any more than I did.

We sat staring at one another for an unbearable length of time until Darlene got up and headed toward the stairs that led down to the cabin.

"Where are you going?" I asked her.

"To find something to write on, things I want to tell the police."

Carl and I looked at each other and shrugged. Had it gotten to the point of calling the police? Even Waffles looked surprised—his eyes open wide and ears pointed straight up.

When Darlene returned, she had a pen and notepad in hand along with another bottle of Dr. Brown's. She fixed her eyes on the blank page.

"When was the last time you saw him?" I asked.

"That's a good place to start," she responded. "I saw him leave the house at about seven-fifteen."

"Look, while you guys put together your list, I'm going to go door-to-door and ask if anyone has seen him. Sound like a plan?" Carl asked.

We nodded and continued with the list.

"What was he wearing?" I asked.

"Navy blue Dockers, dark slip-on deck shoes, no socks. I don't remember what shirt he had on, but he was wearing his blue and white windbreaker. Prada Milano. I bought it for him when we were in Italy last year." She appeared confused.

"What's wrong?"

"You know what they're going to ask me."

"What?"

"If we had an argument beforehand, or if there was any trouble in our marriage, or if I—"

"You've been watching way too many *CSI* shows, Darlene. They're not going to ask you that." But after I said it, I thought she was probably right. They always looked at the missing person's closest relationships first. "So, did you?"

"Did I what?"

"Did you two have an argument?"

She didn't respond.

"Sorry…none of my business."

"This isn't much of a list," she said. "I don't know whether to call or not."

"Why don't we wait until Carl gets back. Maybe he's found out something."

"Good idea. C'mon downstairs. I'll fix us something to eat."

I followed her to the cabin. "Don't fix anything for me. I'm not at all hungry."

"You won't eat with me?" she asked, a woeful expression on her face.

"Well, maybe I could eat a little something."

We settled into the buttery leather reclining chairs that surrounded the large TV screen hanging on the wall. Despite my objection, Darlene filled my glass with more wine and then grabbed her half-empty bottle of celery seed juice for herself.

"Have you heard anything more from Portia?" she asked.

Portia, our twenty-year-old daughter, had dropped out of Ohio State seven months prior in her junior year, without our knowledge until we received a letter from her saying that she'd been living with her boyfriend on a spiritual commune in Costa Rica—a place to rejuvenate their bodies, connect with nature, and find a higher part of themselves.

"Not since she called me on my birthday in March."

"So, no word in over two months? Do you think she's—"

Carl scurried down the steps into the cabin before Darlene could finish the sentence.

"Nothing," he said. "I knocked on everyone's door all the way down to Shaw's to the north and as far as the woods in the other direction. No one has seen him."

Darlene picked up her cell phone and dialed 9-1-1.

Chapter 2

"Do you want us to stay with you for a while longer?" I asked Darlene. "Like the police said, he'll probably show up and explain where he's been, and—"

"No. You guys go home…but not without taking some of this food." Darlene darted around the galley scooping up various foodstuffs into plastic containers. "There, now you'll at least have something for lunch tomorrow."

Carl wrapped his arm around her shoulder. "You sure you'll be okay?"

"I'll be fine. I'm going to lock up the boat and…hey, wait a minute. Was the cabin door unlocked when you guys got here?"

"Yeah. I walked right in," Carl said.

"Hmm. So that means he came here first, then disappeared. I don't know what that means, but I'm going to tell the police that. I'll call you if I hear anything."

"Day or night," Carl told her. "Call us as soon as you hear from him."

"I will, doll."

* * *

As soon as we got home, Carl poured himself a Scotch and buried his face in his laptop, so I retreated to my office to catch up on e-mails. Not unusual to get a couple hundred a day. The bookstore start-up involved a myriad of vendors and service providers who all communicated via e-mail and text messages. Add to that three private Facebook groups and countless online discussion groups comprised of authors who supported each other by helping promote each other's books, and the e-mails could pile up. In addition, I was a mentor to three budding authors, and we used e-mail as our means of communication. I made a mental note to withdraw from some of the author groups.

While I responded to the most important ones—those related to the bookstore—I contemplated how concerned we should be about Lance's disappearance. The police didn't appear very worried at all. Was she overreacting? Were the police underreacting?

Darlene's reaction to my question as to whether they'd had an argument beforehand got me to thinking about my own marriage. Carl and I had been married for twenty-one years. When I met him, I had a lucrative career as the director of clinical compliance for a drug company his employer owned. We met at a business function and married a year later.

Eighteen months prior to meeting Carl, I had lost the first love of my life, Wayne Tauber, to a fatal car accident. We had been together for two years, and I was devastated by the loss. I probably hadn't waited long enough to completely grieve. But then maybe no amount of time would have been enough. I had truly loved that man.

There were times I questioned Carl's reason for wanting to marry me. I wondered whether he was more interested in me the person or me as the incumbent in the director position in the drug company. On more than one occasion, he'd introduced me to someone he knew through business by my title, not mentioning that I was his wife. I went along with it, didn't question it, just like I had gone along with everything else in life—something I'd learned to do quite well since early childhood. Once you have a certain feeling about yourself, it becomes increasingly difficult to change it.

I finished with what I was doing and joined Carl in the sunroom. The builder of this house had done it right—anywhere you sat in the room offered a clear view of the lake and the expansive dense foliage on the far shore. Two giant willow trees flanked each side of our lot, beautifully framing the view.

The room faced west. In the evening, the sun's fiery glow—first reflecting on the water and then slowly disappearing behind the trees—had a way of forcing you to forget about everything else and enjoy the show. I didn't understand why we had to go on all the sunset cruises with the Richardsons—we had a full view of the display from the comfort of our own home—and furthermore, I preferred to spend evenings alone with Carl. The Richardsons were okay…in small doses. Lance, a highly-successful retail real estate developer, was all business all the time—when he wasn't talking real estate, he was thinking about it. Darlene had a lot of free time on her hands and was consumed with local gossip.

"Done with whatever it was you were doing?" I asked him.

He offered a curt nod.

"So, what do you think?"

"About what?"

About anything—just talk to me! Sometimes he reminded me so much of my father—physically in the same room but mindfully not there. Unpredictable and hard to read at times too. Just like dear old Dad.

"About Lance."

"I don't know what to think."

"I feel bad leaving Darlene alone. What she must be going through."

"She'll be okay."

"Do you think those two were having problems?"

"Who knows," he said without looking at me.

"She was worried that the police might ask her if they had an argument before he disappeared."

"All couples have arguments," he said with a brittle smile.

"Of course. But there are arguments, and then there are arguments."

"And then there's what's said and what's not said."

"What does that mean?" I asked.

"Just what it means. What's *not* said can be just as hurtful as what *is* said."

"Are we still talking about the Richardsons?"

* * *

I awoke the next day with a headache, perhaps the result of too much wine the night before. Carl was not in bed, apparently having already started his day.

I lay there awhile thinking about a myriad of things—what I still had to attend to regarding the bookstore, my conversation with Carl the night before, our daughter, and Lance. How dare Carl make me think he'd read all my books all these years! I tried to recall some of the exact words he'd used in the past after he'd said he'd finished one. I distinctly remembered him saying he didn't care for the ending of *Almost Murder*. It left him feeling a little flat. Had he read only the last page?

After leaving the warmth of our bed, I popped an aspirin, got dressed, and found Carl in the kitchen drinking coffee while gazing out the massive glass sliding doors to the patio—an inscrutable expression on his otherwise handsome face. His laptop lay open in front of him—I suspected he had been absorbed in *Forbes* or *FEI Daily* or some other exciting read.

"You look lost in thought," I told him as I put a cup of water in the microwave for tea.

"Three guesses."

"Lance?"

"Him too."

"Portia then?"

He nodded.

When we first learned of Portia's departure, Carl had been vocal about ways she could have accomplished the same things at home—whatever it was that she had supposedly gone searching for in Costa Rica. He blamed her boyfriend for her being there and said if he were to ever get his hands on him, he'd make sure he understood how he felt.

"If it weren't for Dipshit, she'd be here with us right now," he said.

Dipshit—his name for Portia's boyfriend—was the only name we had for him.

"You don't know that for sure. It could have been all her idea."

He shot me a skeptical look. "Does that sound like something she'd do on her own?"

"No, but—"

"Exactly. Maybe he'll fall off a cliff."

"That's a terrible thing to say, Carl. You don't even know him."

"I know enough."

Carl's plan for Portia was to graduate from college and enter law school. For the longest time, I considered it wrong for him to have that plan for her. Before she was even born, he chose the name Portia based on a female character in one of Shakespeare's plays who disguised herself as a male lawyer named Balthazar. I thanked God he didn't suggest naming her Balthazar. My plan, on the other hand, had been for her to do whatever she chose to do, as long as she was happy doing it. Unfortunately, I had won.

"Are you thinking you want to do more about finding her and bringing her back home?" I asked him.

"No. What's the use? She's of age…like we discussed."

Less than a week after we'd received her initial letter, before we'd had time to get our heads around what she had done, she called to let us know she was well and happy. We kept asking her for an address and phone number where she could be reached, and when she wouldn't give us the information, we booked a flight to Costa Rica to try to find her. Carl and I spent ten days traveling between San Jose, Liberia, and Limón, showing her photograph to everyone we saw—but to no avail. Mountains, rainforests, and hundreds of spaghetti-like rivers comprised ninety percent of the small country—a little smaller than West Virginia—making our navigation of the terrain difficult.

"I miss her," I said.

"I know. So do I."

"Maybe she'll call you on *your* birthday."

"If she does, I'm not sure what I'm going to say to her."

"You'll find the right words when the time comes."

"So, Lance and Dar are going to be grandparents, I hear," he said. I predicted he'd change the subject soon. He couldn't stand to talk about his little girl for more than a few minutes at a time these days.

"I didn't think she'd ever stop talking about it yesterday."

"You can't let her be happy?" he asked.

"What are you talking about? I'm very happy for her, for both of them. Why are you—?"

"You seem to want to dampen her spirits, that's all," he said without looking at me.

"What?"

"She doesn't do that to you when you give birth to a new book."

I didn't like his tone. "What are you getting at?"

"Nothing. Just an observation." He got up from his chair and left the kitchen. I followed him into the living room.

"How's the bookstore stuff coming along?" he asked.

"Fine."

"Really? Everything is on track?"

"Pretty much. I'm meeting with the landlord later today to go over some things."

He headed toward the back door. "I'll be back in an hour or so. I'm going to the gym."

"The gym?" Carl never went to the gym.

"Yeah, the gym. You know, the place with all the treadmills and stuff?"

I could have continued questioning it, but his attitude made me realize that would not go well.

"Have a good time."

"I left a message on Mom's voice mail. If she calls back, tell her I'll call her when I get home."

I wondered why he didn't tell her to call him back on his cell phone, but I didn't question him on that either.

"Will do," I said.

Carl's mother Katherine lived in Boca. I had the pleasure of her company three times a year—on her birthday, Christmas, and one other random time. Not only did she call me Mary, Carl's ex-girlfriend's name, for the entire first year we were married, but she sent me a birthday card that year on Mary's birthday. People shortening my name to some annoying nickname was one thing, but to call me some other person's name entirely really annoyed me. We always went to see her—coming to see us apparently was too much for her even though I wasn't aware of anything physically wrong with her. But despite her flaws, she was the closest thing I had to a mother, my own having left my father and me. She'd left with no explanation, no good-bye, just gone—something my forty-eight-year-old brain didn't comprehend any better than my six-year-old one had at the time.

I took Carl's place in front of the window and stared at the calm lake. The shimmering emptiness of the water had a way of stirring up melancholy. I closed my eyes and allowed the tranquility it inspired to wash over me. I thought about the missing pocket watch, the engraved words on the back— TIME IS A GIFT. While I had never given any thought to the concept of time before, I thought about it often now—how it shouldn't be taken for granted or wasted. It was truly a gift, not anything anyone could earn, and no matter what one did with it—whether they used it wisely or squandered it, enjoyed it or retreated from it—it moved on.

After a few minutes, I retreated to my office to check on the number of free downloads my book *Fashion Show Fluke* had received the previous day. Giving an e-book away for a few days usually boosted it into Amazon's top ten in my genre, and that meant a nice spike in sales to follow.

After futzing around with several social media sites, I searched the local theater guide for a movie Carl and I might both enjoy. Even though I had more productive things to do, I thought I'd better make some time for us to be together and give him less opportunity to complain about my burying myself in my work.

The sound of the side door closing indicated Carl's return. As I turned to face the door, my elbow skimmed the keyboard of his laptop and what flashed up on the screen floored me—the cover of *Almost Murder*, my ninth book. I quickly closed the laptop cover and forced my jaw to return to its natural position.

Carl's hat and jacket were wet. I hadn't even noticed it had started to rain.

"Fucking rain," he said as he stripped off his wet clothing.

"Do you want to go to a movie later today?"

"In this?"

"If it lets up?"

"What's playing?"

"The only thing decent is *Every Secret Thing*."

"Is that the one with the missing child?"

"Mm-hm."

"Please. Anything but that."

"Sorry. I wasn't thinking. If the rain lets up, maybe we should take the pontoon out for a spin. Make sure everything is working properly?" A far cry from the Richardsons' forty-foot cabin cruiser, our small pontoon boat was used mainly for taking guests out on the lake, so they could see some of the elaborate homes along the shoreline.

"Nah. Don't much feel like it."

"What *do* you feel like doing today?"

"I don't know."

"Carl, I know you're upset about Portia and Lance, of course, but is something else bothering you…like me, for example?"

He walked over to me, kissed me, and held my face for a few seconds. "No, you're not bothering me, and if it feels like I'm taking out my frustration on you, I'm sorry." He kissed me again. "I don't mean to."

* * *

The rain hadn't let up and in fact worsened throughout the afternoon. By four o'clock, sheets of it pelted the sliding glass doors, making it impossible to see the lake.

I waited for a batch of blueberry muffins to finish baking, all the while pondering what my book *Almost Murder* was doing on Carl's laptop. I had sent it to him as soon as it had been released the previous year. I wished I understood computer technology better so I could tell when he had last accessed it. After thinking about that, I supposed it didn't really matter— nothing I could have done when I brushed up against the keyboard could have opened a closed file, so it had been the last file he'd had open—yet it bothered me at some elemental level. Even the delectable smell of the blueberry muffins coming out of the oven didn't soften what I was feeling about it.

The ringing phone startled me.

"They found him," Darlene gasped over the phone line. "I'm at Mercy Hospital."

"Is he alright?"

"Sort of."

"What do you mean?"

"Do you think you guys could come here? I could really use the company."

"Mercy Hospital. In Lake Geneva?"

"Yes."

"We'll be right there."

Carl and I jumped in our SUV, and as soon as he turned on the ignition, the radio blared a vintage Stones song, not the type of music we'd listened to for years. I checked the dashboard screen—the station was unfamiliar to me.

He drove as fast as he could to the hospital, but what should have taken twenty minutes took longer in the driving rain. Carl, unusually quiet during the ride, parked the car once we arrived at the hospital and exited before I could get my door open.

Darlene stood inside the emergency door entrance. She and Carl were in a hug when I reached them.

"How is he?" I asked, also giving her a hug.

"Let's go sit down over here. It's a crazy story."

Carl handed Darlene a bottle of Dr. Brown's he'd grabbed from the stash we kept on hand for her in our fridge.

"You're a sweetheart," she told him.

"Tell us what happened," I pleaded.

"He went to the boat before I did last night. From what we can tell, he hit his head on something. We don't know what yet, and he must have hit it hard because, well, it took twenty-eight stitches to close up the gash."

"We didn't see any blood or anything on the boat," Carl said. "Where did it happen?"

"This morning, one of the conservation wardens found him, passed out, maybe fifty feet or so into the woods at the end of the street. In the rain, soaking wet. He called for an ambulance. They brought him here. I was at the club having brunch with the girls when the hospital called me."

Leave it to Darlene to not miss an opportunity to socialize with the girls even with her husband missing.

"Is he conscious now?"

"He's conscious, but the doctor told me he has what they call a TBI— traumatic brain injury. I tried to talk to him, but it was like someone else was in his body. It scared me so much that I left his room and called you guys. I haven't been back in there since." She swiped at the tears running down her face. "What if he never snaps out of it?" she wailed.

I understood Darlene's panic. She didn't work, never had, and relied on Lance for everything. Lance took very good care of her, financially and in every other way.

Carl scooched closer to Darlene and put his arm around her shoulder.

"Mags, maybe you can go in his room and see if he recognizes you," he said to me without making eye contact.

Why he suggested that I be the one to go in baffled me—Carl was much closer to Lance than I was.

"I don't think they'll let you in—he's in ICU," Darlene said through her sobs.

Carl gave me a summoning look that impelled me to go to the ICU to find out if he could have visitors outside of the family. When I returned to tell them what Darlene had already suspected, she had her head buried deep in Carl's chest.

Darlene and Lance's son, Edward, and his wife, Melodi, barged into the waiting area.

"Mom! How is he?"

Darlene broke away from her embrace with Carl and stood up to greet them. She hugged her son, a tall, lanky young man with piercing blue eyes and a head of thick red hair.

"He's okay, Eddie, but not okay. Oh, I'm so upset, I can't even talk," she said grasping her scarf and flinging it one more time around her neck.

Carl moved off the sofa to allow the three of them to sit together.

"Calm down, Mom. He's alive and breathing on his own, as you said on the phone."

"I know, but he's not himself."

"What do you mean?"

"I don't think he knows who I am," she blurted out through her tears.

"I'm going in to see him," Eddie said as he dashed off.

Darlene talked nonstop about Lance's condition, Melodi's pregnancy, and her plans for dinner. Droning on and on about the food appeared to have a calming effect on her.

Edward returned in fifteen minutes with a vacant look on his face. "He didn't know who I was," he said as he plopped down on the sofa. "He fucking didn't know who I was."

"Eddie! Your language."

"What the fuck."

Melodi rubbed his shoulder while he talked.

"I called him 'Dad,' and he looked at me as if to say, 'Who the hell are you?' Like he was pissed off that I had even entered the room or something."

"Eddie, can you please watch your language?" Darlene snapped.

"I told him I was his son, and he told me he didn't have a son. When I walked closer to his bed, he yelled for a nurse. Fuck."

"The doctor told me he likely has a form of amnesia, but he was waiting for him to be examined by a specialist to be sure," Darlene said.

"It could be temporary," I said. "One of my characters had a TBI. I had to research it—the amnesia can be very temporary or…"

"Or what?" Darlene asked.

"Or a little longer." I didn't want to tell her it could last years.

"How much longer?"

"Maybe you should wait for the doctor to explain it to you," I said.

Chapter 3

"So, what do you want to do tomorrow…on Memorial Day?" I asked Carl after we had returned from the hospital. "I'm sure under the circumstances, Darlene isn't going to have us over on the boat. I have things to do in the morning for the bookstore, but—"

"On a holiday?"

"There's a lot left to do and—"

"I don't care what we do. We'll figure something out," he said as he walked toward the ringing phone.

After several seconds on the phone without saying anything, he finally spoke. "Mother, slow down. I only got about half of what you just said. How long will you be there?"

Be where? Katherine didn't leave her Boca condo very often—hair and nail appointments, bridge once a week, an occasional dinner out. The condo community where she lived had everything she needed.

"And then what?" he asked.

I was wishing he would put the phone on speaker so I could hear both sides of the conversation.

"But it sounds like—"

Katherine was known to interrupt people.

"But Mother, I—"

Carl continued the conversation, mostly listening, rolling his eyes and shifting his weight from one foot to the other.

"Let me check flights, and I'll call you back. Yes, I know. I'll get back to you as soon as I can. Wait a minute, Mags wants to talk with you."

I took the phone. "Hello, Katherine. How are you?"

"Not good, but Carl is going to take care of things for me."

"Is there anything I can do to help?"

"No. Carl can handle it. It was nice talking to you. Can you put Carl back on?"

"What's wrong?" I asked him as soon as he hung up. "She didn't seem to want to talk to me."

"She fell and fractured her hip. She's in the hospital."

"Is she okay?"

"I think so, but she said they're throwing around terms like *rehab, assisted living,* and *nursing home,* and that's making her hysterical. She said she'd rather be dead than in a nursing home."

"It must be a bad break to be talking about a nursing home."

"I'm not sure, but she *is* seventy-five, so..."

"You're going to fly down there?"

"To see what's going on. Talk to the doctors. Come up with a plan."

"Do you want me to come with?"

"No, not necessary." He said it fast…too fast.

"I know it isn't necessary, but I thought maybe you'd—"

"I should probably do this alone. You know how she can get."

"Okay."

The following day, Carl caught an afternoon flight to Fort Lauderdale, which wasn't far from Boca. He packed enough clothes for several days. I drove him to the airport.

On the drive home, I couldn't help thinking about what little I knew about my own mother. My father, a small-town dentist, had rarely if ever talked about her—why she'd left, where she went, or if anyone had ever searched for her.

I couldn't remember much about my mom, but I remembered the day before she left with utter clarity. It had been a Friday night, and I knew that she would be mad when she came home from her double shift at the hospital where she worked as a nurse. She'd be mad because Amy, the babysitter, had taken me to see *Animal House*—hardly an appropriate movie for a six-year-old. I hated the movie, and I didn't care much for Amy either, so I told Mom about our little excursion as soon as Amy left.

"It was a bad movie," I told her. "And I know that horse didn't really die.

They wouldn't let that happen to a horse in a movie," I said through tears. "Would they?"

But she was not even listening. And didn't seem to notice my tears at all.

"That's nice, Margie," was all she said.

"You're not mad?"

"That you went to a movie?"

"Mom, there were swear words in it, food fights. Sex even!"

"What did you say the name of the movie was?"

"*Animal House*. And it wasn't for kids either, but Amy took me there anyway."

"It's impossible to make a movie that everyone likes, sweetie."

I resented her lack of concern, but being only six, I didn't know how to deal with it effectively.

"One day, I'm going to make a movie that everyone will like!" I said with as much defiance as someone my age could muster.

"That's a fool's dream."

"Daddy says to follow your dreams," I told her.

"Well, Daddy's a fool. And so am I. Don't you be one too."

The next morning when we got up, we couldn't find Mom, but we did find her white nursing shoes in the kitchen waste basket. Dad didn't act the least bit surprised or upset. When I asked him one too many times when she was coming home, he told me she wasn't.

I don't remember much about my mom, but the last words she ever said to me rang in my ears for years.

When I was a teen, old enough and brave enough to ask my father more questions about her departure, all he said was that she had left to pursue another life. For years, I imagined reasons for her leaving, and by the time I left home for college, I had convinced myself that my dad must have done something to her to make her leave. We barely had a relationship after that—then he died a year and a half later.

After my father's funeral, I had to go through his things to decide what to keep, discard, or donate. In doing so, I learned three significant things about my mother. An album containing photos and articles about her before she became a nurse revealed that she had had a prior life as an actress. That shocked me. Dad had never mentioned it. I also found my parents' marriage certificate dated six months before the day I was born, indicating her pregnancy may have prompted their marriage.

And I found what appeared to me to be a hastily written note from her.

I'm walking away from you in exchange for the freedom I so desperately need to be myself. Brutal, I know. Dramatic, that's what you'll think. But honest.

I must have reread that note fifty times before I finally put it down. So had my father, I suspected, as it appeared to have been crumpled up at one point.

What kind of mother did that? The words "in exchange" especially bothered me. You exchanged a purse you didn't like when you got it home—not a family, not a child. "Brutal, dramatic, and honest." Those three words said a lot and made me think that she had carefully thought it through before leaving.

Soon after my father's death, I tried to find her. I had almost no leads but thought maybe she'd gone to Hollywood or New York to pursue her former career. But I didn't get far. Perhaps my resentment over her leaving the way she did prevented me from trying hard.

After I returned home from dropping off Carl, I dove into the bookstore project—something I had taken on against everyone's advice—friends, family, and endless articles on the subject. Frustrated by a lack of opportunity to get my books into retail bookstores, my vision was to open a store featuring solely self-published books, providing a venue for other self-published authors and helping to dispel some of the stigma we self-published "indie" authors had to endure by selecting only fully vetted books—ones that had been professionally edited, formatted, and cover-designed. Fully aware that if I failed, my husband and others would forever have the right to say, "I told you so," I'd conducted a fair amount of research on it and garnered enough information from one bookstore owner in Florida who'd shared her business model on her website to convince me that if she could do it, so could I.

After connecting with a variety of contractors on lighting, plumbing, drywall placement, electrical outlets, paint color, and signage, I took a break to focus on my current book-in-progress, *Stand-Alone Groom*, a missing-persons case. I had finished a first draft of the first half. As I developed the main female character in each of my books, I always fantasized about the book being made into a movie and my mom playing the leading role.

I realized that was a stupid thought, but then that's why they called them fantasies.

The circumstances behind writing my first book had been somewhat fantastical. Carl and I had been married for eight years when the Human Resources Department of my company informed me that they had eliminated my boss's position, offered him his old job back—my current job—and were letting me go. Thirty minutes later, I was standing next to my car in the parking lot with a box of my personal belongings including a three-foot ficus tree, wondering what had just happened. Thirty days later, I made the decision to try my hand at writing novels instead of going back into the corporate rat race. And ten years later, I had nine books under my belt.

After two hours of productive writing, I checked for new e-mails. As I started reading one from my attorney Andrew Wooten, a squeal ushered from my throat that startled even me—a screenwriter was showing an interest in the rights to *Rearview Mirror*. I called Carl on his cell phone, hoping his plane hadn't taken off yet, but then hung up before it had a chance to ring. It wouldn't have been right to share my excitement with him on his way to attend to his sick mother. But damn, I really wanted to.

I could have called Darlene with the news, but I didn't—her frame of mind presumably not fitting to join me in the celebration either. Portia would have been another good choice if I knew how to contact her. I called Lily, my long-time friend in Chicago.

Lilibeth Stokovich came from a family I envied. Her parents were immigrants—she from the Philippines, he from Russia. They'd met on jury duty. After Lily's birth, her mother had been told she couldn't have any more children, so they adopted two—one from Vietnam and another from India. Being from such a large, diverse family was enviable, but not as much as the self-confidence and inner strength that Lily exuded—that's what I held in such high regard when it came to her.

"Way to go, girlfriend!" Lily uttered in a shriek. "I knew you'd get someone interested in at least one of your books."

"It's early in the process, so I'm not getting my hopes up just yet."

"Well, you should. I'd be celebrating if it were me."

"I know you would. You celebrated when your puppy used the training pad for the first time."

"You're damn right I did. That was big!"

"See, I would have waited until he was completely housebroken, but that's just me."

After we hung up, I felt guilty not having told Carl first.

I called my attorney to find out more details about the possible screenplay. I had never used Andrew before but had connected with him years before…just in case.

"Can you come to my office tomorrow so we can discuss it?" he asked.

"I'm in Wisconsin for the summer, but I suppose I could drive—"

"What part of Wisconsin?" he asked.

"Lake Beulah."

"In East Troy?"

"Yes."

"I'm going to be driving to Milwaukee on Thursday. Our daughter is getting married there this weekend. It would be nothing for us to swing by on the way."

"Great."

My book on the big screen—how thrilling! Of course, a million things could happen that would prohibit it from going all the way. Nonetheless, I was excited—soaring sales for my book, a movie deal, a bigger and better retail store. I couldn't stop smiling. I'd come a long way to get to this point— surviving a childhood with a single parent who was almost as uninvolved as the one who was absent, growing up without ever being praised or criticized for what I did, and then feeling like there was something wrong with me to have brought on such treatment.

I was relaxing, listening to the evening news, when Carl called.

"I'm here at the hospital with Mom, but I don't know a whole lot yet. Sunday—limited staff I guess."

"And tomorrow's a holiday."

"Right. All I can tell you is that she's adamant about not going into any type of physical therapy facility or nursing home and…"

"And what?"

"And I'll wait until Tuesday when I can talk to her doctor before I say anything."

To me or to her?

"Okay. How's she doing?"

"Physically, I'm not sure. Emotionally, not good."

"I'm sorry to hear that, hon. Can I talk to her?"

"Hold on a minute. I'm down the hall from her room."

"How's the hospital?"

"It's fine. Very modern. Well, it looks like she's asleep now." He paused. "How peaceful she looks when she's asleep," he whispered. "When she's awake, she's her old feisty self. Told me if I still lived at home, I wouldn't look so thin and tired."

"Sounds like your mom."

"Hear anything from Dar?"

"No. I was thinking of calling her later."

"Good idea. Let me know what she says…about Lance."

"Okay. So where are you going to stay?"

"In her condo, I think. She wants me to bring her a few things from there." He paused. "I'm worried about her."

"Me too. I'd hate for her to be put somewhere she doesn't want to be."

"I was talking about Dar."

"Oh."

"She's going through a lot right now."

"Yes, I know. What kind of rental car did you get?"

"Ford Taurus. It's okay. Mom's insisting I return it and use her car. Hasn't run for at least two years, but you know Mom. I wish I could do more for her."

"Are you referring to your mother now or Darlene?"

"I've never seen her like this."

"Like you said, you'll know more when you talk to her doctor. Then you'll know what to do."

"Right. Well, I need to run over to her place, pick up her things, and bring them back here before visiting hours are over, so I'm going to go. Love you."

"Love you too."

He could have asked how I was doing.

* * *

"Would you like some company?" I asked Darlene later that evening. I could tell by the way she answered the phone that she'd been crying.

"Eddie and Melodi are here right now."

"Well, call me when they're gone, and I'll come over if you want."

I popped on to my Amazon author page—seven new reviews since the previous day. My books were getting pretty good reviews, all averaging four-plus stars out of a possible five. But the last reviewer rated one of my books with only one star. I read that one first.

I downloaded the wrong book. I don't even like cozy mysteries.

Reviews like this used to bother me. Now I just accepted them and moved on.

One of the four-star reviews for *Almost Murder* caught my attention.

Good book except for the ending which left me feeling flat.

Almost Murder was my most recently published book. It had received close to a hundred reviews, and until now, no one had complained about the ending. Except for Carl, who had said the ending had left him feeling a little flat and then later confessed he'd never read any of my books. That was odd.

My cell phone flashed Darlene's name.

"Hi, Darlene. Are they gone?"

"Yeah. Can you still come over?"

"I'll be right there."

I walked next door. Darlene and I settled into her sunroom where the lights were low so we could see out, but no one could see in. The Richardsons' sunroom could have made it into *Architectural Digest* with its twelve-foot domed-glass ceiling and full-length windows with remote-controlled window treatments, an elaborate stone fireplace, and the most gorgeous rattan furniture I'd ever seen.

"You look like you've had a rough day," I said.

"I met with Lance's doctor this morning. His recovery could take months, even years."

"I'm so sorry to hear that."

"His memory has really been impaired, and his doctor told me the preliminary results from the tests they took aren't promising. He may not even be able to come home."

"Ever?"

"He may not be able to take care of himself."

"But there's a chance he'll get better, right?"

"Some. They're going to transfer him to a regular room next week and begin physical and cognitive therapy. We'll know better after a few therapy sessions."

"Any idea how he hit his head?"

"Eddie and I combed the boat for clues, for blood actually, and didn't find anything."

"But the police did that too, right?"

"Yes, but they did it so fast, they could have missed something."

"Do you think someone could have hit him from behind?"

"The police said there was no sign of anything where they found him, not even any blood, which is weird. But it had been raining so hard, who knows what was washed away. The doctor said he lost a lot of blood."

"What about his wallet? Was that on him when they found him?"

She nodded. "And full of money."

One of my characters in *Rearview Mirror* got hit from behind and was left to die. But she didn't die and later identified her attacker—her husband's best friend. I didn't bring that up to Darlene.

"On a happier note, have you come down from the grandbaby news yet?"

"Not yet. Probably never will. I'm not sure how I'll ever get through this pregnancy."

"Darlene, you're not the one pregnant."

"Just wait until it happens to you. You'll understand how I feel."

"I'm not sure I'll ever—"

"I shouldn't have said that. I'm sorry."

"No need. I've come to accept her being gone. It's easier that way."

"She'll be back."

"I hope so."

I told her about Carl's mother.

"I know. He told me. Maybe he'll bring her back here to live with you guys."

I shuddered at the thought.

"Mags?"

"Sorry. I was ignoring your comment for a reason."

"She can't be *that* bad."

I stared at her without saying anything.

"I'll pray for a speedy recovery for her…in Florida."

"Thanks."

"When is he coming back?" she asked.

I shook my head. "Don't know."

Before going to bed that night, I listened to the headlines on CNN. Ireland legalized same-sex marriages. Gloria Steinem led a group of female activists across the Korean border. I closed my eyes and envisioned a third headline—Margaret Manning's bestseller *Rearview Mirror* to go on the big screen next year starring Marilyn Foss Delaney (or whatever name my mother might have been using), Nicolas Cage, and Diane Keaton. The phone plucked me out of my reverie.

"You'll never guess what I found at Mom's," Carl said.

"What?"

"Another woman."

"What did you say?" I asked Carl, thinking I hadn't heard him correctly.

"I found a woman named Sylvia McMasters in Mom's condo."

"What was she doing there?"

"According to her, she's Mom's roommate."

"Her roommate? Your mom didn't have a roommate."

"She claims she did. And she showed me mail with her name and Mom's address on it."

"What are you going to do?"

"Talk to Mom about it, I guess."

"Carl?"

"Yeah."

"Good luck."

Chapter 4

After a fitful night's sleep, I eventually dragged myself out of bed and curled up on the sofa in the sunroom. Barely six o'clock, the early morning sun shone brightly, too brightly for my grogginess. It surprised me that I'd gotten any sleep at all—my mind not ever having had a chance to rest between Lance's condition, my mother-in-law's situation, my missing jewelry—which I was still stewing over—and the fact that Carl sent a Facebook message to say goodnight instead of calling me.

Memorial Day—alone with nothing to do. We had always spent the summer holidays on the Richardsons' boat. The thought of spending it at home by myself, watching everyone having fun on the lake all day long, depressed me. Even being with the Richardsons beat that.

I threw on jeans and an oversized boy shirt before settling into my desk chair. It didn't take long to go through the few e-mails that had come in throughout the night—nothing of much interest there or on Facebook or Twitter. I opened the *Stand-Alone Groom* file and, after a few false starts at writing the next chapter, closed it back up. Trying to be creative when I felt lousy was predictably counterproductive, usually resulting in my deleting most of what I'd written. Having intermittent short periods of time to devote to my writing didn't help matters—allowing longer chunks of time typically resulted in better writing.

After staring out the window for a few long moments feeling sorry for myself, I got the urge to search for the missing jewelry again. I'd checked each room of the house many times already but not with the insane scrupulousness I suddenly felt brewing inside of me.

I had discovered the first piece of jewelry missing at the beginning of the previous summer when I had driven to the cottage alone—a single pearl-drop earring that had been my mother's, one of the few things of hers I owned. I'd kept it in a porcelain Limoges trinket box in the shape of the Eiffel Tower, which was also missing.

The following month, I discovered the second missing item—a thin silver bracelet. I had remembered bringing it up from Chicago and putting it in the locked drawer with the rest of my jewelry, but when I had opted to wear it one day, I found it was gone.

And now the third item, the pocket watch, which I kept in the same locked drawer. Whenever I worked at my PC, I would prop it up in front of me where I could enjoy looking at it. At other times, it stayed in the locked desk drawer. I suppose I locked it up for safekeeping, but I don't know from whom. Carl had often teased me about the ritual.

The bracelet I could get over, but not the earring or the watch. They had been dear to me because they had belonged to my mother. The pocket watch especially held special meaning for me because I didn't know its history, didn't know the motivation behind the person who chose the inscription—TIME IS A GIFT.

Our two-story cottage-style home—a little less than two thousand square feet on the first floor—included three bedrooms, two baths, the sunroom, and a large open area for the kitchen, dining, and general living space. The second floor was nothing but a wide-open unfinished dormered room that would have made a fabulous master suite, man cave, or studio of some sort. Not needing the extra space, we'd left it vacant.

I should have been working on the bookstore business plan. Instead, I began the find-the-missing-jewelry expedition in the bedroom I claimed as my office, starting with the only place I hadn't thoroughly checked before— behind my desk. I moved it away from the windows as far as I could, given the mess of cables and cords back there. Finding nothing but a small pad of sticky notes and a Hershey's Kiss wrapper, I went on to the spare bedroom.

We maintained that room for guests or when Portia came home to visit. Occasionally, one of us would sleep in it if the other one wasn't feeling well or was having a restless night. While I was at it, I unmade the bed and put on fresh linens. As I pulled off the sheets, a small piece of paper flew out—a $178 restaurant receipt from the Le Grille restaurant in Lake Geneva—a place Carl and I had talked about but had never frequented—dated August 29, 2014. The date rang a bell. I thought back to the previous year when I had driven home from our lake home a few days before Carl to keep a book-signing engagement. I made a mental note to check the calendar to see what day that had been.

By noon, I'd combed through every inch of all the rooms except the main open living area. I stopped to have lunch before tackling it. Halfway through lunch, Carl called.

"How is she?" I asked.

"About the same."

"Did you confront her about the roommate?"

"No. They had just given her pain medication, and she was pretty out of it."

"Are you at the hospital now?"

"No. I'm driving to a restaurant. Starving."

"I have some—"

"The cafeteria food here really stinks."

"I was going to—"

"I'll call you later. Gotta go now."

He hung up before I could tell him about the screenplay proposal or ask him about the receipt from Le Grille. Just as well. He had a lot on his mind.

Searching through all the bookshelves took the longest. I picked up every book, checked behind it, and shook it to let the pages flap free. When I had checked every one, I dusted the shelf before putting the books back.

It took me hours to finally get to the last shelf, which contained a dozen or so books that Carl's mother had given us after his father died—all first editions of older books, including Oscar Wilde's *Picture of Dorian Gray* in mint condition. She had been glad to get rid of them, and I had been thrilled to receive them. I found myself thinking that if Carl and I were to ever split up, *Dorian Gray* would be on my want list for sure.

I was removing my mother-in-law's old books from the shelves when it appeared—the missing bracelet—lying there on the shelf like a coiled-up snake ready to strike. As I moved in closer to pick it up, my muscles tensed, causing me to stop briefly. I took a few seconds to compose myself and then, with a trembling hand, picked up the bracelet for closer examination. The lobster-claw clasp that was still fastened puzzled me because my bracelets generally weren't clasped unless they were on my wrist—I had a habit of storing them lying open. I unfastened the clasp and put the bracelet on. The snug fit told me it had not come off without being unclasped.

I felt weak, then nauseous, so I sat down and leaned back in the chair with my eyes closed, wondering how on earth the bracelet had gotten there.

* * *

I must have dozed off because I awoke to the explosive sound of fireworks. It was just after nine-thirty. Carl had said he would call me later, but my phone indicated no missed calls. I considered calling him but decided against it in case he was busy with Katherine.

I glanced down at the bracelet on my wrist. If I had found it unclasped, I could have explained it by saying I had reached into the bookshelf for a book, my bracelet got caught on something, became unclasped, and fell behind the books without me realizing it. Yet it was improbable for a lobster-claw clasp to come undone—the thin chain would have likely broken first if it had gotten caught on something.

The missing jewelry in *Break-In at Buttons and Bows* had shown up in strange places as well. In that book, the owner of the Buttons and Bows resale shop had been robbed of a few pieces of costume jewelry even though many other pieces worth substantially more hadn't been touched. A ring had mysteriously appeared in the mailbox of a man with whom the store owner was having an affair, and she found the missing heart-shaped locket in a small envelope that someone had stuck under the windshield wiper of her car.

Even though I knew it was stupid to compare what happened to my jewelry to the fictional story I had written years earlier, I couldn't help doing it. The culprit in *Break-In*, the protagonist's jealous twin, wanted to make it appear as though her sister was losing her mind so she could assume executorship of their parents' estate.

Carl wouldn't have done such a thing—it was foolish for me to even think that—so I wasn't sure why I allowed my mind to go there. But then, who?

I didn't much like watching the fireworks by myself, so I retreated to my office to check for any new book reviews on Amazon and Goodreads. I read the newest review for *Fashion Show Fluke.*

Two stars – Terrible book. I couldn't wait 'til it ended.

So why didn't you stop reading it before you got to the end? It's a novel, honey, not required reading.

Let it go.

I couldn't let it go. I clicked on her name to see what else she had reviewed—a t-shirt with the words "Always Wash It First" plastered on the front. Now I could let it go.

My computer told me I had a new Facebook message. I smiled at the dancing emoticon.

Still up?

Yep. Catching up on e-mails. How's K?

Same. Hates the bed linens, food, artwork, noise. The list goes on. She wants out.

No one wants in. ☺ Ask her about the roommate?

Not yet. Just wanted to say goodnight. My phone's on charge. Luv u.

Tomorrow you'll know more. It will be a better day. Luv u 2.

I left the conversation with an overwhelming feeling of emptiness but not certain why. I had so wanted to shout out the good news about the screenplay—maybe that was it. Or maybe it was that I missed Carl and looked forward to his call, and all I got was another Facebook message— making it two nights in a row.

In the back of my mind lingered another possible reason for that feeling of emptiness—our marriage. The distance between us did nothing to bolster it. I tried not to think about it, but if I was being honest, I'd have had to admit things were not like they used to be. The first years of our marriage, despite my not having gotten over losing Wayne, had seemed happy enough, although I had to admit that looking back, maybe I had just been going through the motions. Maybe we both had been. The sex was good. We'd said, "I love you" often enough. It all could have been motions.

I honestly didn't know. Sometimes I thought the more time you spend with someone, the more synched up you became with each other's existence, inherently becoming an organic part of each other's lives. Perhaps that was what had happened to Carl and me.

What was bothering me was that while Carl never did anything to cause me to mistrust him, I often did. Lily had once told me I had a knack for ferreting out the negative and distorting the positive. Maybe she was right.

Still, it seemed like he used to care about me more—he would comment on what I had to say instead of just politely listening. Of course, we'd had our share of tiffs but had always quickly gotten over them. Not like now, when even the smallest argument lingered way longer than need be.

I had first noticed the change when Portia had buggered off to Costa Rica. It seemed as though Carl had never gotten past that, and whenever I tried to talk to him about it, he'd change the subject. And now he had his mother's welfare on his mind. Maybe he had other things on his mind too. Whatever the cause, it felt as though the many layers of our marriage were gradually wearing away. Perhaps I had been naïve enough to believe that in time our marriage would eventually morph into something better than it had ever been.

I pulled up my personal calendar from the previous year to see what day we had closed up the lake house to return to our primary home in Chicago. August 28, the day before the date of the Le Grille restaurant receipt. I had driven home alone. Carl had stayed for the Labor Day weekend. I examined the receipt again—it didn't include an itemization of what had been ordered, just an amount. $178.00. I Googled the menu for Le Grille and studied the prices. Two people could have had a nice dinner with a couple of glasses of wine for that amount, or one person could have had one hell of a meal with multiple drinks.

Thinking I had probably read too much into it, I went to bed, a vision of my future Indie Book Nook storefront the last image I remembered before falling asleep.

Chapter 5

The call I had been awaiting with trepidation came the following evening.

"Well, I talked with her doctors today," Carl said.

"And?"

"What concerns me the most is what the occupational therapist said. Rehab could take months."

"I think I know what you're thinking."

"You do?"

"About bringing her up here until she's back on her feet again?"

"I can't leave her, not like this."

"So is that what you're thinking?"

"No. I can work from anywhere, you know that. I feel like I should stay here until she's able to take care of herself."

"But you just said that could take months."

"She can't function on her own, and she's been very clear to everyone that she will not go into a nursing home or assisted living."

"Carl, you're talking long-term here, what about—"

"What about what?"

"What about...us?"

"I don't...um..."

"She couldn't come up here and stay with us? We have room in both places, and I'm sure whatever care she needs would be just as good up here."

"I couldn't do that to you."

"But you could leave me."

"I wouldn't be leaving you, I'd—"

"Same effect."

The uncomfortable silence lingered for several seconds until Carl spoke.

"You never liked her. How would that work?" he asked.

"I never said I didn't like her."

"You didn't have to."

"I thought she never liked me."

He didn't respond. He didn't have to.

"It's your decision to make, but my preference would be to have your mother live with us and save our marriage."

"I didn't know it needed saving."

"How could it possibly survive living a thousand miles apart?"

"That's why they have airplanes, dear."

"Like I said, the choice is yours."

"Thanks a—"

"By the way, Miles called to tell me a studio is interested in producing *Rearview Mirror.* I have a meeting with my lawyer on Thursday."

"That's—"

"I gotta go. I'll talk to you later."

After I clicked the phone off, I meandered my way into the dark sunroom and sunk into Carl's favorite chair where I sat for I don't know how long, regretting how I had ended our conversation. The more I agonized over it, the more I believed that maybe a short separation wouldn't be such a bad idea.

* * *

Halfway through my morning ritual of checking for new reviews of my novels and reading e-mails, Darlene called.

"Lance is going into residential rehab tomorrow."

"Did they say for how long?"

"They don't know. Some things are coming back to him, but he's got a long way to go."

"What's coming back?"

"He asked about his precious boat."

"Well, that's something."

"He didn't ask about me. *Little Shitsy* he cares about."

I chuckled. "Darlene, you can't be upset over that. He has no control over what he does and doesn't remember. Is that what you really call his boat?"

"Only when I'm mad at him. Like now. Like most of the time lately."

"I suppose that being hit on the head—looks like it was pretty hard— can mess up a guy's thought process."

"Really?"

"I don't know, but that seems logical, doesn't it?"

"To someone who's not married to him, maybe."

I didn't understand why she was being so hard on him.

"Was that the only thing he remembered?"

"No. He remembered a piece of real estate he wanted to buy outside of Milwaukee."

"See? If he recalls that, everything will come back to him eventually."

"Maybe in the long-term, but I'm living in the short-term. So have you two decided what's going to happen with Carl's mother?"

"What's going to happen with her?"

"You know…since her fall and all."

I explained the situation, making no mention of how it was affecting our marriage.

"I'm trying not to think about it too much," I told her.

"How much longer will Carl be down there with her?"

"I'm not sure."

"Another week? Longer?"

"Like I said, I'm not sure."

"Would you like to go with me to lunch at the club tomorrow?"

I wasn't into the yacht-club scene, but as we were both husbandless for the time being, I said yes.

I finished reading the book reviews that had come in overnight. Someone named Not Your Average Reader loved *Blue Bonnet Hoers*, saying it was, "delightfully entertaining beyond my expectations." I clipped it from the Amazon site and put it in my Reviews to Post on Social Media file. The previous day had been the last day of the *Fashion Show Fluke* free e-book promotion—it had been downloaded more than forty thousand times, and the reviews that had come in during the promotion were all good, something that doesn't always happen with a free-book promotion even if you've written a good book. Of the forty thousand people who downloaded it, maybe ten percent would actually read it, and some of them would read a few pages, decide it's not for them, and leave a bad review. It's a risk we authors had to take when offering a book for free.

* * *

We arrived at the club at eleven-forty, ten minutes late for our reservation. Darlene showcased her ample breasts by wearing a skin-tight leopard-print tank top that I wouldn't have been caught dead in even to lounge around the house.

"You never arrive on time," she told me. "A few minutes late shows them they're not the most important thing you have on your schedule." Then I saw a big smile take shape on her face as she waved to someone who must have been behind me.

Whatever.

The hostess led us to a table next to the window overlooking the lake.

"Do you mind if we take that table over there?" Darlene asked.

After we were redirected to the table of Darlene's choosing, I asked her what was wrong with the table by the window.

"Better view from here."

Of the people, I assumed.

We opened our menus, and after a couple of minutes of chatting about the items on it, I could tell she wanted to order for me. I let her, hoping I would recognize at least one or two of the ingredients in whatever dish would be put in front of me.

"So do you miss being on the boat?" I figured she hadn't gone out on it alone—she depended on Lance for that and, from what I could gather, everything else, except for gossiping.

"What?"

"I said, do you miss—"

"Did you see who Aretha Longhorn just walked in with?"

"No." *And I don't really care.*

"Sarah Fields."

"Is that a problem?"

"Aretha's daughter left Sarah's son standing at the altar a few years back."

"Looks like they've put it past them then."

"What did you say?"

"I said it looks like—"

"I'm glad our Eddie never had to go through *that*. They dated for a while."

"Who?"

"Aretha's daughter and my Eddie."

"Looks like it turned out well for him in the end—Melodi seems like a lovely daughter-in-law."

"Who?" she asked, her gaze focused on everyone but me.

"Melodi."

"Mm-hm. What were we just talking about?"

"Are you okay?" I asked her.

"Yes. Why?"

"You seem to be, I don't know, preoccupied with something."

As soon as the waiter brought our food, Darlene got up from the table. "I'll be right back," she said.

I watched Darlene sway her hips as she wove her way over to the bar where Aretha and Sarah were standing before I peered down at my plate of Moroccan Wiki-Wiki Volcano. Under the "lava" that had been drizzled over the top of a mound of couscous, I recognized chickpeas and chunks of pineapple, but nothing else. I willed the meal to be a grilled cheese sandwich with tomato and bacon, but of course nothing happened.

"Looks yummy. Have you tried it yet?" Darlene asked when she returned.

"No. I was waiting for you."

"Well, dig in. There's a surprise at the bottom of the volcano you know."

"Can't wait for that."

I had managed to extract a few forkfuls of the meal when Darlene asked me a question that caught me off-guard.

"Do you trust Carl?"

"Well…of course. Why do you ask?"

"No real reason."

"*Something* must have spurred you to ask that question."

"Not really. Curious, I guess."

"Do you trust Lance?"

"With some things."

"Like?"

"I trusted him to take out the garbage every day."

"That's huge," I said with an eye roll.

"Do you feel Carl would support you…no matter what?"

"Okay, Darlene, why are you asking me these questions? What's up?"

"Nothing's up! I'm just making conversation."

She wasn't just making conversation, and she knew that I knew it.

"Mm-hm."

"Sorry I asked."

We ate our meals in silence. Before I had a chance to discover the surprise at the bottom of my dish, she signed off on the check.

The painfully quiet ride home seemed to go on forever. I couldn't wait to get back to my bookstore work.

* * *

When I got home, I had an hour to get ready for my next activity of the day—a book-signing by a fellow author. I decided to leave the house a half an hour early and stop off at my as-yet-unopened storefront, for the pleasure of seeing it again and reimagining all my plans for it. The lease commencement date was July 1, but the owner of the building allowed me access so I could take measurements or the like. My hope was to pull off a grand opening by Labor Day. Getting the physical space ready was the easy part. Finding authors, getting consignment agreements signed, and refining the business and marketing plan presented bigger challenges.

The store was in a good location—in the heart of Lake Geneva's quaint downtown business district on a busy side street visible from Main Street. With parking in the rear and the nearest Starbucks far enough away as to not interfere too much with my coffee bar, I figured it had a fair chance at attracting sufficient customers. The square footage lacked space for a separate room for lectures, book signings, and book clubs to meet but included space for everything else I wanted—ample shelving for new and used paperbacks, computer terminals for customers to order the Kindle or Nook versions if they wanted, a couple of overstuffed chairs for customers to peruse books, a bathroom, an enclosed cashiers island in the middle of everything, a coffee/ wine bar area, and a storeroom. Even enough room for a few racks for bookmarks, reading lights, bookends, and other reading-related items.

After cruising the perimeter of the fifteen-hundred-square-foot empty space a few times, I sat in the folding chair I had brought and envisioned the different sections of the store I intended to set up. If I closed my eyes, I could picture the store's layout down to the smallest detail. I daydreamed about the opportunity I would be creating for my fellow self-published authors and the gratification for myself. But if I had been completely honest with myself, I would have seen that the more genuine reason for the bookstore may have been that everyone had told me I couldn't make it work. My father—girls should stay out of business. My financial advisor—the failure rate for start-up retail stores was extremely high. My husband—the long hours would kill you. My fellow author-friends wished me luck without much encouragement. I never did like being told what I couldn't do.

On the way to the book-signing, I pondered Darlene's offhanded questions about Carl. At first, I thought she wanted to know some things about Carl and me to compare to her own relationship with Lance. But then, why wouldn't she have just said so? No, she wanted to know about Carl— did I trust him—but it puzzled me why.

When I arrived at the book-signing, I immediately saw my author-friend Vineta standing behind the checkout counter looking out at twenty-five or so guests milling around the bookstore. I had met Vineta at a book fair the previous year. She and I had shared a table and discovered we lived a mile from each other and had a love for literary fiction in common. We waved to each other.

When the store proprietor asked for everyone's attention, I took a place toward the back of the room where I was soon joined by a man about my age, quite handsome, sporting a baseball cap with a fish patch on it. I did a double-take—he looked a lot like Wayne, my first true love, the man I would have married but for the accident. "I just came in here to buy a book," he whispered. "Didn't know there was a presentation going on."

"A book on fishing?"

He looked at me puzzled.

I peered up at his hat.

After I caught him glancing down at my left hand, he adjusted the brim of his hat and smiled. He had a nice smile, boyish like Carl's had been when I'd first met him. "So, what's going on here?" he asked.

"A book-signing."

"Is that the author?" he asked nodding toward Vineta.

"Yes. Her name is Vineta Atkins."

"What did she write?"

"Fantasy fiction."

"I'm afraid I don't even know what that is."

Before I could explain, Vineta began her presentation. Instead of talking about her latest book, *United in the Mist*, like most authors would have done, she talked about the process she had undergone when writing the series—how she went about creating a new world for the setting, the challenge of developing fantastic characters that appeared real, and the research she had to do on the myths and legends that she'd woven into the stories. She ended with a statement that I had heard her make before.

"The fact that there is no shortage of outlandish ideas in my head for future books is both gratifying and scary at the same time," she said.

I stood in line to buy her book with fish-hat guy directly behind me.

I turned to face him. "So, are you going to buy her book?" I asked him. His smile seemed to engage every feature of his face.

"Not sure. I have a niece who's read all the Harry Potter books. Would she like this one?"

"Probably—they're both contemporary fantasy."

When I reached third in line, I turned around to face him again, only to find him gone.

"You didn't have to buy a copy, Marge. I would have given you one," Vineta whispered as she signed my book.

"*Now* you tell me," I whispered back.

After leaving the bookstore, I headed down Main Street to pick up a few things before going home, thinking more about my life in my twenties than anything else.

At my first stop, a hardware store, I ran into fish-hat guy again.

"You're not following me, are you?" I asked him through a grin.

He barely touched my arm—yet enough to bring a flush to my cheeks. "I could ask you the same thing, you know."

"I was here first."

He laughed. "Well, I'll tell you what. From here, I'm going to the post office. That way you'll know where I am so you can go in the opposite direction."

"Okay, thanks for the warning."

He went east. I went west to a small boutique that I liked to browse.

I bought a couple of things at the boutique and headed toward my car. That's when I observed him once again, on the other side of the street. He was standing with his back to me. I shook my head and walked to my car, wondering what he was all about and if he found me as attractive as I found him.

The uncanny resemblance to Wayne made me think back to that more carefree era of my life, though it was painful to do so. We'd met in college. It had taken him a year to work up the courage to ask me out. I liked that about him. Six feet tall with jet-black hair, he was good-looking, even sweat-soaked after shooting hoops with his buddies on campus. I had loved his easy demeanor, his intellect, his respect for other people even when he disagreed with them. I had loved everything about him.

His death was so unfortunate, so unfair—being hit head-on by a woman who'd suffered a heart attack while driving to her weekly Bingo game. Gone in an instant. Both of them.

I shoved both Wayne and fish-hat guy out of my mind. I was a happily married woman.

Chapter 6

Carl had been gone for four days, and I missed him. Missed his company. Missed being with someone. Anyone. I thought of calling Darlene but figured it was too soon to call after that awkward lunch we'd had. Plus, I couldn't decide who should call whom first. Who was at fault—her for asking those impertinent questions or me for confronting her on them? After consuming a chopped salad for dinner, I called her, deciding it was the proper thing to do regardless of who was at fault.

"Hi, Darlene. It's Margaret."

"Aren't we being formal!"

"I'm not being formal. It's my name. I know everyone calls me anything but Margaret, but Margaret is my—"

"I got it."

Glad she couldn't see the muddled look on my face, I began my spiel. "Look, I called to apologize for questioning your motives at lunch today. I—"

"So now I had motives?"

"Motive just means—"

"I know what motive means. You're not the only one who knows words."

"May I start over?" I asked, wondering how the conversation had spun off in this direction.

"Do what you like."

Before I had a chance to speak again, she hung up on me.

After I got over the shock of being hung up on, I fell into one of our cozy club chairs and watched the fiery sun ball disappear through lazy clouds scattered in the sky before it slowly descended behind the tree line, a pink and gold watery sky trailing behind it.

Tomorrow would be a better day. It had to be.

* * *

I awoke the next morning after a dream-filled night with an annoying fusion of unwanted emotions running through me—lonesomeness, guilt for putting a damper on the friendship with Darlene, fear of not being able to meet the bookstore-opening date, and anger because Carl hadn't called me when he'd said he would.

Not that long ago, I'd been a happily married author with a screenwriter interested in one of my books—every author's dream. Now everything in my life seemed off.

After breakfast, I stood for a few minutes in my office gazing out over the unruffled lake, watching a ghost-gray layer of mist creep away from me and disappear into the shrubbery on the other side. My notebook in hand, I moseyed out to the patio to catch up on the news. The fragrant smell of damp grass early in the morning before the sun had a chance to dehydrate it always brought me back to my childhood and the aroma that went along with watching my father cut the lawn before he went to work. A successful dentist, he could have easily hired someone to mow but preferred to do it himself. Unfortunately for me, it added to the time he didn't spend with me.

The faint echo of a squawking crow contributed to the shimmering emptiness of the lake. Feeling more melancholy than I wanted to be, I retreated inside and sat down at my computer to work on the bookstore marketing plan.

After a while, I began to zone out on the marketing plan details and decided to switch to something else. I had been struggling with a climactic scene in *Stand-Alone Groom*. I had a handle on the climax itself—the groom impatiently waiting at the church for his bride-to-be to arrive— but was having trouble building up to that pivotal point. After an hour of unproductive writing, I jumped to the climax of the story and hoped that something would inspire me later to fill in the rising action. By noon, I had a decent rough draft. Now, in a far better mood than I'd been in first thing that morning, I called Carl to see how he was doing.

"We're home now," he said.

"Just you and your mom?"

"Hold on. I'm going to go outside. Keep talking. Tell me about your day. No, tell me about your yesterday. What happened?"

What did he think happened yesterday?

"Mags?"

"I'm here."

"I'm outside now so she can't hear me. I hired a home health aide to take care of her personal needs, someone to come in first thing in the morning and again before she goes to bed. She'll have to see an occupational therapist three times a week, and we'll have strengthening exercises to do each day."

"Can she walk?"

"With a walker, yes. I removed all the throw rugs she had around and rearranged some of the furniture so there won't be anything she can trip over or run into."

"What about the roommate?"

"When we got here, she was gone."

"Did you ask Katherine about her?"

His sigh was audible. "No, I didn't. All her things are gone, so…"

"Why do you think she left like that?"

"Maybe because I walked in on her and startled her. She'd said she didn't know Katherine had a son."

"Makes you wonder what else we don't know about what your Mom's been doing on her own."

"I know. Her mind isn't right—I'm not sure if I could even have an intelligent conversation about it with her. The roommate, that is. You know what, she's calling for me. I have to go. I'll call you later, hon."

"Okay. Give her my—"

He hung up.

* * *

Despite knowing better, I allowed Carl's "tell me about what happened yesterday" comment to eat away at me for the rest of the day, to the point where I had to stop working. Not understanding what he meant by it and thinking about the worst scenarios possible had caused my writing to take on an entirely wrong tone. Was Carl in cahoots with Darlene? Had she told him every word of our conversations? Not hungry, I opted for a glass of wine instead of dinner while I watched the sun make its gradual descent behind the tall pines across the lake.

Carl's greater allegiance to his mother than to me was bothersome too. But they were bonded by blood, he and I only by a piece of paper. That and an estranged daughter. At one time, I'd thought that a marriage license transferred primary loyalty away from a parent and on to a spouse. Now I wasn't so sure.

I considered my own mother—the little bit I knew about her. After digging out the file I had assembled years ago when I had tried to find her, I retired to the chaise lounge in my office, fantasizing again, like I'd done so many times before, about having some connection with her.

Instead of responding to the electrician as to where I wanted the outlets in the bookstore, I opened the file on my mother—it was smaller than I had remembered. I reread the articles about her acting career, first the one from 1969 that talked about her role in ABC's TV film *Honeymoon with a Stranger* starring Janet Leigh. A separate photo of her and the cast accompanied it—she had been quite the looker back then. Other articles that talked about various musicals, plays, and movies made no specific mention of my mother in them, so I assumed her roles had been too minor to warrant any discussion.

I could still picture Mom coming home from work in her bright white nurse's uniform and clunky nursing shoes. Dad had teased her mercilessly about those shoes, asking her if she'd purchased them at an army surplus store. Funny how certain things stick in your memory.

Back in the eighties, when I had done my initial search for her, I didn't have the benefit of the Internet. Now I did. By dinnertime, I had registered her name and mine on several missing-relatives bulletin boards, checked public databases, and made a connection with the National Center for Missing Adults. After registering with a Family History Center associated with the LDS church, I checked social media sites and did a broad Internet search on her name. Unfortunately, there were hundreds of Marilyn Fosses in the world. Even using keywords such as "actress" and "movies" didn't result in any usable information about her whereabouts.

The further I got, the more futile it seemed. If she didn't want anyone to find her, she would have likely changed her name.

The search at least served to occupy my time when I wasn't in the mood to write—and that was a good thing. After thinking it through, I came to a decision—if I assumed she was dead, it would eliminate the aggravation that gnawed at me every so often. Probably easier said than done but worth a shot.

I called Lily to share with her the recent revelation I'd had about my mother.

"So you won't try to find her anymore?" Lily asked.

"If she's alive, there's this underlying level of anxiety, feeling of rejection more than anything else, I suppose, that just hangs on me, like a ball and chain. I always feared that I'd let her down as a kid and that was why she left. Maybe not the whole reason, but a contributing factor. If she's dead, I think that guilt may go away. That, and the hurt of never getting a birthday card or Christmas present."

"You sound like you're still angry with her."

"No matter what was going on inside her head, she couldn't have stayed…for my sake? I wasn't worth it? I'll bet she has no idea the effect her leaving had on me. The fact that I went through years of thinking maybe I'd done something wrong…so bad that it caused her to leave. I used to go to bed praying she'd come back, and when she didn't, I thought maybe I hadn't prayed hard enough or maybe God was punishing me by not answering my prayers. There's another reason to assume she's dead—it serves no purpose being angry with a dead person."

"Maybe she thought you'd be better off without her."

I pondered those words.

"I've never looked at it that way."

"Have you forgiven her, Margaret?"

"Not yet. Someday."

After we ended the conversation, I admitted to myself that the real reason I hadn't expended much effort in trying to find her probably stemmed from fear of what I'd find.

* * *

After dinner, I relaxed on the patio with a novel I'd been reviewing for an organization that vetted self-published books, occasionally gazing at the lake to watch the boats cruise by on their way to…wherever. Under normal circumstances, Carl and I would have been on the Richardsons' boat doing the same thing.

"You look like you're a thousand miles away."

Her voice startled me so that I dropped my Kindle on the hard, stone floor, causing the page I'd been reading to disappear. I stared at the blank page, afraid to glance up.

"Mom?" she said.

There she stood, not exactly as I remembered her from almost eight months earlier—a little heavier, no makeup, dishwater-blond hair that hadn't seen a stylist in a while—but unmistakably Portia.

I stood up and held out stiff arms, unable to speak during our lengthy hug. When I could finally get myself to talk, the words came out through muted sobs.

"You're home. For good? I hope for good. Tell me it's for good, Portia."

She nodded.

"Sit down. Tell me everything. Do you want anything to eat? Drink?"

"Water would be fine."

When I returned with a glass of water for her and eighteen-year-old Scotch and water over ice for me, we stared at each other for a long moment.

"Where's Dad?"

"In Florida with Grandma. She fractured her hip."

"Is she okay?"

"She will be."

"How long will he be there?"

I shrugged.

"Is everything okay with you guys?"

"Sure."

"Mom?"

"What?"

"Something's wrong."

"Nothing is wrong, sweetie."

"He's pretty pissed at me, isn't he?"

"Mmm."

"So maybe I should tell you everything first, and then you can tell Dad a filtered version of it?"

"Ugh, let's let him decide."

I texted Carl with the news and asked him if he wanted to be patched into the conversation.

Great news! Can't wait to talk to her, but now w/Mom and her doctors. Will call u back.

"Proceed. And start from the beginning."

For the next two hours, Portia told me about the recent months with her boyfriend Enrique at the commune in Costa Rica, with Carl calling in periodically to catch parts of it. She talked about the diverse culture of the hundred or so people who lived there, the spiritual awareness they gained through togetherness and aloneness, and their self-sufficiency through gardens and permaculture. She described the crudely built casita in which she and Enrique cohabited—five hundred square feet of living space in the middle of the rainforest with no electricity or indoor plumbing. She talked about the importance of simplicity, meditation, and living in harmony with the earth. And she talked about how behind our different personalities and cultures, we were all one, and explained that to fulfill our human potential we had to break away from our real self and move toward our ideal self.

"Why did you leave?"

"I hated it."

I took a long sip of Scotch.

"You hated it. But you just got done describing a—"

"Mom, can we agree on something?"

"That depends."

"That now that I've told you what a stupid thing I did, we can forget about it and go on from here. Except for organic food and maybe the colon hydrotherapy. And the liver cleansing."

"And your father? You think he'll be able to forget about it and go on from here?"

"Can't you talk to him? You're good at that."

Maybe the old me had been good at talking to the old Carl. Now, I wasn't so sure.

"What's wrong, Mom?"

"Nothing is wrong, Portia. I told you that."

"What are you going to tell him when he calls back?"

"I'm going to hand the phone to you. He wants to talk to you."

"I don't know…"

"What are you afraid of," I asked.

"Nothing, I guess."

"Where's Enrique?"

"He went back home."

"He hated it too?"

"Just as much as I did."

"So, are you still a couple?"

"That didn't work out so well either."

"Now, would you like to explain what colon hydrotherapy is?"

"Trust me. You don't want to know."

Chapter 7

"What's going on with Dad? He didn't call back yesterday after he was done with Grandma."

"I'm sorry honey. I forgot to tell you that he did. But it was late, and you'd already gone to bed. He said he'd call again today."

"I'm starting to think he doesn't want to talk to me, just him and me."

"Absolutely not true. He said he'll call you later today."

"Why does he have to take care of her down there? Why can't she come up here until she's better?"

"I suggested that, Portia, and he said that she wanted to be at home. So that's what he's doing."

"He doesn't care about us."

"Of course he does." I put my arms around her.

"You maybe."

"Right. Why do you think he was so upset when you disappeared with no way to get in touch with you?"

Her hands flew to her hips. "You said you'd let that go, Mom."

"Sorry, but it fit right into the conversation that *you* started."

She waved off the apology. "Do you feel okay?" she asked.

"Sure. Why?"

"You don't look so good."

"Maybe I'm tired." I told Portia about the bookstore.

"I thought you agreed that bookstore idea was a bad one."

"I never said that. Everyone else may have, but I never did."

"You don't have to get defensive about it. Anyway, I'm going to call Dad. Can I use your cell?"

"May I."

She rolled her eyes, bringing back memories of the teen years.

"I think that's a good idea. Here," I said as I handed her the phone.

After leaving the kitchen so she would have privacy for the call, I tried getting some work done, but I couldn't concentrate on anything for very long. With Portia home, my brain automatically focused on her—whether she'd be going back to college and how she would re-establish her relationship with Carl.

And while I didn't feel very good about it, I couldn't stop fantasizing about fish-hat guy—the way he'd looked at me with those soulful eyes.

I examined myself in the small hallway mirror. A stranger stared back. Portia was right—I didn't look good. Maybe that was why Carl didn't care much about me anymore.

A wave of inadequacy swept over me—in my marriage, in dealing with my twenty-year-old daughter, in keeping on track with the bookstore project, in my wounded relationship with Darlene. I looked at the now-wilted yellow rose Carl had brought home the previous week—something he often did when he'd been in the vicinity of the local florist. I had stuck it in a vase of sorts but failed to add water. I couldn't even nurture that right.

I fully realized Portia had been through a stressful ordeal in Costa Rica, and even though I'd tried during her homecoming, I didn't feel like I'd been emotionally there for her. I resolved to make it up to her after the call with her father. I opened my office door and heard her talking with Carl. When I heard her raise her voice, I crept closer for a better listen.

"Well, I'm sorry you feel that way, Dad. I thought maybe you'd be just a little understanding." She paused. "No, *you* be reasonable!" she said before dropping my phone on the kitchen table.

"Portia, is everything—"

"Can I borrow your car?"

"Sure. Where—"

"Just give me your keys. I'm outta here."

"Where are you—"

"Can I have your keys or not?"

Her disagreeable tone was enough to cause a tightness in my chest.

"Portia, I'm not sure you should—"

"Forget it then! I'll borrow Dar's," Portia screamed before snapping her head around and stomping away, leaving me and my phone behind in her acrimonious wake. When did she start calling her Dar? Only Carl called her that. What happened to Mrs. Richardson?

I collapsed into one of the club chairs and allowed the tears to fall without restraint. My mind drifted back to when Portia and I had such a great relationship—one I would have sworn would never change. She and I had forged so many relishable memories over the years—especially after we got through those early teenage years when I accepted the fact that purple hair and black-painted fingernails weren't the worst things in the world, and when she learned that responsibilities came with independence.

I thought of the time I drove her to college for the first time. We took Carl's SUV to move all her stuff, and even then, she had to do some picking and choosing because not everything fit. Carl followed in Portia's new Ford Mustang, our high school graduation present to her—the same car she sold to spend six months in Costa Rica with what's-his-name. I learned from my father that when you give someone a gift, it's theirs to do with as they wish. Accepting that premise when it came to Portia's car hadn't come easily, especially for Carl.

We talked about her career plans during the 350-mile drive to the University of Michigan, a school Portia had chosen because of its political science program, an area of study for which she'd had, at least back then, a deep passion.

"Tell me again why you think you want to get involved in politics after you graduate," I said to her. "You won't give any thought to something like teaching or nursing or interior design maybe? Politics is so…"

"Stressful? Complicated? Full of controversy?"

"Exactly."

"But, Mom, that's what's drawing me to it. You know what I loved most in high school? Being on the debate team. I loved going up against people with opposing viewpoints. You always said to do something in life you're good at. Well, I never lost a debate."

"So you're all about winning. What about learning something from the people with opposing viewpoints?"

"That's the beauty of being a politician—you have your own views and those from your constituents as well as the voters. Mix it all together, and you get to the truth."

"You make it sound easy. What about public scrutiny from those who don't agree with you?"

"I have a thick skin."

"The pay is not that good."

"Yeah, but the perks are."

"Whatever you choose to do, I'm sure you'll do it well."

"I'm not looking to change the world or anything, but maybe I can make a difference in the world on some small scale."

"I'm sure you can and will."

Looking back, I realized that was probably the first adult-to-adult conversation we'd had together. While what she had to say may have been somewhat naive, I found it interesting. Here she was talking about making a difference in the world someday, and I still thought about her as my little girl. Time to stop doing that.

We talked about so much during that car ride—about goofy things that had happened in her childhood, her best friends and where they were going to school, her old boyfriends, and the new horizons that lay ahead of her. I would never forget that trip and longed for those days to be back again.

The phone rang, making me jump.

"Is Portia there?"

"Hi, hon. No, she isn't. She stormed out of here right after your call."

"So, it's *my* fault?"

"I didn't say it was your fault."

"Sounded like it to me."

"Why are you taking this out on me? I'm the one who had to deal with the aftermath of your call."

"And how did that go for you?"

"Why are you being such a—"

"A what? An ass?"

"Carl—"

"So where did she go?"

I took a deep breath, determined to not let Carl goad me into an argument. "I don't know. When I didn't give her my car keys fast enough, she said she was going to try Darlene. I assume that's where she went."

"And so you called her?"

"Who?"

"Dar."

"No, I didn't."

"Why not?" he snapped.

"What exactly did you and Portia talk about that made her run out of here and you so ornery?"

"Ornery? You think I'm being ornery? Well, toots, you're making this really easy for me."

He hung up.

His words echoed in the room and then inside my head for the longest time. I reran the conversation in my mind trying to figure out what I'd said to deserve this reaction. Finding none and needing to release the tension that had built up inside me, I flung my phone, sending it across the room to smash into the expansive window overlooking the lake. When it hit the limestone tile floor with a thud, the phone went in one direction and its protective case went in another.

Get hold of yourself.

He had called me "toots." He'd never called me "toots" before.

Hey, wait a minute. Wait a goddamn minute.

I raced to my office and pulled *Blue Bonnet Hoers* off the shelf and furiously flipped through the pages searching for the pivotal restaurant scene. That took too long, so I sat down at my PC, opened the *Blue Bonnet Hoers* file, and searched for the word "toots."

"I knew it!" He'd read my books alright. I read the whole sentence out loud.

"You're making this really easy for me, toots!"

I stared out the window at the motionless lake and forced myself to soak in the calm for a moment, until the last tensed-up muscle in my body relaxed. I longed to call someone. But who? I thought of calling Lily, but then decided against it. Maybe being alone was better at a time like this.

Hoping I'd find something spirit-boosting in my e-mail Inbox, I waded through fifty meaningless messages, half of which would end up in the Junk folder when I reclassified them. But one from my attorney, Andrew Wooten, caught my eye. I clicked it open.

I'm sorry to inform you that the studio that was interested in *Rearview Mirror* has backed down, and without their commitment, the screenwriter isn't willing to risk buying the screen rights. If anything changes, I will let you know.

I reread the message in case, by some miracle, I had read it wrong the first time. I hadn't.

So much for spirit-boosting. At least I didn't have to tell anyone the deal had fallen through—only Carl had known about it in the first place, and at the moment, I didn't care much about telling him anything.

* * *

The man behind the counter took one look at my cell phone and said it wasn't fixable and suggested an upgrade rather than a replacement, something I was sure all cell-phone salespersons had been taught to say in such situations.

The tangled thoughts I had about Carl on the way home frustrated me. A month earlier, I would have brushed off his boorish behavior, thinking it was another one of his short-lived lapses in good judgement. But his recent ill-mannered conduct seemed to be his new norm, and I didn't understand it. Sure, he was under pressure regarding his mom, but that didn't excuse his rudeness toward me. I was his wife. I was on his side. At least, I thought I was…most of the time.

That S.O.B. had read my books, for sure. But denying it made no sense. It wasn't the first time I'd suspected he was trying to make me think I was losing my mind so he could…could what? I didn't know what. Leave me. Have me committed. Something. What would he gain if I wound up in a mental institution? Nothing. Maybe self-satisfaction, gratification, a sense of accomplishment. Or freedom. But a divorce would do that too.

I couldn't believe my thoughts had gone to divorce—our relationship surely hadn't deteriorated to that level. Though it may as well have since we were essentially separated.

Nothing stopped me from hopping on a plane and being with him to take care of his mother. I imagined he'd be very surprised to see me. But then Portia would be left alone. And the bookstore project would be delayed.

Portia. I didn't know whether I wanted her to be home when I got there.

After a quick visit to city hall to check on one of my bookstore permits,

I pulled into the driveway to find Darlene sitting on my front porch. I joined her as soon as I parked the car.

"Hey," I said as I sat down in the other chair.

"Hey," she said, her face void of any expression.

The strands of glittery black beads that layered her chest glinted in the sunlight, but there was nothing glittery about her expression.

"How are you?"

"I've been better."

"Not feeling well?"

She ignored my question.

"Look, about what's happened between us," I said, trying to lessen the tension in the air. "If it's because of something I said or did, I apologize. I didn't mean to. I don't know how it even got to this point, but I'd like for things to go back to how they were."

"Portia borrowed my car. I wish I hadn't said yes now. I need it."

So much for the olive branch.

"Why did you lend it to her? She could have borrowed mine or Carl's."

"I told her on Friday if she needed to borrow my car, she could. She always loved my car." Darlene drove a sporty red Porsche.

"What do you mean 'on Friday'?"

"The day she came home."

"She came home yesterday, Saturday."

Darlene's facial expression showed regret.

"Was it yesterday? I'm getting my days mixed up. Nothing has seemed right since Lance has been gone."

I let it go despite my wanting to know if Portia had arrived in town the day before she showed up at our door.

"How is he?"

"I suppose he's doing as well as expected."

"Is his memory coming back?"

"Some."

"His speech?"

"Not good."

"Where is he? Are you able to see him often?"

"The rehab place is in Lake Geneva. Half hour in good traffic," she said. "I won't go every day because he's always in physical therapy, or occupational therapy, or some damn therapy. And there's no set schedule.

Yesterday, I waited in the hallway for an hour and a half to see him for ten minutes. Waste of time."

"I'm sorry to hear that. Would you like something to drink? I have a bottle of Dr. Brown's in the fridge with your name on it."

"No, I'm just waiting for Portia. I need to go to the club, and I don't like driving Lance's car."

"I could drive you there if you want."

"No, that's okay."

"Did she say when she'd be back?"

"How's the bookstore coming along?"

"Fine. It's a lot of work."

"More than you anticipated?"

"Yes."

"Are you going to go ahead with it?"

"Yes, of course. Why do you ask?"

"Just curious."

For the next half hour, we each fought to invent enough small talk to fill the long stretches of silence. Finally, I looked at my watch. Three-thirty. Even though I generally followed the five o'clock rule when it came to drinking alcohol, I craved a glass of something. Darlene must have sensed my restlessness.

"You don't have to stay out here with me. I can wait for her alone."

"Don't be silly. Would you like to come in? I was thinking of pouring myself a glass of wine."

"No, thanks."

Things clearly weren't the same between us. We managed to keep a conversation going, albeit lacking in substance, for another fifteen minutes until Portia appeared on foot from around the hedge that separated our two yards. She handed the keys to Darlene.

"Thanks, Dar. You don't know how much I appreciated that." She walked past me without any acknowledgment.

"Any time, Portia. You know that."

Darlene got up to leave. I said, "See ya later," but she didn't respond.

I followed Portia into the house.

"So, where'd you go this afternoon?"

"What, I have to check in with you for my every move?"

Shades of her teenage years again flashed through my mind.

"Of course not. I asked because—"

"Because you want to keep an eye on me. I know."

"Portia, that is so not the case. What's gotten into you? I can't even talk to you."

She went to the kitchen and grabbed a beer from the fridge. "Oh, brother. Dar said you'd react this way."

"Since when did you start drinking beer?" Portia wouldn't turn twenty-one for another six months.

"Get real, Mom. How old were you when you had your first drink?"

"We're talking about *you*. And what do you mean by Darlene saying I'd react this way?"

"Never mind. I don't suppose Dad called back while I was gone."

"I don't know. I was out buying a new phone."

"What's with your old one?"

"Oh, I don't know. Maybe something happened to it when I threw it up against the wall earlier today." My voice may have been calm, but there was a storm going on inside my body.

I retreated to my office and called Carl.

"Can I call you back? There's a nurse here right now."

Of course there is.

Chapter 8

I stayed holed up in my office working on the bookstore marketing plan, leaving my safe haven only to fetch a bottle of wine and a glass. I had poured my second glass when Carl finally called back.

"What's up? You sounded upset," he said.

His voice triggered an emotion I wasn't expecting. "Things are falling apart here, Carl," I blurted out through my sobs.

"Okay, sweetie, get hold of yourself. What's going on?"

Before I could think it through, the words came out in rapid-fire succession, and once they started flowing, I couldn't stop. "Everything. You're there. I'm here. I've let things fall through the cracks for the bookstore. Then there's Portia, who I can't even talk to anymore. Darlene is giving me the cold shoulder. I don't know why. I broke my phone, and I don't know how to use half the stupid features on this new one. I haven't eaten all day, but I've had two glasses of wine. And you. You've read my books, every goddamn one of them. I *know* you have! I don't know where our marriage is headed. Maybe you do, but…"

"But what?"

"I think I'm done."

"Do you want to take these issues one by one?"

It irritated me that he was so in control when I felt like my life was falling apart. "Whatever," I said, now regretting the wine.

"I've only been gone a week. What's going on?"

"I don't know. You don't call very often, and when you do, we don't talk much. Not like before."

"Would you like to know how my typical day goes down here between taking care of Mom's needs and trying to work too? Not exactly a piece of cake, Mags. You know my mother—she isn't the easiest person to deal with in good health. It's harder now, believe me. There have been many nights I've collapsed on the bed too tired to even get undressed."

"I'm sorry. I know it hasn't been easy for you. I shouldn't have said anything about that."

"As far as Portia, you've got to give her some leeway. Imagine what she's been through. No wonder she seems like a different person—she probably is. Let her get angry—my guess is that she's angrier at herself than anyone else. And let her be herself, not the person you want her to be."

This didn't sound like the same Carl who was pushing for her to go to law school.

"I'm not— But what about her arriving in town on Friday and not showing up here until Saturday? And contacting Darlene before me?"

"I'm not surprised. She was probably unsure of how we'd react to her return and hesitated coming home."

"You knew she was at Darlene's the day before she came here?"

"Yes, I knew."

"How'd you know that?"

"Dar told me."

"She called you?"

"We talked."

"When?"

"I don't remember the exact date and time, if that's what you're asking."

"I'm right next door! Why didn't she contact me? Why didn't you tell me?"

"That was right after you'd insulted her at lunch. I suspect she wasn't feeling the love."

"What are you talking about? I never insulted her! And how'd you know that?"

"That you insulted her?"

"I didn't insult her!" I felt my face redden. "How'd you know we had lunch?"

"She told me, of course."

"She called you?"

"Or I called her. I don't remember."

"Must have been on one of those evenings you didn't collapse on the bed with your clothes still on."

"Look, Mags. Lance is my closest friend. And I'm worried about him. Very worried. I can't very well call him when he doesn't even remember who I am, so I call his wife, *our* friend. I don't understand why you have an issue with that."

I had no response. None that made any sense.

"Mags?"

"I'm still here." I was tired. Too tired to continue the conversation. Too tired to try to understand the mix of emotions I was having. "Maybe I just miss you."

"I miss you too. I'll be honest with you, when I came down here, I was sort of afraid you'd like it that I was gone so you could get more writing done—no interruptions, no one else to deal with. You could write like crazy, day and night, if you wanted."

"And the bookstore."

"Yeah, that too. Or you could give it up now. Cut your losses early."

I hung up on him, regretting it soon after.

* * *

The new day brought with it a serious headache but also a clearer understanding of the aggregate of Carl's recent conduct. He had lied to me about reading my books. His demeanor of late had been more than a little offish. He and Darlene had developed a close relationship and appeared to be hiding it from me. He thought I should give up on my dream, my aspiration, the most important thing in my life.

Carl had defended Portia's bad behavior. In fact, he had defended just about everyone in that conversation—his daughter, his best friend, his best friend's wife, himself—everyone but me. Not one bit of compassion for me—his wife—the one who was upset and crying.

If I were to have used such a narrative in one of my books, it would have been to spur the reader into thinking the husband was doing something sinister, like having an affair. And for all I knew, he and Darlene *were* having an affair, and Portia knew about it and maybe even supported it! That would explain why Darlene asked me those questions about whether

I trusted Carl. It would explain why he and Darlene talked on the phone so much, and why Portia went to her first when she came home. Well, maybe not that last one. It was understandable that Carl would gravitate to her—she was far more attractive than I, more fun to be with, and probably lonely with Lance gone. It all fit.

Carl had supposedly flown to Florida the day after Lance wound up in the hospital. Now I wondered if he was even in Florida. What if his mother never had an accident, that he'd made up the whole thing so he could be with Darlene. What if he'd had something to do with Lance's so-called accident? And what if he'd been next door this whole time, sleeping with Darlene?

While I showered and got ready for the day, I stewed over the thought of them being together. She was probably better in bed too.

* * *

At noon, I finally emerged from my bedroom, not feeling at all like myself, but not able to pinpoint exactly why. I peeked into the spare bedroom for Portia—the bed wasn't made. She had always been good about making her bed, even during those god-awful teen years. After checking the kitchen to see if she'd left a note, I called Darlene.

"No, she's not here, Mags."

Normally, she would have invited me over for a cup of coffee or something. Not this time. After all, how could she look me in the face if she was sleeping with my husband?

While certain Portia wouldn't have taken either vehicle without asking, I checked the garage just the same. Relieved I'd been right about that, I settled into the sunroom. That's when I discovered her—sitting on the edge of our small dock, half-hidden by shrubbery, with her knees tucked up under her chin staring out onto the water, like the answers to her problems were out there somewhere. Torn between going to her and leaving well enough alone, I opted for the latter. If the conversation didn't go well, the outer limit of our relationship would surely be tested.

A few minutes passed before Portia walked up the stone path toward the house, her pace slow and deliberate. I waved her inside.

"What?" she asked.

"Nothing. Just wanted your company, that's all."

"Right."

"Want to talk about it?" I asked her.

She slumped into the chair next to me, her long leg draped over the arm. "Talk about what?"

"What's bothering you."

"Nothing." Her gaze drifted out the window. "Everything."

"I know that feeling."

"Do you?"

"I think so."

We sat in silence for a long moment as we watched a line of sailboats lazily glide through the pristine water, each one barely leaving a wake.

"I slept with Eddie," she said. Her words came out fast, all run together. At first, I didn't think I'd heard her right.

"Eddie?"

"Eddie Richardson. Dar's son."

"What? How'd that happen? Never mind. I think I know how it happened. When was this?"

"Friday."

"This past Friday?"

"Mm-hm."

"Why?"

She let out a deep sigh. "When I got into town, I had the cab driver drop me off in the next block so I could gather my thoughts while I walked home. I saw Eddie going from his car to Dar's front door, and I stopped to talk to him. When I told him how nervous I was about coming home, he invited me in and we had a long talk."

"Where was Darlene?"

"At the hairdresser or someplace. Eddie had come over to take her shopping for something for the baby—I don't remember what."

"Go on."

"Anyway, we had a couple of beers, enough to get a good buzz going, and one thing led to another, and…"

"And you had sex?"

"Yeah."

"Portia!"

"What?"

"For starters, he's married."

"So?"

"So? How can you say that?"

"No one cares about that anymore, Mom. Get with it."

"Well, I do. I still care about that. Where did this take place?" For some reason, I pictured them rolling around on the living room floor.

"On their boat."

"That was so wrong, Portia."

"Spare me a lecture, okay? It's not like I make a habit of it or anything."

Apparently, that was supposed to make me feel better.

"Then why did you do it this time?"

"I don't know. I always kind of had a crush on him, that hair of his, and he was saying all the right things, and I guess I was pretty vulnerable, and the alcohol."

I shook my head. "Now what?"

"Now what, what?"

"How'd you leave it with him?"

"His mom called him from in the house right afterward and asked him where he was. He told her I had stopped by and we were checking out the boat. She invited me in the house, and we talked a while."

"And you didn't feel uncomfortable talking with her after what you'd just done?"

"Nope."

"I don't understand how— So where did you go after that?"

"They dropped me off at the Quality Inn."

"Instead of coming here."

"I wasn't ready."

"I see. Well, no, I don't. Anyway, you haven't talked to him since?"

She shook her head.

"He never called you or—"

"It was just a booty-call, Mom. Get over it."

In my mind, there was no such thing as "just a booty-call." There was always something more to it than that.

I tried to focus on the positive—it was a pleasant surprise that Portia had chosen to confide in me. I didn't want to blow it by being overly judgmental. And confessing to me seemed to allow her old self to reappear.

During the days that followed, in between my meeting with myriad contractors for the bookstore, Portia and I had many more talks—about her life at the commune and her relationship with Enrique. The Portia I knew and loved slowly emerged. But she didn't talk about her future plans, how long she intended to stay at home, whether she'd be returning to college. Finally, after a few days, I confronted her about it.

"Look, I came home to what I thought was a soft place to land after what I'd gone through, and all you keep asking about is when I'm going to leave. Where's the love, Mom?"

"I just want you to have plans, that's all. Get back into some good routine. Like school."

"Do you know that 25 percent of kids my age return home after having been out of the house? Many of them stay well into their thirties."

"No, I didn't know that."

"They call us the boomerang kids."

"Wouldn't you rather be part of the majority—the non-boomerang kids?"

"More than 50 percent are still financially dependent on their parents even after leaving home."

"Something is wrong with that picture."

"It's life, Mom."

"Not when I was your age."

"Oh, please, am I going to get a lecture about how you and Dad—?"

"No, I'll spare you. Besides, you already know how it goes."

"Next you'll be giving me a curfew."

"The thought did cross my mind. Along with you contributing to the household some."

"Like what?"

"Some chores, maybe? Like maybe you should do something to help keep this place neat and clean."

"Really, Mom?"

I hadn't intended to make a big issue of this, but I wasn't about to back down either.

"You didn't even make your bed this morning. And I found an empty milk carton on the—"

"You're something else, you know that?" Portia shrieked before leaving the room.

I didn't know which one of was being unreasonable. Portia had changed since Costa Rica. But, so had I.

* * *

Later that day, Carl called to tell me he had spoken with Lance over the phone, and he had sounded good—acknowledging Carl, Darlene, and even asking about me.

"That's great. I'm so happy for him."

"And what about Dar?"

"What about her?"

"You're not happy for her?"

"Of course I am. Why would you ask that?"

"She's going through a lot too, you know."

"Of course she is."

Trying to steer the conversation back on track, I asked him if Lance remembered what happened to him.

"Dar doesn't think so."

"We may never know what happened," I said.

"And maybe that's better," he said airily.

I thought that an odd response but didn't call him on it.

"I just got off the phone with Portia," he said. "I'm glad she's decided to go back to school."

"What?"

"College. Ohio State."

"When?"

"September. She said you two talked."

"Right. We did."

I hoped I'd been influential in her decision in some way.

"How's Katherine?" I asked.

"The same."

"Is she available?"

"She's napping."

"Well, tell her I said 'hello.'"

After hanging up the phone and thinking about our conversation, I wasn't sure if I even wanted Carl to come home. He never asked how I was doing. Didn't seem to care about me—just his mother, Portia, Lance, and Darlene.

I couldn't help but think about Carl and Darlene having an affair. Sort of ironic—Darlene having an affair with my husband, and her son with my daughter. Lance and me getting together would complete the absurd circle.

Feeling guilty that I hadn't talked to Darlene lately to see how Lance was doing, I called her.

"You must be so relieved." I told her.

"Yes, of course," she said, her voice teetering on the edge of indifference.

"His memory must have come back suddenly, then."

"On everything related to real estate it did. He still has lapses for most everything else."

"Will he be coming home soon?"

"Maybe as soon as Friday. That's when he sees his primary doctor."

"I'll bet he's eager to come home."

"I suppose."

Chapter 9

"I'm flying home tomorrow," Carl said.

"Really?"

"Mom's doctor has given her a clean bill of health, and she's agreed to having this one nurse's aide she befriended come each morning to check on her."

"That's wonderful, Carl. What time does your flight get in? I'll pick you up."

"Portia's going to pick me up. That way we can talk on the way home. We need to do that."

"Sure. I think that's a good idea." Portia hadn't mentioned that to me. "I guess I'll see you tomorrow then."

"Bye. Hey, have you given any more thought to the bookstore?"

"Yes, I have. Bye."

I found it amazing how one man, in one brief phone call, could have such an adverse effect on me. To prevent my mind from going places I didn't want it to go, I threw myself into *Stand-Alone Groom* and by five o'clock had written an entire chapter. I spent the next hour gathering end-of-the-month sales figures for each of my books.

Most of my book royalties came from Kindle books, and most of those came from royalties I received from the Kindle lending library. For every page read, I received approximately one-half of a cent. That didn't sound like much, but when your readers collectively averaged more than a million pages a month, like mine did, it added up quickly. I was surprised that the month of May did not disappoint me, as I'd spent so much more time with the bookstore than I did promoting my books.

I joined Portia in the kitchen.

"I saw you had a whole roast in the oven, way too much for the two of us, so I invited Dar to join us for dinner," Portia said.

Portia loved pot roast, and I had planned the meal with her in mind… her alone. Darlene was the last person I wanted to dine with.

"That's nice, dear, but won't you—"

"You're still not over that, are you?"

"No, I'm not."

"Dad once told me that the best way to hide an indiscretion is to act like it never happened."

Really? Carl actually said that?

"Did I say something wrong?" she asked.

"No. Not at all. I'm a little surprised she accepted though. Lance is coming home tomorrow. I would have thought she'd have to prepare for that."

"Well, she said she'd love to, so…"

"When did you tell her to come over?"

"Seven."

"I had it planned for six."

"It'll stay hot. No problem," she said before leaving the room.

I called Darlene to see if she could come at six.

* * *

Darlene didn't talk much during dinner, and when she did, it was to ask something about Carl or Carl and me, making me extremely uneasy…and suspicious. But not as suspicious as when she asked me if I was going to continue with plans for the bookstore.

After Darlene finally left, I said something to Portia.

"You're reading way too much into it, Mom. She didn't mean anything by it."

"Why would she ask me if I was going to continue with the bookstore? I never said anything about not continuing with it."

"C'mon, Mom. Even you must admit, it's a crazy idea. Nobody reads books anymore, not in paper form anyway. And you've said yourself there are too many bad self-published authors out there."

"Gee, thanks for your support."

She came to me and gave me a hug.

"Sorry, Mom. Just trying to be real with you."

After I cleared the table and loaded the dishwasher, I joined Portia as she nursed a beer. We watched an episode of *The First 48.*

"So, you're going to pick up Dad at the airport tomorrow?"

"Yep."

"Are you two okay?"

"Sure. Why do you ask?"

Because your lying father led me to believe you weren't.

"No reason. Can I ask you something, Portia?"

"Sure. What?"

"Why didn't you let us know when you dropped out of school and went to Costa Rica? I thought we had a better relationship than that."

"I knew you and Dad would be pissed, and to be honest, I was so into Enrique that going with him without stirring up things with you guys was my focus."

"Would you say you were a little blindsided by him?"

"Maybe."

"And while you were there with him, the same thing?"

"I don't know. Maybe. But you know how it is—once you're into it up to your knees, it doesn't make much difference if it rises up to your thighs."

"I guess that's one way of looking at it. If you had it to do over, would you do it the same way?"

Portia shrugged. "Maybe. I don't know."

I didn't like her answer…at first. But the more I thought about it, the more I thought I should be more like her. Carefree. Live for the moment. Don't worry about what others think or feel. "There's a happy medium that exists in most things," my father used to say to me. Maybe. But not when it came to sleeping with another woman's husband.

* * *

The following day, when a local culinary shop offered a series of wine-pairing classes, I jumped at it. Carl knew his wines. I didn't, something that had been confirmed the previous winter when I'd used a $300 bottle of cabernet sauvignon in a beef bourguignon recipe.

Taking small breaks from writing had its benefits as well—they tended to clear my head, giving me the ability to write fewer words of higher quality that required less revision later. The first class was being held on the same day Carl was coming home, and when Portia called from the airport to tell me his plane had been delayed, I had to decide whether to go to the class as planned or skip it and be home when he arrived. Portia encouraged me to go to the class, and so I did.

The small group consisted of two men and four other women. Normally, I was a social person in groups, and I even thought maybe I could have befriended someone there, but on this night, I had little interest in talking to the others in attendance. It had nothing to do with them—they appeared to be nice enough people—it was all on me. The class was moderately interesting, but I was eager to get home to see my husband for the first time in almost two weeks.

As I was walking back to my car, I noticed a pawn shop Carl had recently mentioned. I often went into pawn shops in Chicago—finding them inspirational in my writing, especially if the proprietor was talkative. One of my best plots had been hatched while browsing a pawn shop.

When I got home, Carl and Portia were engrossed in some horrific video game and initially ignored my greeting. When I repeated myself, Carl stopped playing and jumped up to give me a hasty kiss. Then he went back to playing.

"Game's almost over, hon," he said.

There was a time when I was the most important thing on his mind.

I went to the kitchen to toss a tissue in the garbage when I noticed an empty bottle of Dr. Brown's in the can.

"So, was Darlene here while I was gone?" I asked him.

No response.

I headed to my office and busied myself with work, hoping it would distract me from my worries, which I was beginning to fear could make me physically ill.

A recent reviewer had given *Almost Murder* five stars and said, "The whole book played out with fluid intrigue and left me wanting more with every page." Now that was the kind of review I liked to receive. Unlike the one directly beneath it submitted by someone called Lover of Good Books.

This book does not rate even one star. It deserves nothing. It is the worst book I have ever read. It is boring, like a very poorly written story by a five-year-old. I would not give this book even one star but the only way for me to comment was to tick a star! I will never read another book by this author ever again. Absolute rubbish.

Almost Murder had more than five hundred reviews averaging 4.3 out of five stars, making this review clearly an outlier. But it still irritated me. I dug a little deeper into the reviewer's identity—she (I don't know why I assumed it was a woman) offered no information about herself. I searched for her other reviews and Amazon wish list. Nothing there except my book. When this sort of thing happened, I had to wonder if it was a competitor of mine who thought trashing my book would make hers look better. Unfortunately, that happened in the publishing business.

I read the other new reviews, which were all good, and then focused on e-mails. Afterward, I joined Carl and Portia who were watching the news.

"So, how was the class?" he asked.

"It was okay. Covered basic wine facts. The next one pairs wine with seafood, so I hope it's a little more exciting."

"Big class?"

"Seven of us."

"Where do you have to park for that class anyway?" he asked.

"There's a lot in the back."

"Did you walk out together? There's not that much activity in that section of Main Street this time of night. May not be that safe."

"I've never heard of anything happening right in town like that."

"Says here the last murder in East Troy was in 2007," Portia said, peering down at her cell phone. "Four rapes and two other assaults here last year though."

"Those must have been on the bad side of town," I said.

"I didn't know there *was* a bad side of East Troy," said Portia.

"There's a bad side of every town, sweetie," Carl explained. "And sometimes bad things happen on the good side of town. Just be safe when you go there, hon."

"Why all this talk about crime all of a sudden? I went to a wine class on Main Street in a perfectly safe area."

"We were playing a *Hunger Games* video," Portia said. "That may explain things."

"Well, don't come crying into our room when you wake up in the middle of the night having nightmares," I told her.

"Mom, I haven't done that since I was seven."

"Yeah, well. I'm tired and going to bed," I said, hoping that would be a clue for Carl to follow me into the bedroom. It didn't work.

* * *

Over the next few days, things continued to feel strained between Carl and me—his actions and dialogue passed the "being nice" test but were too rote and shallow to be genuine. Like when I mentioned feeling tired lately and said I planned on getting a physical when we returned to Chicago. That day, he came home with Chinese carry-out for dinner and a bouquet of flowers. He'd never picked up carry-out on his own before, and he usually brought me one rose, not a whole bouquet. And he spent more time away from home than before, saying he needed to meet with someone, or go to the library, or the gym. When he was at home, he was present physically but seemed to be somewhere else mentally.

When he came home one day from a local men's clothing store with a shopping bag that contained two pairs of washed-out jeans and a bomber jacket, I commented on his new taste in clothes.

"Can't a man buy some new clothes every once in a while?" he asked.

Even his body language seemed different to me.

"You've never bought clothes like that in your life. Why now?"

"Maybe I need a change," he said.

* * *

Lance came home the day after Carl got back. I called to invite him and Darlene over for a happy reunion, but Darlene told me it was too soon. After several days, I still hadn't seen either of them. But Carl managed to go next door many times, always when I wasn't home.

"How is Lance doing?" I asked him one evening after dinner. Portia was out shopping for clothes for school, and Carl and I were watching TV.

"Doing well, I think."

"You think? You've been over there enough times since he's been home. Don't you talk to him when you're there?"

"Of course I do." He mumbled something under his breath I didn't catch. "Maybe I should have said, 'Doing well, *in my opinion.*' I should be more exact with my words when I'm talking to you."

"No need to get sarcastic. What do you two talk about when you're there? Is he back to being the normal Lance? Talking Shakespeare. Any plans for his boat?"

"Something like that."

"None of my business, in other words."

"What's with you? He had a terrible accident. He's home now, and all I've done is check in with him a few times. What's wrong with that?"

"How's Darlene? I haven't talked to her since he's been home."

"Call her. Walk over there. See for yourself."

The tension present in his tone, in the whole room, was unsettling.

That evening, I poked my head out the patio door and told Carl I was leaving for my wine class.

"So early?"

"I want to stop in that pawn shop near there to see what they've got."

"Have fun."

Comprised of a half-dozen or so tall glass cases and four waist-high ones that doubled as a counter, Casa de Pawn didn't occupy much more than five hundred square feet. Before walking over to the first case, I said hello to an older man with a large pot-belly and gin-blossomed nose sitting behind the counter.

The Polly Pretend doll caught my attention and brought back unsettling memories. My father had given me that doll the first Christmas after Mom left. The doll came equipped with a trunk full of mommy shoes, hats, curlers, jewelry, and other stuff you could put on the doll to dress it up like a mommy. Why he'd bought that particular doll baffled me. Perhaps it was the first doll he saw in the store, and he grabbed it.

"Looking for anything in particular, Miss?" the proprietor asked as he cleaned under the nails of his cigar-like fingers with a pocketknife.

"No. Just browsing. I suppose you get some pretty interesting things in here."

"Sometimes."

Nothing of interest in the next few cases—musical instruments, electronics, video games. The cases that served as a counter separating the proprietor from the customers displayed guns, coins, baseball cards, and a variety of jewelry. I perused the jewelry.

"Lots of wedding rings in here," I said. "Sad."

"Yep."

My eyes focused on an item in the far corner of the case, behind all the jewelry—a hand-painted porcelain Limoges trinket box shaped like the Eiffel Tower. My heart raced.

"May I see the Limoges box please?"

He unlocked the case and handed it to me. The first thing I did was open it to see if there was an earring inside. Finding it empty, I asked him how much it was.

"Two seventy-five."

I'd paid two hundred for the same box several years earlier.

"That's a little high, don't you think?"

"It's market value, and it's firm."

"May I ask you where it came from?"

"I can't tell you that."

"Why not?" I knew darn well why not, but I wanted to see if he did.

"FTC rule."

"I see."

"Can you tell me if you bought it outright from him or—"

"No."

"I'll give you two hundred for it," I found myself saying without thinking it through.

"Two fifty."

"Two twenty-five."

"Two fifty."

"Do you accept credit cards?"

"Yep."

I left the shop with a painful tightness in my chest. I had just bought back my own trinket box—I was sure of it. And Carl had something to do with it being there. I walked toward my car at a fast pace—every muscle in my body now tense—when I remembered the wine class. With the key already in the car door, I hesitated before pulling it back out. The classes had been paid for, and if I came home early, I'd have to explain myself.

After class ended, I walked into the freedom of the still night air toward my car, the only one parked in the dimly lit lot behind the shop. With no reason to feel unsafe, still I clutched my handbag—which contained the precious Limoges box—tightly under my arm and hurried to my car. Then, feeling slightly foolish, I took my time unlocking the door.

"Gimme your purse," he demanded. Dressed in dark clothing and wearing sunglasses, the man appeared to come out of nowhere.

"No!" I said loudly, my voice quivering. I slipped the rest of the way into the driver's seat and attempted to close the door, but he grabbed the door handle, preventing the door from closing. Small for a man, he was nevertheless stronger than me, and I couldn't pull the door all the way closed.

"Don't be stupid, lady. Hand it over to me."

My hands trembled as I reached over for my purse, which I'd thrown on the passenger's seat. I pulled out my wallet. "You can have all my money, but not my purse."

"Hurry up!"

In a move that surprised even me, I threw all the bills from my wallet at him, and when his guard was down, I slammed the door shut and locked it. I fumbled with the car keys in the ignition for what seemed like an eternity, and when the car finally started, I threw it into drive and rammed my foot against the gas pedal until I reached a safe distance. My beloved Limoges box was safely in my possession—the box that now had cost me over five hundred dollars if you counted the first time I'd bought it and the money just stolen.

I stopped in a grocery store parking lot to collect my thoughts, white knuckles still gripping the steering wheel. The attempt I made to calm the trembling that wracked my body failed as I considered whether to report the incident to the police.

The protagonist in *Rearview Mirror* had been faced with the same dilemma—whether to report a mugging. She didn't because she suspected she knew her mugger, and she had bigger issues with him. I didn't recognize my mugger, but someone I did know could have been behind it—someone who wanted to make a point about it not being safe to park in a desolate parking lot late at night.

My first instinct told me to not report it. I wasn't hurt. He hadn't threatened me with a weapon or anything. And I didn't want Carl or Portia to know.

On the other hand, if Carl had had something to do with it, he'd expect me to tell him what happened and report it. But would Carl have actually gone that far?

I realized I was foolish to think like this because Carl would never have done such a thing.

Chapter 10

"How was class?" Carl asked as soon as I walked through the door.

"Fine."

"Find anything at the pawn shop?"

You know damn well what I found there.

"It's a small shop. Not much inventory."

"Dar and Lance came over while you were gone," Portia said.

"Did they? How's Lance?"

"He looked good to me. Knew who I was and everything."

"Is he back to work yet?"

"He's still home and driving Dar a little crazy."

"Darlene said that?" I asked.

"When is your next class?" Carl asked.

"Friday." I hadn't made up my mind yet if I wanted to continue with the last three classes, not only because of the mugging but also because I didn't feel much like spending time with those people. Any people really, outside of my family, and even them at times.

"The Richardsons asked us if we wanted to go out on their boat on Friday."

I had so hoped that custom had died.

"He feels up to it?"

"I don't think he would have asked if he didn't."

"Well, I can either skip the class or maybe join you afterward." Or maybe try to start rebuilding my relationship with Portia, which was much more important to me than being with the Richardsons. It felt empty with her home without the connection we once had.

"Up to you," Carl said without taking his eyes off his laptop. "But if you come late, you'll miss the sunset, sort of the whole point of going out on the boat."

If it was really up to me, he wouldn't be making a case for me to go out on their stupid boat. The wine class was the lesser of the undesirable options.

"We'll see."

Before going to bed that night, I slipped the Limoges box into the locked drawer where I'd always kept it. Lying there sleepless for about an hour, I came up with a slew of different ideas about how to handle Carl, most of which I discarded after thinking them through.

* * *

We hadn't had sex since Carl had come home. He had been away for twelve days, and that had been the longest we'd ever gone without it. Twice I had tried to initiate it, and each time he'd come up with some excuse. The first time, he told me he was expecting a call from his mother's doctor, who tended to call late in the evening. Sure enough, her doctor did call. The second time, I tried after a lengthy call with his mother, and he said he wasn't up to it. I could appreciate that too.

The next day, I vented my concerns to Lily, telling her I wanted the old Carl back, the man I married.

"Did you really have that good of a marriage?" she asked.

"Yes. Sort of."

"Are you sure?"

"I think so. I don't know. No, I'm not sure."

When I brought up the issue of his lack of interest in sex, she responded without hesitation. "Give him time to get back to his normal routine," she'd said. "Men are like lab rats—mess with their normal routine and they get stressed out over the smallest things. In the meantime, enjoy your time off." Lily, who had been married for ten years before discovering her preference for women, didn't always have the highest regard for men or their habits.

* * *

"I hope you don't mind, but I think I'm going to keep my wine class tonight," I told Carl.

"Fine. I'm sure the Richardsons will miss you," he said flatly without looking up at me from his precious laptop.

"Where's Portia? I'll ask her if she wants to go."

"She doesn't."

"You asked her?"

"Mm-hm."

"Where is she anyway?" It was noon, and she wasn't in her bedroom. I had not seen her yet that day.

"Out."

"Is something wrong, Carl?"

"No. Why?"

"Do you think you could drag yourself away from that thing for a minute and talk to me?"

Our eyes held each other's briefly, but I couldn't read him, couldn't make out the unspoken words I knew lurked below the surface of his gaze.

"I'm working against a tight deadline," he said calmly.

"Sorry. I won't bother you again."

"Wait, Mags. I—"

I left the room before he had a chance to finish his thought.

Carl had not ever had a "tight deadline" like this before. Sure, annual budget deadlines plagued him every year and there were occasional project deadlines, but none of these had ever interfered with our relationship. I considered whether I should check his call history but quickly realized how difficult that would be since he never parted with his phone. When I'd commented on his new habit of wearing his cell phone in a belt holster, he'd said he didn't want to miss calls about or from his mother.

Curious deadlines, excessive concern for his mother, lack of interest in sex. None of it passed the smell test.

Having no intention of attending the wine class, I parked my car in the far corner of the local movie theater parking lot, purchased a ticket for *Manglehorn*, and settled in for a relaxing evening.

After the first twenty minutes of watching Al Pacino play the part of a small-town locksmith with a dark past, I was wishing I'd chosen something else. This movie didn't seem to suit him. I took in the film with only half of my brain, while the other half ruminated on my unsettling relationship with Carl. I thought way back to the beginning. We'd met shortly after I had turned twenty-six and he thirty-four. We married a year later. The only knowledge I had about his past was based on what he'd told me. He'd brought no friends into the relationship and no relatives except for his mother. How would I know if any of what he'd told me was true? None of what he'd ever told me sounded suspicious at the time, but now I wasn't so sure.

When I arrived home, I found Portia glued to the TV and Carl to his laptop, which he shut off as soon as I walked into the room.

"How was class?" he asked.

"Fine."

I headed toward my office.

"Hey, come sit with us for a while. Can I pour you a glass of wine?"

"No thanks. I had one in class."

He laughed. "Since when do you stop at one glass of wine?"

"Since when do you grill me on it?"

"Mags, what's—"

I dashed out of earshot before he finished his sentence. I regretted not being more prepared for what I was going to say when I got home.

"Do you want to tell me what's going on?" Carl asked when he entered my office.

"Nothing's going on."

"The place where you signed up for the wine classes called to say the class had been cancelled. The instructor was sick."

"I know, I—"

"Tell me what's going on with you," he said in a calm voice. He scooted over to me and reached out to hug me, but I didn't want to be hugged, so I jumped up and ran into the bathroom, choking back the tears and slamming the door behind me.

"May I come in?" he asked through the door. It bugged me that he correctly used the word "may." Carl was not a stickler for proper word usage and normally would have said, *"Can* I come in." Another indication he'd read my books. He was such a liar.

"Mom?"

Portia must have heard the door slam.

"I need to be alone for a minute," I told them through the door. "Okay, guys?"

"Okay," Carl said. Portia said nothing.

* * *

The next morning, I awoke early, alone in bed with a tight stomach and feeling feverish. After a quick shower, I made myself a cup of tea and went to work in my office, hoping to take my mind off Carl and my stomach. Before I turned on the PC, I removed the Limoges box from the locked drawer and put it next to the monitor where I could gaze at it while I worked.

"Hey, Mom."

Startled by Portia's abrupt greeting, my hand jerked the teacup I held, spilling some of its contents on the papers on my desk. I grabbed a tissue to mop it up.

"I'm sorry, Mom. I didn't mean to—"

"That's okay. I—"

"Your Limoges box! I thought you'd lost it."

"Who told you that?"

"Dad."

I hadn't remembered telling Carl about the missing Limoges box.

"I never lost it."

"But something happened to it, right?"

"Yes. It was stolen, but I found it in a pawn shop."

"Stolen? You guys had a break-in? He didn't tell me that!"

I shrugged.

"How do you know it's the same one?"

"I know it is. Too many coincidences. Mine goes missing, and then one shows up at the local pawn shop? C'mon."

She stared at me for a long moment without saying anything. I stared back.

"Well…I'm glad you found it."

"Me too."

"Where's Dad?"

"I don't know. I woke up this morning, and he wasn't in bed. I haven't looked for him."

Portia's eyes widened.

"What?"

"Don't you care where he is?"

"He's a big boy. He doesn't need me to look after him."

She left without saying anything more.

I wasn't his keeper.

Letting several minutes pass, guilted by Portia's disapproval, I searched the house for Carl. When I observed him talking to Lance and Darlene out in the yard, I took the opportunity to snoop on his laptop.

He had cleared his Internet search history. What didn't he want me to see? I opened Excel and tried to access the most recent file he had opened—password protected. I did the same in Word—same thing.

It occurred to me that I'd left my fingerprints on his laptop, so I went to the kitchen to find something to use to wipe it clean. When I returned with a microfiber cloth, I found Carl sitting in one of the club chairs.

"What's that for," he asked.

"What?"

"The wadded-up cloth you're clinging to."

I walked over to the sliding glass door and pretended to wipe something off of it. "A smear mark that was bugging me. Got it." I sat down in the other club chair. "So, what did Lance and Darlene have to say?"

"They asked if we wanted to join them at the club for dinner tonight."

"What did you tell them?"

"That I'd talk to you first."

"Hmm."

"Eddie and his wife will be there. And Portia if she wants to."

"Special occasion?"

"No. Or maybe there is. Another step closer to normalcy for Lance?"

"Oh."

"You want to go?"

I hated that place. "Sure. How was he last night on the boat?"

"Like his old self. Well, almost. He slipped and called me Craig once. Then he laughed, caught his error right away."

"What time is dinner?"

"Seven."

"Good. That gives me all day to write." I got up to leave.

"I thought maybe we could take in a movie this afternoon. I see *Manglehorn* is playing locally. Al Pacino."

"Why that film?" I asked in a raised voice I couldn't control.

His blank stare annoyed me.

"Why that—"

"Why are you shouting at me?" he asked. "I thought you liked Al Pacino."

"You're too much, you know that?"

I left the room before he could say anything more. "I see *Manglehorn* is playing locally." He *never* knew what was playing in the theaters—he *always* relied on me to find that out and suggest a movie. That lousy— He *knew* I'd been at the movies the night before. And another thing, he had never asked me where I was when I was supposed to be at the wine class— one more indication that he knew.

I went to work, and before I realized it, I'd written two chapters in *Stand-Alone Groom*. A rap on my office door caused me to jump.

"You need to be ready to go in ten minutes," Carl said through the door.

"Fine."

I waited for him to leave, and when I opened the door, Portia stood before me, a funereal expression on her face.

Chapter 11

"What's the matter, Portia? You look like you just lost your best friend?"

"I did," she said, a distant empty stare on her face.

"Who?"

"Enrique."

"Talk to me while I get dressed. What happened?"

"He went back to Costa Rica. I don't know, maybe I do know. I don't know," she said through sobs.

"Portia, you're not making any sense."

I put my arm around her and led her into my room.

"Apparently, after he got there, he was gathering wood for a campfire when he slipped and fell down a ravine. His sister said he hit his head. Never came out of it."

"He died?"

"Yes," she said, swallowing hard.

"Maggie!" Carl yelled from another part of the house. "I'm ready to go."

"I'll stay here with you if you want. We don't have to go to dinner with them."

"No, you go. I'll be fine."

"No, I don't want to leave you at a time like this."

"It's no big deal."

"Yes, it is."

"But this is the first time that you guys are going out with the Richardsons since his accident. I'll be fine, Mom. Really. In fact, I'd rather be alone for a while."

"If you're sure."

"I'm sure. Give the others my regrets. Maybe next time."

"We'll talk more when I get back then." I gave her a long hug. "I'm so sorry, Portia."

"Wait. Don't go. I haven't been truthful with you."

I turned toward her.

"While I was in Costa Rica, I..."

"What honey?"

"I had a…"

"What? You had what?"

"A baby."

"What?"

A cold, heavy sensation expanded through my core as she spoke.

"A girl."

"Portia, why didn't you say something? We could have— We would have—"

"C'mon girls," Carl said in a loud voice before entering the room. "Let's go."

"We're not going," I said. "Portia is—"

"I'm not feeling well, Dad. You go on ahead."

"Mags?"

"I'm going to stay here with her. Give our regrets to Darlene and Lance."

"Fine."

"He sounds perturbed," Portia said.

"He'll get over it. Tell me what happened."

When Portia told me she'd found out she was pregnant shortly after arriving in Costa Rica, I felt like the worst mother in the world—I should have been there for her. If I'd raised her better, she wouldn't have hidden it from me.

"She was premature—I never got to see her."

"Why not? They didn't let you see her?"

"I was in so much pain. I didn't know what was happening. And Enrique was by my side, concerned about me. We just let the people there take care of her until I felt better. Stupid, I guess, looking back."

"Where did you have her? In a hospital?"

"In a birthing center."

"Where's the baby?"

"She died three days later. Or so that's what we were told."

"Portia!"

"I know. It all sounds so, I don't know, surreal."

"You sound like you're unsure whether she died."

"We weren't at first, but days later, when we caught wind of the human trafficking and illegal adoption problems there, we started to question it."

"Was there a funeral?"

"Where I was, they were mostly Evangelicals. They don't believe in embalming dead bodies, so burials happen really fast, sometimes the same day the person dies. Little Evangeline was buried the day after she died when I was still hurting. I never actually saw her—the little coffin was closed, and I was still feeling so lousy…"

"Evangeline. What a pretty name."

"Mm-hm."

"This had to be devastating for you."

"Still is."

She put her head in her hands and sobbed.

"That's why Enrique went back there—to find out the truth."

I sat next to her, but comforting her was impossible.

"What do you think now?"

"I don't know what to think."

"I wish I could say something to make you feel better, but—"

"That's not the worst of it," she said, now bawling.

"What? What is it?"

"I never wanted the baby. It wasn't planned. I wasn't ready. It's all my fault!"

"Sweetheart, you can't blame yourself."

"If I'd wanted her, maybe none of this would have happened."

Her words unnerved me—I'd never told her the whole story about my mother. I so wanted to be there for her, protect her. I didn't want to be like my mother.

"How many weeks was she premature?"

"We think ten weeks."

"That's a lot, sweetie. Three or even four weeks early is generally not a problem, but ten…"

"I know. That's what everyone told me."

Portia jumped up from her seat. "I want to go back there, Mom. She may be alive."

"Honey, what makes you think you'll find out any more than before?" All I could think about was what had just happened to Enrique when he had gone back there.

"I have to, Mom. Don't you see?"

"Did you receive medical treatment there while you were pregnant?"

"The local *buhuitihu* saw me."

"The who?"

"That's what they called the doctors in the little village we were in."

"Sweetie…maybe you should see a doctor here, just to make sure you're alright."

"I'm fine."

"Just to make sure."

"I'm going to go back there. I need to find answers."

"Could you try calling them first?"

"I suppose, but going there would be a lot better."

"Then I'll go with you," I said before I comprehended the full impact of my words.

"No, I'll go alone. I got myself into that mess. It's my responsibility. And besides, you'd hate it there."

"I'm not going to let you go back there by yourself, Portia. And that's final."

"But what about the bookstore? You have a date set for the opening and everything."

"That can wait. It's a thing. You're you."

"I'll call first. There was this one local woman who worked at the U.S. Embassy we befriended but who was out of the country when all this happened. Maybe she can find something out for me."

"Okay, but if you end up going back there, I'm going with. No more discussion."

She saluted me.

"Don't get smart with me."

"I take it your father doesn't know about any of this."

"Are you kidding? It was hard enough telling you."

"Tell me something, Portia. Is that why you didn't keep in touch with us while you were there?"

"That was part of it. I didn't know how to deal with it on my own, so how could I involve someone else?"

"But that's when you *should* involve someone else," I said, knowing I probably would have done the same thing.

"I know."

"You said that was just part of it."

"I didn't want you to know about Enrique."

"Why not?"

"You guys wouldn't have liked him."

"Why not?"

"Well, he was into campanology and stuff."

"Something to do with camping?"

"Bells."

"What?"

"The art of ringing bells."

"There's a field dedicated to that?"

"It's more complicated than you think."

"Okay, so that's not a reason we wouldn't have liked him."

"He had a lot of tattoos."

"So?"

"Of bells."

"I can think of worse tattoos."

"Like the Taco Bell logo on his ass."

"I see. Well, no, I don't see. I don't want to see. I mean—"

"You wouldn't have liked him, Mom. Just take my word for it."

* * *

I couldn't help thinking about how Portia, my own daughter, went through her ordeal—being pregnant in a foreign country, not receiving good medical treatment, and then losing the baby—without her family, without her mother. She hadn't trusted me enough to let me in on her life at that time. That was on me—a burden I'd have to bear.

The next day brought an e-mail from my attorney, Andrew Wooten, that surprised and confused me.

Congratulations, Margaret. I received a contract from screenwriter Bennett Crandall for rights to *Rearview Mirror.* If you want me to handle this for you, please sign and return the attached attorney/client contract. You must be very excited!

Andrew

How could this happen without my knowledge? I didn't know any Bennett Crandall. My first thought was that it was a scam—the publishing industry was full of them—but my guess was that Wooten would have been able to figure that out. Unless he was in on it. I'd spent a considerable amount of time vetting Wooten, so I believed him to be on the up-and-up but didn't know for sure. I responded.

Thank you, Andrew. Before I review the contract, may I ask you if you know how this deal came about? I know nothing about it.

Margaret

He responded immediately.

I'll get back to you.

"There doesn't seem to be—" Carl's voice made me jump.

"I wish you wouldn't sneak up on me like that," I snapped at him.

"Sorry. I just came in to say there doesn't seem to be anything in the fridge for lunch. Do you want me to go get something, or do you want to go out?"

"Where's Portia?" I asked.

"In her room, I assume. The door's been shut all morning."

"I'll go check on her. She was very upset last night. Sure, why don't you go pick something up at Dolly's?" Dolly's Deli was our favorite place to get sandwiches. "Get Portia tuna salad on wheat." That was always her favorite. "I'll have the City Girl special on pumpernickel."

"Do we have stuff to grill outside for dinner tonight?"

"Not defrosted."

"I'll get that too."

He was awfully willing to run these errands. He was wearing a denim shirt and a pair of his new faded jeans. His butt looked good in them. I don't know why that bothered me.

I knocked on Portia's door, then opened it. "Are you okay, sweetie?"

She was seated on her bed with her back to the door.

"Portia?"

When she turned around, I could tell she'd been crying. I lowered myself beside her on the bed and wrapped my arm around her.

"He was going to go back to Ohio State just like me," she wailed. "We were going to pick up where we'd left off. I wish he hadn't gone back to that godawful place."

I was surprised to hear the two of them had reconnected—she hadn't mentioned that before.

She handed me her phone. "This was the last thing he texted to me."

See you in September pothead.

"Portia?"

"C'mon, Mom. Everyone does it."

"Not everyone."

"Okay. Everyone but you and Dad."

"Don't be ridiculous." I paused before deciding to tell her this. "We both smoked in college, by the way."

"Pot?"

"Mm-hm."

"No way."

"Way."

"Do you want to smoke one now? I'm dying for some."

"No! My pot-smoking days are long gone, and I wouldn't smoke an illegal drug with my own daughter anyway. What would that say about me as a mother?"

"That you're cool?"

"Nice try. And you're not to smoke it in this house either. It's not legal in Wisconsin."

"This would be for medicinal use."

"Oh. So the pot you have was prescribed by a doctor?"

"Well, not exactly."

"Look, you're a big girl. You know the consequences. The choice is yours. Just don't smoke it here. Any luck with your embassy friend?"

"Not yet."

After Portia told Carl about Evangeline, he persuaded her to go with him for ice cream. While they were out, I scoured Portia's room for the pot and found it in her backpack—six perfectly rolled joints in a plastic case. I confiscated one of them.

Five minutes into fingering the joint in my pocket, the phone rang.

"Portia and I were thinking of taking in a movie after ice cream. To get her mind off things. Want to join us?"

"What movie?"

"We're thinking the new *Jurassic Park*."

"No. You go. I've got plenty to keep me busy here."

As I continued to finger the joint, my mind kept wandering to Carl's phone call about me joining them when he knew I wouldn't like a movie such as *Jurassic Park*.

Carl and Portia would be gone for a few hours. Let them be alone. Without me. I didn't care. It was a stupid movie anyway. I didn't need to be with them 24/7. I was my own person.

I liked being alone.

* * *

What harm would a few tokes do?

After slipping a Rachmaninoff CD into my office stereo, I situated myself on one of the loungers on the patio, leaned back, muscles slacked. When I felt completely relaxed and comfortable, I closed my eyes and thought about what I was about to do—illegal, sneaky, and stupid.

I choked on the first toke—it had been years since I'd inhaled a joint or even a cigarette. The second one came easier. The third one brought back memories of that indescribable earthy fragrance that one hardly notices after a few hits. I used to love that initial smell, how it magically went from pungent to powerful to insignificant in such a short span of time. It appeared as though I still did.

I didn't feel much of anything for the first ten minutes or so—just more relaxed, a little melancholy. I allowed my mind to drift to happier times, the early days with Carl, when Portia was born. What a happy day that had been when we brought her pink little body home from the hospital—experiencing that range of emotions that I suspected every new parent went through, not realizing how life-altering the event would prove to be. And now I knew that Portia almost went through it herself. That made me sad.

I hadn't realized how quiet it was outside—no birds singing, cars going by, or sounds coming from boats on the lake. The silence rang in my ears like noise, but it felt good, like I was under water, away from the rest of the world. It scared me a little, yet I felt no need to interrupt the silence with anything else.

I inhaled the last two puffs, and without warning, scads of images flooded my brain—each one trapped in a separate freight car on the fast-moving train that roared through my head. One by one, they flew out of the cars and settled in my mind.

I envisioned Carl's mother falling down the stairs and before she lost consciousness flashing a kind of death stare at me like only Katherine could. Carl came to her aid as one of the paramedics. I left as soon as he came. But I had nowhere to go.

I refused to accept any blame for Katherine's situation but still worried what she thought of me. I worried what everyone thought of me. Especially Portia, but also Carl and Darlene and Lance and the new neighbor across the street who I hadn't yet met. Or had I? I couldn't remember. All I knew was that they were up to something sinister. I could tell that even without meeting them. Maybe I hadn't raised Portia the best way possible. Look at her—she's a college dropout who smokes pot and had an unwanted pregnancy. Could pot have caused her baby to die? I'd have to Google that. I prayed she wouldn't die from an accidental overdose. Could that happen? I prayed, even though He had never listened to me before. Probably didn't even know who I was. Google was a funny word. I wondered how they'd come up with that.

I envisioned Carl's mother in a hospital bed, slowly fading away. Then I envisioned myself in a hospital bed, slowly fading away. Then I envisioned everyone I knew in the same hospital bed—a big square one with bright yellow sheets but no pillows—slowly fading away. I glanced down at my hands to make sure they were there. They were, and that surprised me because I couldn't feel them.

Maybe Katherine would be better off if Carl had stayed down there.

Maybe? Of course she would have. What was I thinking? If it hadn't been for me, he'd still be down there with her. His mother, the person in the world who meant most to him. His precious mother.

I opened my eyes and focused them on my body for several seconds before I decided that I was sitting in an awkward position. I rearranged my legs and tried to straighten out my torso. But as much as I tried to sit like a normal person, it still appeared wrong—flawed. Flawed like the rest of me. Especially my mind. I clearly didn't fit in.

After reflecting on my body for I don't know how long, I came to the realization that I must really be screwed up. I thanked my mother for that. "You can't do this. You can't do that. Better marry well, Margie, so you have someone to take care of you." I could picture her saying this to me even though I had never had that memory before. Was it real? Hard to tell.

I didn't need anyone to lean on—not Carl or anyone else. And I knew that wasn't the pot talking. Or was it? I'd have to revisit that later. If I remembered. I wished I'd come out with paper and a pencil. No, a pen. That way no one could erase it. Either one would have worked. Of course, crayon would have worked too. It didn't really matter what type of writing utensil I used. And crayons were coming back. For adults. I didn't feel like an adult. I felt more like a six-year-old child.

And another thing, I didn't like the way my mother had treated me as if I was a bother to her. She needed a lot of "me time," as she had called it. I remembered that very clearly. I spent more time with the TV than with her. Of course, maybe I was a bother to her. Of course I was—that's probably why she left.

I'd made some bad decisions in my life. Sometimes I thought marrying Carl was one of them. And giving up a lucrative career to write novels? Who does that? But then, hasn't everybody? Made bad decisions that is. Speaking of everybody, where was everybody? I surveyed the patio and the far corners of the lawn. Had they all gone home? What—they didn't want to be around me? I scratched my head and questioned why I did that. It hadn't itched. Now it itched, so I scratched it again. It itched deep.

A sailboat floated by, mast up but no sail, going too slowly for my liking. He had to be up to something. I assumed a male to be at the helm because I'd never seen a female sailor. Of course, that didn't mean there couldn't be one. I wondered how many times I had said "of course" to myself in the past few minutes. A lot, I thought. Maybe all mothers were like mine and told their daughters they couldn't be sailors. Wouldn't have surprised me.

Suddenly, I realized I was a big shooting target for the people on that boat. I got up and dragged my chair closer to the house so as to be less out in the open and then pulled over a heavy planter—the one with the arborvitae tree and Creeping Jenny cascading down the sides—to serve as a shield. I had to protect myself. No one else would. Creeping Jenny. Who was the poor sap they named that plant after? Had I just ended a sentence with a preposition? I couldn't remember if that rule was real or some myth I'd learned in school. And if it was a rule, did it apply when you were just thinking it and didn't say it out loud? After I said the word *just* out loud a few times, I wondered how it was spelled, and then I wondered why I'd chosen the word *just* to reflect on. Shit. Another preposition.

There had to have been something wrong with me to have been thinking like this after only a few tokes. I let my mind drift back to my college days when Carl and I used to get high together. Sometimes I had weird thoughts back then too. The next day, Carl had to remind me what they were. He could have been lying to me. Like he was lying to me now. About my books he said he hadn't read. He had read them. He had read every damn one of them. He had probably even read what I'd written so far on *Stand-Alone Groom*. I wouldn't have put it past him. He was probably playing mind games with me to force me into writing a certain ending. One that suited him, not me. Well, I was not going to let him manipulate me like that. I tried to spell *manipulate* but couldn't get it right.

What if I actually was an insane person deep down, and pot brought that part of my personality out of me? I had already smoked the whole joint. Too late now. The good thing was that I knew enough about weed to know that I probably wouldn't remember any of this later on anyway. But how later on was later on? And was there a point of no return?

I was smoking much higher quality pot than what I'd smoked in college. I didn't know why that was important to note to myself, but I did.

A blackbird danced among the boxwood bushes. When the bird stopped and shot a mocking look at me, I envisioned him in on Carl's little escapades. I didn't trust it. The same one kept coming around. Never with another bird. Always alone. Something must be wrong with it that no other bird wants to be with it. Like some people. When I turned my focus back to the bushes, the bird had vanished. Sneaky little bastard.

I looked down at my watch, but the hands spun around so fast, I couldn't catch the time. Why did they make watches so hard to read? I turned around to study the house behind me and couldn't remember whether I lived in it or someone else did. If someone else did, I knew I'd better leave before they found me on their patio.

Chapter 12

"Hey, where are you going?"

"Who, me?" I asked.

"Well, you're the only one here besides us," the man said.

"I didn't do anything. Honest. I was just leaving," I told him.

He approached me, and when he got too close, into my personal space, I backed away.

"Mags, what's wrong?"

"My name is Margaret."

"She's high, Dad. Look at her eyes."

"I smell weed!" he said.

"So do I," I said. "I wonder where that's coming from."

"It's coming from you, Mags!"

"My name is Margaret. I already told you that."

He grabbed my arm. "Let's get into the house."

I turned toward the house to which I thought he was referring. A Rachmaninoff piano concerto that I recognized could be heard from within. Whoever lived there had good taste in music.

I yanked my arm out of his grip. "No. I want to go home."

"To Chicago?"

"Is that where I live?"

"You live here. At least in the summer."

"Is it summer, then?" I asked.

"Can we please go in the house?" he asked. "Maybe have a cup of coffee or something."

I turned toward the street and started walking. "I don't drink coffee. And my name is Margaret."

"Dad, do something!"

I didn't want them to call the police and report me on their property, so I quickened my steps, all the while afraid that I didn't know where to go. Heavy footsteps behind me caused me to run.

"Stop her! There's a car coming!"

* * *

I peeked through partially closed eyelids to observe my surroundings—obviously, a hospital room.

"Hey, hon. It's me, Carl."

"Hey." My mind raced, looking for an explanation as to why I was there. "What happened?"

"You were almost struck by a car. Fortunately, you lost your footing and fell, giving the car time to swerve out of the way. How do you feel?"

"I have a terrible headache."

"You hit your head on the curb."

"How long have I been here?"

"Just overnight. You have a concussion. You're under observation." He paused for a moment. "You don't remember anything?"

"Not too much."

"They found marijuana in your system."

"I smoked a joint of Portia's," I said, rubbing my forehead. "How is she?"

"She's fine."

"Can we talk about it when we get home? When can I go home?"

"I'll go see when the doctor is expected in to see you. You'll be all right?"

"Of course. I'm fine."

When Carl returned, he said the doctor would be in to see me in a few hours.

"I'm starving," Carl said. "Do you mind if I go grab something in the cafeteria and come back here with it?"

"What about me?"

Carl pointed to a tray of sorry-looking food beside my bed.

"Could you bring me a milk shake if they have it? Chocolate."

"Sure."

Something in my chest tightened. I didn't remember a thing past having a strange vision of everyone with whom I had ever been acquainted in life lying in a giant hospital bed. And now I was in one.

After Carl returned, a doctor came in and told me they had run a battery of tests, found nothing seriously wrong, and I could go home. Before he left, he handed me a page of instructions that included potential warning signs that something was wrong. Carl helped me get dressed and walked beside me as I was rolled to the front door of the hospital in a wheelchair.

Once home, Carl asked me why I felt the need to smoke pot.

"Because it was there?" I said.

"Mags?"

"I don't know, Carl. It just seemed like a good thing to do at the time. Maybe I was feeling stressed or maybe I was angry. I don't know. You and Portia decided to spend the afternoon without me, and—"

"Wait a minute. I called you to see if you wanted to join us."

"To see a movie that you knew I wouldn't like."

"We could have seen a different movie."

"You didn't offer that."

"So you got wasted on pot."

"Like you never have?"

"Not in the last twenty years. Come to think of it, not ever. A little high maybe, but never wasted like that."

"Like what?"

"You were quite…delusional."

"And you're so perfect."

"Mags—"

"Can we change the subject, please?"

"Fine. What would you like to talk about?"

"Anything but this."

"How about what's got into you lately?" he asked.

"Meaning what?"

"Meaning what happened to the girl I married? The sweet, always positive, fun-loving girl I married? Where is she?"

I got up and retreated to my office without responding. Right then, I hated him. And myself. I wasn't sure whom I hated more.

* * *

The next day, Carl left early in the morning, saying he had to drive back to Chicago for a meeting and wouldn't be home until late. Funny how he hadn't told me about that the previous day—he must have received notice of this very important meeting in the middle of the night. I didn't believe a word of it and was glad he'd be gone for the day. At least Portia would be home with me in case I developed any of the symptoms I was supposed to look out for following my fall.

Shortly after breakfast, Darlene called to ask if Portia and I wanted to join her for lunch at the club where they were holding their annual auction for charity. Having no interest in it but not wanting to do anything to further undermine our relationship, I said I'd go and would check with Portia.

I decided to spend the hours before lunch working on *Stand-Alone Groom*. While I was deeply into writing a pivotal scene, Portia knocked on my door.

"Can we talk?" she asked.

"Sure. C'mon in."

Portia sat down on the chaise lounge, arms crossed over her chest, a tense smile on her face.

"I just wanted to tell you that I was worried about you the other day."

"Imagine how *we* felt when we didn't even know where you were for all those months." As soon as I said them, I wished I could have taken those words back.

"That's why I came in here. It took Sunday's incident for me to realize how you felt, and I feel terrible for what I put you through. I'm sorry I did that, Mom."

I rose and hugged her. "You're home now. That's what counts most."

She shook her head and smiled, then wagged her finger at me.

"What?"

"You were flyin' *so* high."

"That's some pot you have, sweetie. I hope you're careful with that stuff."

"High-quality Jamaican ganja. Can't beat it. I don't know where Enrique got it, but he always seemed to have a stash. I've never smoked a whole one by myself."

"Well, I did."

"And you almost got killed."

"I don't remember much. Any news about Evangeline?"

Portia teared up.

"What is it, sweetie?"

"Helena found her grave. She's dead."

I hugged her tight. "I'm so sorry."

She pulled away from me and, through her sobs, said, "Thank you for offering to go with me to find her. That meant a lot, with the bookstore going on and all."

"I'd do anything for you, you know that."

"I do now." She swiped the tears from her cheeks. "I have to go. I told the neighbors across the street I'd watch their two-year-old this afternoon while they play a round of golf."

"You've met them?"

"I met her, not him. She's nice."

"Do you feel up to it? I'm sure they'll understand if you cancel."

"I'm okay."

"What's their name?"

"Fivgard. Her name is Flora. I don't know his."

"Flora Fivgard?" What kind of name was that? "How well do you know them?"

"Not very, but I'm only going to watch their kid for a few hours."

"Darlene asked us to go to a charity auction at the club this afternoon."

She gave me that you've-got-to-be-kidding look.

"I was hoping you'd go with us."

"I have no money to buy anything, not that there would be anything there I'd want to buy. And those people really irritate me."

"Tell me you'll be careful across the street."

"Why are you being so— Never mind. I'll be careful."

She kissed me on the cheek and headed out the door.

I had just enough time to shower and find something appropriate to wear to the club. As I got ready, I thought about how much it bothered me that Portia would be spending time in some stranger's home. She said she hadn't met him yet. I Googled Fivgard to see the origin of the name. Nothing came up. No such name.

I wanted to run after her, but I didn't.

* * *

"So, what new gossip do you have from the neighborhood, Darlene?" I asked her on our way to the club.

"Gossip? You know I don't gossip."

Right. By now I was sure that at least half the neighborhood knew about my pot-smoking episode, thanks to Darlene's big mouth.

"I suppose you heard about—"

"Now that you mention it, I did hear that Tammy and George Montgomery are splitting up," she said. "She's staying here. He's moving back to Maine."

"That's nice. What's Lance doing today, and how's he feeling, by the way? Things pretty much back to normal?"

"Kind of. He made his official retirement announcement on Friday."

"Oh, really? So what's he going to do with all his free time?"

"Golf. Boating. Poker games at the club. He'll keep busy. And he'll do some consulting, I'm sure. And then there's—"

"And then there's what?"

"Um, I don't know. I lost my train of thought," she said as she pulled into the club parking lot.

After making sure that everyone who Darlene wanted to see her saw her and we had perused the items up for auction, we sat down at a table that had been reserved for us, in front near the podium. I managed to eat most of my lunch, which included three things I didn't recognize.

"What's Lance doing today?" I asked her for the second time.

"Shh. They're starting the auction."

I hadn't intended on bidding on anything and didn't. Darlene bought a one-week timeshare in Aruba for $2,500. She appeared thrilled over the purchase. I had no idea if that cost was typical, a generous charitable contribution, or a steal. Whatever—it made her happy.

On the ride home, I asked Darlene for the third time what Lance was doing while we were at the auction.

"My goodness, Mags, you seem awfully interested in what my husband is doing today. What gives?"

"Nothing. Nothing gives. I was just trying to make small talk, that's all. Carl drove to Chicago this morning for a meeting."

"Lance went—"

"Lance went where?"

"I'm not sure, actually."

Before parting ways, we talked about going out on their boat the following Friday. I dreaded the notion of having to suffer through another boring evening but kept up a good front.

Back home, with Portia and Carl out of the house, I was guaranteed quiet time to delve back into chapter 15 of *Stand-Alone Groom*—the chapter that included the climax of the story line, at least it did according to my outline. I didn't always follow the outline—sometimes after writing a few chapters, the stories I wrote took on a life of their own, in which case the outline would go by the wayside. I typically wouldn't feel that coming on until it actually happened—an inexplicable phenomenon that often happened to us fiction writers.

Not having had a break for hours, I welcomed the ringing phone at nine o'clock.

"Hi, hon. I'm stuck here at the house. The meeting has been continued into tomorrow, so I'm going to sleep here tonight. Hope you don't mind."

What if I did?

"No, of course not. What's the meeting about that it's taking so long?"

"I'll spare you all the boring details. What are you doing?"

"I'm busy writing, and Portia went out with some friends."

"Good." He laughed. "No more pot smoking?"

"Very funny."

"Good night, hon. Love you."

"Love you too."

If I hadn't been so tired, I would have driven to Chicago to spy on him.

* * *

"I'll be home by six," Carl said the following morning. "I've invited the Richardsons to join us for dinner at Le Grille." I hadn't heard that kind of excitement in his voice for a long time.

"Pretty fancy place for a Wednesday night."

"I thought you'd like it."

"*I've* never been there," I told him.

"I have, and I know you're going to love it. I made reservations for seven-thirty."

"Fine."
"Is everything okay?"
"Of course. Hurry home."
"Can't wait to see you," he said.
He was up to something.

Chapter 13

Carl's fidgety behavior while we readied ourselves for dinner with the Richardsons finally got to me.

"What is the matter with you?" I asked him. "You're acting like you're expecting something to happen."

"Nothing like that."

"What's going on?"

"Okay, so I wasn't going to say anything until dinner, but we've been thinking—"

"Who's been thinking?"

"Lance, Dar, and me. We were thinking that there's no way you can pull off this bookstore thing all by yourself, so we're going to help." His wide grin annoyed me.

I allowed time to fully digest his words. *We've stood by and watched your incompetence long enough. We're coming in to take over.*

"I'm incompetent?"

"I didn't say that. I said—"

"That's what I heard."

"Well, you heard wrong. C'mon, Mags. You've done nothing but angst over all the work involved in starting this thing up. Why wouldn't you welcome the help?"

"Maybe it was in the presentation. And I'm not 'angsting' over anything. That's not even a verb."

"Well, I think you know what I meant. Look, you need the help, and here are three able-bodied people offering to do just that."

"Because I'm incapable of doing it on my own."

"Will you stop with that? That's not what I said."

"It was inferred."

"I ought to know what I meant, and it wasn't that."

"How about this? If and when I need your help, I won't hesitate to ask for it."

He stared at me like I'd just insulted his mother or something.

"That's a little ungrateful, don't you think? What am I supposed to tell Lance and Dar? We talked about this at length and they, being the nice people they are, offered to help, be part of the team. I already told them 'yes.' You can't turn around and say 'no' to them. That wouldn't be fair."

I stood up to face him. "I'll tell you what's not fair," I said waving my finger in his face. "My growing up with a father who did everything for me, never showing me how to do things for myself or explaining things to me. He just came in, took over, and did them himself. He tied my shoes, made my bed, cooked all my meals. Why? I don't know. Because he thought I wasn't smart enough, or strong enough, or whatever."

"I didn't—"

"It took a long time for me to figure out that I didn't need someone else to do things for me, that I was capable of doing things for myself. I wasn't stupid. I wasn't incapable or incompetent. And now, when it comes to doing the most important thing in my life, you want to step in and do it for me. You want to set me back thirty years. *That's* what's not fair."

"You never shared any of that with me," he said with a dazed look on his face.

"Well, maybe it was something I preferred to keep in the past. I'm sure you can relate to that."

"Does it really—"

"I've pretty much lost my appetite. Why don't you go on without me."

"Maggie, don't be this way. All we—"

"Please don't tell me how to be," I said before going into the bathroom and closing the door.

After he left, I remembered an incident from my childhood. I had to have been fifteen or sixteen years old. Dad wasn't home when a panic-stricken Mrs. Sullivan from next door came looking for him—her toilet was overflowing, and she didn't know how to shut off the water. I didn't either, but I offered to help her anyway. I waded through an inch of water that had accumulated in her bathroom, took off the toilet-tank lid, thinking I'd see some kind of off/on switch in there. When I didn't, I stared at the toilet trying to figure out logically where the water was coming from. When I peered behind the toilet, near the floor, I saw the shut-off valve and turned it until I heard the water stop gushing.

It took us a while to mop up all the water, and when we finished, Mrs. Sullivan told me how smart I was to have figured out the solution so quickly. I never forgot her comment—it was a kind of praise I'd never heard from anyone before.

* * *

When I woke up the next morning, the unfairness of things came down hard on me. I didn't know where Carl had slept the night before—it hadn't been in our bed. An hour later, I still didn't know his whereabouts as I sat on our patio allowing the gradual warmth of the new day to penetrate my skin.

I closed my eyes and before long pictured myself floating over the surface of the lake, not caring about anything except how delicious it felt to be suspended above the large body of pristine water. My short-lived state of serenity shattered when Carl slid open the patio door and joined me.

"Can we talk?" he asked.

I didn't answer.

He sat near me and leaned in close enough to take one of my hands in his. "I thought about what you said last night, and I shared it with Lance and Dar. We're sorry we handled it the way we did. We were…I was thinking of what I could do for you instead of supporting you in what you wanted to do yourself, and that was wrong. I hope you can forgive me. Us."

It was a nice speech. I had to give him that. It sounded a bit rehearsed, but I decided to accept it.

"Fine, and if I need help, I'll ask for it."

"Right. Even if we see you're in trouble, we'll stay out of it."

Now he was going too far, but I chose to let it go.

"Okay."

"You can be sinking in a pit of quicksand, and we—"

"Stop with it, okay?"

"Just wanted to make sure we're on the same page," he explained.

"We're good then."

"Are we?"

"What do you mean by that?"

He got up and turned to leave.

"Nothing," he said without looking back.

The tightness in my chest caused me to let out a chirp that seconds afterward I wasn't sure I'd made. Carl was never one to talk about what he was feeling, but he was also never one to be cryptically suggestive about it either. Was he referring to our agreement, our relationship, or our marriage when he questioned whether we were "good"? Before I had a chance to mull that over, the sound of the garage door opening and closing swayed me in the direction of thinking he meant our marriage.

The first sob rose in my throat too quickly to stop. More followed, provoking me to run inside to the sanctuary of my office. I didn't want my marriage to end. Not now. Not this way. Not because of me. I didn't want it to be my fault.

I spent the rest of the day going through the motions of writing and preparing for my next book promotion, while my mind played the *what if* game for every aspect of my life that would be affected by a divorce. I thought about fish-hat guy, what it would be like to be in bed with him, have him hold me and tell me repeatedly how he loved me, like Wayne used to do.

I saw no one except for Portia, when she came in to my study to ask if she could borrow my car and my credit card to finish shopping for school things. Carl stayed out for hours. I thought maybe he had gone next door to cry on the collective shoulders of the Richardsons. Or maybe just Darlene's bare, nicely tanned shoulders.

I finally called Carl, to see where he was, but more importantly to get a sense of his attitude.

"I can't talk now. I have Mom's doctor on the other line. I'll call you back."

At least he had put his mother's doctor on hold to take my call, if in fact he really was on the other line.

Minutes later, he called back.

"Where are you?" I asked him.

"Just out. I'll be home in a bit."

"How's your mom?"

"Apparently, she wandered out in the middle of the night, couldn't remember where she lived, and when the police found her standing in the middle of the street, they took her to the hospital for observation. We need to decide where she'll go after they release her. She can't live by herself anymore. I don't know what we should do."

"We?"

"You and me…that is, if we still are a 'we.'"

"I want us to be a 'we.'"

We both chuckled at the awkwardness of my statement.

"Should I bring something home for dinner?"

"Please."

My work didn't seem so important now. I took a quick shower, put on a fresh outfit, dabbed a little makeup on my face, and waited for Carl.

Portia came home first carrying two large shopping bags.

"Did you get everything you need?" I asked her.

"I think so."

"When do you go back?"

"Classes begin the third week of August, but I have an opportunity to—"

"I'm home, and I have pizza!" Carl hollered from the kitchen.

"I'll explain later," Portia said.

After dinner, Portia disappeared into her room, giving Carl and me privacy to talk.

"So, what do you want to do about Katherine?" I asked him.

"Here are what I see as the options. I can hire someone to live with her in her home. I can find assisted living for her in Florida. I can find assisted living for her up here."

"Or she could come live with us," I said with mixed motives.

"I didn't want to impose that option on you," he said.

"I appreciate that, Carl, but let's throw it out there anyway. We want to do what's best for your mom first."

He moved closer to me and held my hand. "I still love you, Mags. You know that, don't you?"

I lost sight of Katherine for an instant as I reveled in the moment. "I know. I love you too," I said.

"What to do," he said.

"What do you think she'd want to do?"

"Live with us, but—"

"You didn't even have to think about that, did you?"

"What?"

"You answered that question so quickly. I don't think we should consider the other options."

"Not so fast. Do you know what you're agreeing to?"

"Of course, I do. And if it were my mother, you'd react the same way."

He laughed. "I don't know your mother, so… Are you sure?"

"What are you sure about?" Portia asked as she entered the kitchen.

"Grandma Katherine is going to come live with us," I told her.

"You're kidding."

"Not kidding."

"When?"

I looked at Carl. "We haven't gotten that far yet, but soon."

"This is the perfect segue for what I need to talk to you guys about."

"Sit down. Take a load off," Carl told her.

"Flora and Fred asked me if I would go with them to London for all of July to take care of their kid. I'm going to do it."

"Flora and Fred?" I asked.

"The Fivgards, across the street."

"Portia, you don't even know them," I said.

"Yes, I do. Mom, they're nice people. And we'd be going to London, not some third-world country run by terrorists, for God's sake."

"There are terrorists in London, by the way," I said.

"There are terrorists here, too," she responded.

"She has you there, hon," Carl interjected.

"You're of age, you can make your own decisions, but—"

"And that will free up the room for Grandma," she added.

"She has a point, Mags."

"What nationality are they?" I asked.

"Who?" Portia said.

"The Fivgards."

"What difference does that make?"

"I'm just curious."

"I can call and ask them."

"Don't get smart."

"Mom, it doesn't make any difference to me where they were born or where their ancestors were born. They're nice people. And little Noah loves me."

"Okay. But I expect frequent phone calls. Video chats."

"How frequent?"

"Twice a day. Three times on weekends."

"Very funny."

Portia got up and bent over to give me a kiss on the cheek. "I love you too, Mom."

"Mom could be here in less than two weeks. Are you still sure you want to do this?" Carl asked.

"Of course. It's the right thing to do."

Chapter 14

During the next two weeks, Carl's days were filled with chores related to his mother's move— pulling from her how she wanted her room in our home furnished and decorated, getting rid of most of her stuff and shipping the rest, closing on her townhome, and transporting her to Wisconsin.

We had to decide whether we would keep our two homes—the Chicago brownstone and our Lake Beulah home—or consolidate our households into one. Would Katherine be able to easily move between the two twice a year—once in the spring and again in the fall? After much discussion, we decided to keep both, with Carl traveling back and forth between the two homes and Katherine and me staying in the lake house.

By the time Portia left for London, everything that would make the room special for Katherine had been shipped by Carl and piled in the living room—her bedroom furniture and linens, most of her clothes, and several pieces of her artwork. Despite being busy with dealing with contractors and developing my business and marketing plans, I agreed to get her room ready while Carl flew to Florida to pick her up. Since Katherine refused to fly, the plan was for Carl to rent a car and drive her to our home—a twenty-hour trip if driven straight through. Carl planned to do it in three days.

Mentally, I tried to prepare myself for Katherine's arrival—visiting her a few times a year was one thing, but living together would obviously be different. Not knowing what to expect, I prepared myself for the worst.

On the day of her arrival, Katherine walked through our front door in a rumpled pantsuit and a haggard expression on her face. Rawboned with a hawk-like nose and thinning, obviously dyed black hair, she seemed to me a female version of Ebenezer Scrooge.

"Where's my room?" she shrieked as soon as she entered our home.

"Right this way," I said. "How was the trip, Katherine?"

"Long. That's how it was. Very long."

Welcome to your new home, Katherine. I hope everyone survives your stay.

I led Katherine to her room and asked her if she wanted to lie down for a while before unpacking and getting settled in.

"I slept most of the way here. The last thing I want to do is lie down."

"Are you hungry?"

"We just ate."

I offered to help her unpack. She nodded.

I told her it would go faster if I could hang things in the closet as she pulled them out of her suitcase. What didn't need to be hung, she could put in the dresser drawers. The system worked.

"Carl said your bedroom at home is painted yellow, so I hope you like what we've done with this room."

"It's okay," she said as she handed me a dress.

"And I think your artwork goes well in here too."

"Mm-hm."

"A lovely breeze off the lake comes through this window, so feel free to open it if you want."

She walked over to the window. "I don't see the lake."

"Well, you can't really see it from this room. When we're done here, I'll give you the grand tour and then you'll see our little piece of the lake."

"Okay."

I struggled to find more things to talk about—one-sided conversations were difficult.

"Do you like pasta, Katherine? I thought that's what I'd make for dinner."

"You mean spaghetti?"

"Actually, what I have is some cappelletti…stuffed with minced—"

"I like spaghetti."

"Okay, spaghetti it is, then." I peered at the empty suitcase. "Is that it?"

"Mm-hm. I think I'll lie down now."

After leaving her room, I sent Portia to the store to buy some spaghetti.

* * *

During the days prior to the Fourth of July holiday, I was so overwhelmed with the bookstore start-up that at times I wanted to throw in the towel or resort to seeking help from Carl and others. Either way, I felt like a loser. I called Lily for advice.

"Take a step back, girlfriend, and breathe. Let go a little. Release the pressure. You sound like you're wound up tighter than a drum."

"I can't afford to do that, Lily. I have a million things to do and a short time to do them in. Everything is new to me. I've never felt so unprepared for anything in my whole life."

"You can't afford *not* to take a step back, hon. Are you getting enough sleep? Eating right? Exercising?"

"No, no, and no."

"So, your energy is low. That's part of the problem. When's the last time you and Carl went out on a date?"

"Ha! That's a laugh."

"Look, just relax a little, look at your to-do list—and I know you have one, or two, or ten of them—and prioritize the tasks. If you focus on one at a time, instead of allowing them to occupy your mind all at once, you'll do fine. I know you."

I knew she was right, but I also knew myself well enough to know I probably wouldn't follow her advice, not all of it anyway. But I didn't want it to come down to me failing or having to admit I couldn't pull it off, so I knew I'd better follow some of it. Lily was a smart girl.

Ever since I had declined Carl's help with the bookstore, things hadn't been quite the same—stilted conversations between the two of us and him spending his spare time with his mother. The distance between us was widening.

* * *

By Fourth of July weekend, while still feeling slightly overwhelmed, I had calmed down enough to enjoy the holiday. The work ahead of me seemed to be almost manageable. Katherine had settled in. Life began to take on a semblance of normalcy. The Richardsons invited us to join them on their boat the afternoon of the Fourth, but Katherine said she would rather stay home. What to do with Mom when both of us were out hadn't been considered.

"We can't trust her alone," I told Carl. We had observed her doing too many potentially perilous things, like mistaking eardrops for eyedrops, asking for medication twenty minutes after having taken it, and walking toward the front door for no apparent reason.

"I agree. But we can't be expected to give up our social life entirely either."

"That's true too," I said, even though giving up being a guest on the Richardsons' boat wouldn't have bothered me in the least. "And she still thinks she can manage by herself, so whatever we do isn't going to sit well with her."

"I know."

"Can't you make her come with us when we go out?"

He shot me a look that answered my question better than any words could have.

"Did you happen to see the way she reacted to Waffles when Dar brought him over the other day?" he asked.

"Seemed to me she liked him well enough. Petted him. Let him lick her. Why?"

"It was more than that. Her eyes lit up when she saw that dog, and then she was immediately concerned about one of his ears. She thought it looked a little red inside."

"Did she ever have a dog?"

"We had a dog when I was a kid. Fluffy. We had that dog for more than ten years. Broke her heart when it died."

"The last thing we need in this house is a dog, Carl. So let's not go there."

"It would be something to keep her busy. Out of trouble while we're gone. We'd never be gone for that long, and we could even install one of those nanny-cams that allows us to tune in with our phones to see what she's doing."

"I'm against it," I said. It wasn't that I had anything against dogs, although I preferred cats, but adding a pet to our already-uncertain family dynamic spelled trouble, in my view.

We passed on the Richardsons' invitation, explaining to them the issue with leaving Mom alone. Instead, we invited them, including Waffles, to join us for a cookout on our patio. They accepted.

The morning of the Fourth, Carl left early to buy a few more groceries for the cookout. Katherine, an early riser, joined me in the kitchen where I was preparing the potato salad.

"Carl likes poppy seeds in his potato salad," she told me. "I always add poppy seeds."

"Well, Katherine, I don't have any poppy seeds, so he'll have to be okay without them."

"You could call him," she said.

I stared at her, trying not to give away what I was thinking.

"Just a suggestion," she said through pursed lips.

"You're right. I could." I picked up my cell phone. "Hey, Carl. Are you still in the store?"

"I'm in the checkout line. Why?"

"Your mom thought maybe the potato salad could use some poppy seeds."

"I hate poppy seeds."

"Okay, so if you can't find any there, maybe you could go over to that small store on Cleveland where they have a larger selection of…seeds."

"She's right there, isn't she?"

"That's right."

"Screw the poppy seeds."

"Okay, hon. I know you'll find them."

Katherine shook her head. "I wouldn't have asked him to check at another store. Not that important."

I kept mixing.

"It's getting too smooth," she told me. "Carl likes it chunkier."

"Oh, that's good to know." I'd only been married to him for twenty-one years. What did I know?

"Are you making coleslaw next?" she asked.

"I wasn't planning on it."

"Hmm."

"Do you like coleslaw, Katherine?"

"Yes, I do."

"I'll make it sometime, then."

"Not for today?"

"Well, I don't have the ingredients for it."

She glanced down at my cell phone.

"Carl, are you still in the store?"

"I'm pulling onto our street. Why?"

"Katherine was wondering if we could have coleslaw today. It's one of her favorite dishes."

"How's it going, hon? Ready to change your mind about Mom yet?"

I stifled a smile. "No, but I'll ask her." I turned to Katherine. "Do you know off-hand what all goes into coleslaw? Carl, I'm going to put you on speaker so your mom can tell you what to get."

"I'll get you for this."

"I love you too, hon."

"Hi, honey. You'll need a nice head of cabbage. Pick out a firm one, not one of those soft spongy ones. And don't get one too small. Sometimes the small ones are too…cabbage-y."

"What else do we need, Mother?"

"I like a little shredded carrot in mine."

"One shredded carrot coming up."

"Don't buy it shredded. She'll cut up a whole one. Fresher that way."

"Her name is Mags, Mom."

"I know that."

He laughed. "Okay. What else?"

"Mayonnaise, the real thing, none of that fake stuff. Vinegar. White-wine vinegar. Don't get the other kind. A little sugar. You don't need much. Maybe you already have that. And salt and pepper. I'm sure you have that here somewhere. Oh, and celery seed. I always put celery seed in my coleslaw."

"No poppy seeds?"

"In coleslaw?"

"Sorry. What was I thinking? Mags, are you still there?"

"Yes, Carl."

"Do we have any of those ingredients in the house?"

"Only the salt and pepper."

"Okay, darling. I'll see you in a bit. Bye, Mom."

"Bye, son."

"Is that what you're going to wear today?" Katherine asked me.

Chapter 15

I planned for a Labor Day weekend grand opening for the bookstore—on a long holiday weekend when Lake Geneva visitors were getting in their last visit before winter. Even though I had made connections with hundreds of authors and had everything ordered—computer equipment, shelving, display racks, fixtures, coffee equipment, and supplies—I was only halfway down my to-do list with Labor Day just eight weeks away.

Katherine continued to, well, be Katherine with her frequent "poppy seeding," as Carl and I called it. "I wouldn't do it that way," she would say. Or "You could do this, or you could do that." It was always something. Carl bore the brunt of it, so I didn't care. In fact, I egged her on from time to time.

One day, when Katherine and I were alone in the house, she told me something that could not have surprised me more.

"Has Carl been in touch with his father lately?" she asked. "He hasn't said anything about him in the longest time."

"Katherine, his father died years ago." Carl and I both thought she had been exhibiting early signs of dementia, although she hadn't been medically diagnosed with it.

"Peter died years ago. Not Howard."

"Who's Howard?"

"I assumed you knew."

"Knew what?"

"That Peter wasn't Carl's real father."

As soon as I became aware of my mouth hanging open, I quickly shut it. Carl had never said anything about this to me.

"Oh, dear. Me and my big mouth."

"Who's Howard?"

"I told you. Carl's biological father."

"I know, but…is he someone you were married to at one time?"

"Ages ago. I divorced him when he went to prison. Peter adopted Carl when he was two years old."

What? How could Carl not have told me something this important?

"Prison—is he still there?"

"No. He's out now. That much I know. Lives in Milwaukee I think."

"What was he convicted of?" I asked, afraid of her answer.

"A Ponzi scheme, I think they call it—money-laundering, mail fraud. There may have been other charges. You can't tell him I told you all this. That would cause too much turmoil in this household, and we don't need any more of that."

I didn't dare ask what she meant by that.

"I won't tell him if you don't want me to." As soon as I'd said it, I wished I hadn't. What about Portia? She had the right to know. I couldn't believe Carl had never shared this with me.

"I'm sure he didn't mean anything by it, not telling you, that is. He's probably just being private about it."

Did she slip in telling me, or did she want me to know for some reason? Half-jokingly, I asked her if there was anything else I should know about Carl.

She didn't answer.

I planned to confront Carl about what Katherine had told me, but the time had to be right.

* * *

"Hi, you guys!" Darlene said as she rounded our house and leapt onto our patio. Waffles trailed close behind her, and when the dog saw Katherine, he ran to her for some attention. Darlene carried another small, white furry dog in her arms.

"Who's this?" I asked.

"This is Brenda. Do you remember Mrs. Cassidy on the corner?"

"I went to her ninetieth birthday party a couple of summers ago," I said.

"Well, she died, and this was her dog. Now her daughter Kristen is looking for a good home for her."

I peered at Carl, who quickly looked the other way.

"So you're going to take it in? How does she get along with Waffles?"

"No, it's not for me," she said. "It's for you."

"No, it's not. We don't want a dog."

"You got something against dogs?" Katherine snapped.

"They're too much work. We're both too busy."

"Well, I'm not," Katherine said.

Darlene sauntered closer to Katherine.

"Look at that face," Katherine said. "How could anyone hate that face?"

"I don't hate her, Katherine. They're a lot of work, that's all," I said.

"No, they're not," Katherine quickly responded.

"If Mom wants a dog, let's let her have it, dear. Is she housebroken?"

What? Whose side are you on?

"Yes, she's housebroken. She's three."

"And where is she going to do her business?" I asked. "In our backyard?"

"I trained my Fluffy to wee-wee on puppy-training pads inside the house. Never missed, not even once."

Good grief.

"So, it's a done deal?" Darlene asked.

"Yes," said Katherine. "Hand her over to me."

"See y'all later," said Darlene. "I'll give Kristen the good news."

Carl continued to avoid my look.

"So, you got yourself a dog, Mom," he said. "Brenda."

"That's the worst excuse for a dog's name I've ever heard," she said. She held the small pooch high in the air and said, "This is Fluffy."

"Mom, that was your other dog's name."

"More than one dog can't have the same name?" Katherine rose from her chair and walked away. Before she left the patio, she turned toward us and said, "I'll need dog supplies."

I stared at Carl until he finally met my gaze. "You had that all planned out ahead of time with Darlene, didn't you?"

"We talked about it, but I didn't know she was going to come over with it I swear. Would you like me to undo what has just happened?"

"You can't do that, not now."

"Sure, I can. Just give me the word."

"And then I look like the bad guy. No, thanks. Let her have the damn dog."

"Okay. I offered, remember."

"I know."

* * *

I couldn't believe it when August arrived. Four weeks until the grand opening of The Indie Book Nook, and while things were falling into place, I still had a ton of stuff I had to do. So that I could be there for deliveries, I brought my PC into the store and developed my website and social media pages in between dealing with a steady stream of big, strapping men hauling in shelving, furniture, and various equipment. It didn't take long for the ten- and twelve-hour days to take a toll on me.

I had struck a deal with a local art dealer to hang several of his pieces in the store. As I scanned the walls for places to hang them, Portia, who had faithfully called me almost every day while in London, walked into the store.

"Sweetie!"

She ran to me and gave me a hug. "Hey, Mom."

"I didn't expect you until next week."

"I thought I'd surprise you. We managed to get an earlier flight. Noah was having frequent meltdowns, and the Fivgards thought he may have been homesick."

"Well, whatever the reason, I'm so glad you're home."

"Some place you got here. Need any help getting it ready?"

"Are you kidding? I'd love the help. But I thought you were going to stay at the Fivgards and be the nanny until you went back to school."

"I am. I have weekends off."

"But it's only Thursday."

"They're giving me a long weekend. Said I deserved it."

"Their loss. My gain. C'mon, you can begin inventorying these books."

"How's life with Grandma?"

"And Fluffy. Don't forget Fluffy. We're managing. She's full of surprises. I found her vacuuming her room the other day, and the vacuum wasn't plugged in."

Portia howled. "How can you keep a straight face when she does something like that?"

"It's not easy."

"Is she still trying to help you manage the household and plan meals?"

"Not as much now. Fluffy keeps her busy. Thank goodness. Just about everything she wanted me to make or buy because Carl liked it so much was something Carl hates but his father liked." I stopped short of calling him his stepfather—telling Portia the identity of her real grandfather was something Carl had to do.

"That's creepy."

"I know."

Portia and I talked while we worked. We talked about her mostly— more about her experience in Costa Rica, the unfortunate loss of her child, and the effect it had on her, her future. It felt good having her back and things heading toward normal.

* * *

"What on earth?"

Portia and I entered the house that evening to find pots and pans strewn all about the kitchen. More ominously, a scorched dishcloth lay on the stove top. Utensils crusted over in food lay in between empty cans and boxes on the counter. I almost fell when I stepped into a puddle of something on the floor.

"Carl?" I yelled. "Katherine?"

No one answered.

"Portia, will you please start cleaning up this mess while I find out what's going on?"

I checked around for Carl, and when I didn't find him, I searched for Katherine. Her door was closed. I knocked on it.

No answer.

I knocked again, this time louder.

Still no answer.

I opened it a crack and found Katherine lying on the bed with her back to me, Fluffy cuddled up against her.

"Katherine?"

No answer.

I walked over to her and peeked at her face. Her eyes were open, her lips tightly pursed.

"Katherine, are you okay?"

She took her time sitting up on the bed. "I was taking a nap. What's all the fuss about?"

"Are you alright?"

"Of course I am. Don't I look alright to you?"

"What happened in the kitchen?"

"How do I know? I've been in here all afternoon with Fluffy."

I left her room and called Carl.

"Where are you?" I asked him.

"I had to meet with an attorney. I'm in Waukegan. Why?"

"You left your mother alone."

"So?"

"And you didn't think to check in on her from the nanny-cams?"

"I was busy. It slipped my mind."

"She could have burned down the house, Carl."

"I'm on my way home."

"Bring something home for dinner. Our kitchen is a disaster."

I hung up without saying goodbye and checked in on Portia, who had the kitchen halfway back to normal.

"What was she trying to make?" I asked her.

Portia opened the cupboard door and slid out the waste basket.

I peeked inside. "What is it?" I asked.

Portia shook her head. "All I can figure is maybe an omelet. There are egg shells in there, an open can of mushrooms, cheese, and bread."

I picked up the burnt hand towel. It appeared that Katherine, who was used to a gas stove, had placed the towel on the electric cooktop, probably without realizing the burner was on.

"What are you going to do?" Portia asked.

"I don't know, but something has got to change because this certainly can't continue."

Chapter 16

"Carl, you can't leave for long periods of time without checking in on your mom."

"I know. I know."

"First her wandering out of the house the other night while we were out, then her trying to do a load of laundry with my cell phone still in the pocket of my sweater—a sweater that required dry cleaning. And now this. We need a better plan."

"Obviously."

"A better plan for what?" Katherine asked. I hadn't heard her come into the kitchen.

I looked at Carl. He looked at me.

"What's going on?" she asked.

"Nothing, Mom. I brought home some Chinese for dinner. Are you hungry?"

"No, I had something earlier. What were you two talking about when I walked in?"

"Nothing. We're just talking."

"You're talking about me. Do you think I'm stupid?"

"Of course not, Mother. Sit down with us, will you?"

Katherine joined us at the table, her face tightly drawn. A shiver ran down my spine while I waited for Carl to say something.

"Mom, we almost had a serious accident here today when—"

"Really? What did she do?" she asked, referring to me.

"It was you, Mom. You tried to fix something to eat in the kitchen, and you put a dishcloth on a hot burner. We're lucky it didn't catch on fire and burn the whole house down…with you in it!"

"Wasn't me."

"You said you had fixed yourself something to eat earlier. What did you fix?"

Katherine stared blankly at the space between Carl and me. "I don't remember. My memory isn't as good as it used to be. I'm tired now. I think I'll go lie down."

After we heard her door close, we took the conversation to another room.

"What do you think we should do?" I asked. "She seems to be fine when she's under supervision."

"To be honest, even when I'm home and working, I don't know what she's doing most of the time."

"So you could have been home earlier and the same thing could have happened?"

"Possibly. You know how it is—you get engrossed in what you're doing and kind of shut everything else out."

"We can't afford to do that anymore, Carl."

"I know. I agree."

Carl and I spent the next couple of days brainstorming ways to get Katherine the help she needed in our home—the thought of putting her somewhere not yet an option. Without another bedroom or my giving up my office, we didn't see how we could add another person, a caregiver, to the household. The way we left it for the time being was that one of us would always be home, no matter what, checking in on her often.

* * *

Nine o'clock and still no Portia. She had said she'd be at the store early to help, but her definition of early and mine apparently differed. I had wanted her to finish stocking the used-book shelves so she could move on to the new ones. With twenty-one days until the grand opening, I needed her help, someone's help, as I was expecting several deliveries and knew I'd be tied up with them. And I saw it as an opportunity to build on that mother-daughter relationship that had once been so powerful.

When the toilet and sink arrived, I called the plumber, who said he could install them along with the coffee equipment the following Monday. He asked me if they were still crated. I told him they were. He said he didn't do uncrating. Fine.

I grabbed a box cutter and slit the sides of the boxes that held the toilet and sink. Twenty minutes and one nicked finger later, the fixtures were out of their boxes.

My heart sank when I discovered both pieces damaged—the sink chipped in a visible spot and the toilet base cracked. I called the seller, who instructed me to take pictures and e-mail them to him, which I did. Then I called the plumber and asked him to hold off coming on Monday.

Noon—still no Portia.

I wrongly thought I could install the operating system for the cash registers myself. Eventually, after numerous swear words and two calls to the Geek Squad, the issues I faced were resolved, and I had three operating cash registers—two in the bookstore and one in the coffee shop.

Portia walked in the front door at two o'clock with a sourpuss face.

"What's wrong with you?" I asked her.

"Do you have to yell?"

"I'm not yelling. Where have you been all day? I needed your help."

"I'm in no mood, Mother."

"No mood for what?"

"Your interrogations."

"What's gotten into you?"

She covered her face with her hands and mumbled something.

"What did you say?"

"Too much beer. And Tequila shots."

"Portia!"

"Stop yelling!"

I clenched my jaw to avoid saying something I'd regret later. "Go home, or to the Fivgards…wherever. I don't need your sorry-looking face in here while I'm trying to get work done."

"Fine."

"Fine."

I proceeded to pick up stocking the shelves where Portia had left off the day before when my cell phone indicated an incoming text message.

Repackage the toilet and sink in the same boxes they came in. They will be picked up on September 2 and replacement ones will be delivered on the same day.

I glared at the mangled boxes. September 2 was two days before the grand opening.

My phone rang as soon as I closed out of the message.

"Hey, hon. How's tricks?"

"Shut up."

"Hey, what did I do?"

"I'm sorry. I'm having a bad day, and your daughter isn't helping matters."

"What did Portia do?"

"Got drunk last night and came in here bright and early as promised, at two, hungover, and looking like something the cat dragged in. I sent her home, or to the Fivgards."

"Why'd you do that? You could have gotten a few hours of help from her."

"Not in her condition. Hold on a minute." I turned to the delivery man, who had just walked in the door. "Can you put it over there, please? Do you uncrate or just deliver?"

"Just deliver, ma'am."

"Okay. Sorry, Carl. The coffee equipment just arrived."

"What did you wind up ordering?"

"A semi-automatic La Pavoni."

"Sounds like an Italian assault weapon."

"Very funny. I'm opening the carton while we speak. How's your day going?"

"Okay."

"Shit!"

"What's wrong?"

"They sent the wrong machine. What else is going to go wrong today?"

"Are you sitting down?" he asked.

"Why?"

"Because I'm about to tell you what else went wrong today."

"What?"

"Your mother came to our front door."

I dropped the box cutter on the floor. "My mother?!"

"And *my* mother answered it."

"Why are you pausing? What happened?"

"Well, my mother sort of told your mother that no one by the name of Margie lived here."

My excitement skidded to a halt. "What! And where were you?"

"I didn't know this was even going on until it was too late. She was gone."

My entire body froze. I held my breath as my eyes darted from one corner of the store to the other looking for…something. I didn't know what. A soft place to land perhaps.

"I told you to sit down. I hope you're doing that."

"I'm sitting." My voice sounded shaky even to me. "So you never saw her?"

"No."

"How do you know it was her?"

"She asked for Margie. You told me once that she was the only one who ever called you that."

"That doesn't prove it was her."

"Mom said the woman was looking for her forty-eight-year-old daughter."

"Shit. When did this happen?"

"From the best I can tell, about three hours ago."

I took in a long breath. "I'm going to kill your mother."

* * *

She was out there. My mother, the one who ran out on me when I was six, was trying to find me. The person I had tried to forget by pretending to be someone else when I was a kid, in some other family, one with two parents and brothers and sisters. I did that until I was old enough to realize how stupid and pointless it was. It was better to try to forget that she had even existed. Marilyn Foss Delaney, or whatever name she was going by these days, could be anywhere by now—sitting on a park bench a block from our house or on a bus heading to some other city. It crossed my mind to go search for her, but I didn't even know what she looked like.

I wanted so badly to go home, to talk to Katherine, but three more expected deliveries prevented me from doing that. It didn't help my state of mind that I had to reposition some of the books that Portia had previously arranged because she hadn't followed my instructions for filing books first by genre, then by author last name, and then by title.

Carl must have been reading my mind because he came to the store with Katherine in tow.

"Have time to take a break?" he asked.

"Sure. I can't offer you much, not even a chair." I retrieved a box of books for Katherine to sit on. Carl remained standing.

"I hear you had a visitor today," I said to her.

"Mm-hm."

"Can you tell me a little about her?"

"Some old lady. She had the wrong house."

"Actually, Katherine, I think she had the right house. She was looking for me."

"No, she was looking for someone named Margie."

"That's my name."

"Oh."

"My name is Margaret. People call me Maggie, Mags, Margie, all sorts of things for short."

"So what I did was wrong?"

"Well, you didn't know…" Carl said.

"You must think I'm stupid."

"Of course not. It's just that—"

"I'm ready to go now," Katherine said as she rose from the box.

"Please don't go," I said. "I'd like to hear about the woman who came to the door. It's important to—" No use finishing my sentence with Katherine halfway out the door.

Five minutes later, Carl texted me.

Sorry

The notion of cancelling the grand opening ran through my head as I finished straightening out the used-books section. Labor Day felt too soon, now that my mind was elsewhere.

I got back to work, constantly adjusting the drugstore cheaters I wore for reading, reminding myself that I should go to an optometrist to get fitted for full-lens glasses. After an hour of internal grumbling over the inadequacy of the glasses, I locked up the store and marched down the block to Lake Geneva Opticians where I hoped they could take me without an appointment. They had just had a cancellation and took me right in.

I left the optometrist's office at least feeling like I had accomplished something more for the day than getting used books on the shelves, especially since I didn't have very many of them. Most used indie books came from reviewers who had no use for them after they reviewed them.

As I drove home at nearly seven o'clock that evening, the idea of having leftover Chinese for dinner fit the miserable day I was having, and the likelihood of eating it alone made it even more fitting. Carl, Katherine, and Fluffy were on the patio when I got there. Before joining them, I checked the fridge but found no leftovers and then noticed the four empty white cartons on the counter. I went to pour myself a glass of wine to find that stash gone as well.

"No more Chinese left?" I asked Carl.

"I'm sorry, hon. I thought when you didn't come home for dinner, you'd grabbed something in town."

"No more red wine either?"

"Sorry. Mom and I polished off the last bottle."

"I don't suppose there's any Glenlivet left."

"I doubt it, but you can check."

Without saying a word, I marched back to my car, threw it in reverse, and gunned it out of the driveway, not even sure of my destination.

He *knew* about the bad day I'd had. He *knew* what his mother had done had upset me. He *knew* the fridge was empty. The wine. The Scotch. Heartless little—.

I drove four blocks to the nearest grocery store. Finding something to eat that was both comforting and healthy presented a challenge. Finding the wine and a bottle of my favorite Scotch proved easy.

I drove toward home, past a small park, mindlessly drumming my fingers on the steering wheel to the tune of "Uptown Girl." If I'd had a corkscrew with me and a glass, I would have eaten dinner on one of the benches. Maybe just a corkscrew—forget the glass. Actually, a hammer would have sufficed given my frame of mind.

I found Carl waiting for me when I got home. Katherine must have been in her room.

"I'd like to speak with your mother before she forgets everything that happened with my mother today," I said to him.

"I think it's best not to disturb her," he said. "I filled Portia in on your mother's visit by the way."

"Why can't I talk to her?"

"She's having a bad day."

"*She's* having a bad day?"

I couldn't believe he'd said that. I threw the already-made salad I'd bought onto a plate, poured myself a healthy glass of wine, and retreated to my office. After plopping down in front of my notebook, I unlocked the drawer that held my beloved Limoges Eiffel Tower and placed it on my desk. I didn't know why, but having it there with me, especially at that moment, made me feel better.

But not for long. The more I stared at it, the madder I got over how he'd stolen it from me and pawned at a shop he knew I might frequent. He had expected me to find it. God only knew where my pearl earring was.

The salad provided no comfort. The wine did, so I stuck with that. A host of emotions rose in my body until I had to swallow a sob to keep it from spilling out.

"May I come in?" Carl asked through the door.

"No."

"Please?"

"No."

He opened the door and came in anyway. "We have to talk."

Chapter 17

"Fine. Say what's on your mind," I told Carl against my better judgment. I knew not to have a discussion with him when I was in this bad of a mood.

"I'd rather you say what's on yours," he said.

"You don't want to hear what's on my mind."

"Try me."

I took a sip of wine and put the glass down beside the Limoges box. "Let's start with this."

"I'm sorry we drank the last—"

"Not the wine."

"What then?"

"The Limoges box. You took it and sold it to a pawn shop where you thought I'd find it. You even told me about the pawn shop, so I'd be sure to go in there."

"That's preposterous. Why would I do that?"

"You tell me."

"I can't, because I didn't do it."

"Then how did it go missing and happen to end up there?"

"You bought it back?"

"See? You just admitted it."

"I did no such thing. Yours went missing. You found a similar one at the pawn shop, and you bought it."

"Like you had nothing to do with it."

"I *didn't* have anything to do with it!"

"Where's the pearl earring?"

"What pearl earring?"

"You know the one—my mother's."

"How much wine have you had?" he asked.

"Not enough. And what about the bracelet?"

"What bracelet?"

"You know damn well what bracelet. The one I found mysteriously hidden behind some books. That bracelet."

"I don't know anything about it."

"And what about you saying you never read any of my books, and then I find one on your laptop? Why did you lie to me?"

"I didn't lie to you. You're the one who sent me all the pdf files of your books. I tried to read each and every one, but I just couldn't get into them. But then after you made such a big deal of it, I tried again. I'm sorry, Mags, but I'm not a 'cozy mystery' kind of guy. So shoot me."

"Don't tempt me. And why all of a sudden are you using passwords to protect all your files? You never did that before?"

"You tried to get into my files?"

"Yes, I did. Want to make something of it?"

"That's a new policy at work. We were hacked last month, and some sensitive data got into the hands of the wrong people. We password-protect everything now."

"And clearing your Internet search history? I suppose that's a security thing too?"

"As a matter of fact, it is."

"And why are you keeping your phone glued to your side? You never did that before."

"Because I missed an important call from my boss a few weeks ago, and he gave me a hard time about it. Mags, what has—"

"And who were you with at Le Grille restaurant on August twenty-ninth of last year?"

"What?" He glared at me, his eyes suddenly empty tunnels. "A frickin' year ago? How the hell do I know?" The tone and volume of his voice reached levels I didn't like. So did mine. "What were *you* doing on August twenty-ninth of last year?" he asked.

"I'll tell you exactly what I was doing on August twenty-ninth of last year. I was at a book-signing in Chicago while you were up here playing footsies with someone at Le Grille! And what about your father? Your real father. Why didn't you tell me about him?"

"How did he get into this conversation, and how do you even know about him?"

"I have my sources. Why were you hiding him from me?"

"Because he's a fucking criminal, but I suppose you already know that. I didn't want anyone to know we're even related. And, for your information, it was him I was with at Le Grille."

"I don't believe you. It was a woman."

"It was him!"

"If you don't want anyone to know you're related to him, then why have a relationship with him at all?"

"Because he asked for one. I thought I was doing the right thing."

"You have a warped idea of what is the right thing. I suppose you think cheating on me is the right thing too."

"You're fucking crazy, you know that? I've never cheated on you in our entire relationship. But I'll tell you something—you're making it look awfully tempting right about now!"

"Go ahead! Go over to Darlene's. I know you two have a thing going on."

"You're nuts! Why would I try anything with her? Our next-door neighbor of all people. I think of her like a sister, for God's sake."

"A sister. Hmph."

Carl got up. "Let me know when you've stopped being such a lunatic. Maybe we can talk again then." He stormed out. Within seconds, he returned.

"This is probably the worst time I could ever choose to tell you, but I found this earlier today." He reached in his pocket and pulled out a pocket watch, *the* pocket watch.

"Where did you get that?"

"It was in one of our dresser drawers."

"Which dresser drawer?"

"The top left one," he said as he placed it on my desk. "You must have forgotten you'd put it there."

Bastard.

Carl had an explanation for everything, and I hated that. I wasn't stupid. I didn't imagine things. I wasn't crazy. It was *him*. *He* had the issues. I picked up the pocket watch—it felt good in my hand. TIME IS A GIFT. I thought maybe it was trying to tell me something.

And how dare he keep the truth about his father from me and our daughter.

After stewing over our fight for a while, I marched into the kitchen, threw away the rest of the salad I'd been eating, and refreshed my glass of wine. A scrap of paper on the kitchen counter caught my attention.

Mother and I have gone to a movie

I balled up the note in my hand, wishing I could have balled up the resentment I felt toward Carl at that moment. Carl had intentionally removed Katherine from the house to make sure I didn't ask her anything more about the visit from my mother. And he'd keep Katherine and me apart until all memory of it had completely escaped her feeble mind. I hated that man.

The more wine I consumed, the more I brooded over Carl's malicious ways. If he wanted out of the relationship, he should have just left. But in between feeling hurt by his incendiary words and actions, I did think that perhaps he *was* telling me the truth, the godawful truth, and that maybe I *was* losing my mind.

My father's Aunt Rosie, whom I'd met a few times, including one time as a teenager after my father had heard she had cancer and was in a nursing home, was insane by his account. She obviously had one or more mental illnesses—it didn't take a professional to come to that conclusion. She'd lived alone in a tiny house in an unincorporated area of a small suburb northwest of Chicago that was hard to find even with a GPS. She had furnished her house with an odd assortment of things one wouldn't normally see inside a home—a beat-up plastic car bumper in the living room, the top half of a cemetery monument in her bedroom, a rusted grocery cart in the kitchen.

But it was her behavior that was most concerning. One time, she asked my father to remove a cheap framed print from her wall because she said there were bad people lurking behind the bushes in it just waiting to do something harmful to her. Another time she was in the hospital for chest pains and told the staff she lived in Canada and wanted to know why her medical bills weren't going to be paid by the government. She wouldn't eat anything out of a can because she thought they were trying to poison her, but she didn't know who "they" were. He talked about finding her hiding in a lilac hedge one time when they went over to see her. She'd often lose it during their visits, causing them to turn around and go back home after only minutes of having arrived.

I knew enough about mental illness to know it was sometimes genetic, and my greatest fear in life had always been that I would take after Aunt Rosie.

To gain a better understanding of mental illness, I did an Internet query on the symptoms. Twelve types of mental illnesses were listed on one site I found. After studying the lists of symptoms, I left the site freaked out and scared—no one wants to believe they're mentally ill. After taking a moment to calm down, I convinced myself that those descriptions could have fit anyone.

When I realized I had downed three quarters of the bottle of wine, I decided I'd had enough and lay down on the chaise lounge in my office to think things through while I still had a clear head. But all I could think about was the distant past, times I had to face things without the benefit of a mother. Like the time I noticed blood in my underwear at school. I didn't know what the hell was wrong with me, so I went to the school nurse, and she said I was having my period. I didn't even know what that was or how to deal with it.

Mom hadn't been there for me for other important things—my first date and kiss, selecting a college, my wedding. Neither had Dad. He didn't know how to deal with any of that. My graduations. Let's not even go there. He showed such lack of interest that I usually made plans to go to various events—events that were important to me—with other families.

I closed my eyes, but sleep didn't come easy for me.

* * *

I awoke to Carl, Katherine, and Fluffy glaring at me through the sliding glass door. My head hurt, and my mouth felt like I hadn't brushed my teeth in days. Peering down at the clothes I had worn the previous day, I realized I must have fallen asleep in the chaise lounge the previous evening. My darling husband apparently had left me there so he would have the entire king bed to himself.

Carl and Katherine shook their heads and walked away. How dare they stare at me while I slept. I swung both legs over the side of the lounger and sat up—angry at them, at me, at the world. Even at Fluffy who still stared at me through the window.

"Go away!" I shouted at the dog.

The long, tepid shower I took was mildly refreshing. After drying my hair and fingering it into a reasonable style, I journeyed out into the main part of the house to see what unpleasantness awaited me. The stillness of an empty house and a peek into the garage told me that Carl and his mother had taken his car somewhere. Perfect.

After leaving a curt note for Carl, I grabbed my purse and a breakfast bar from the cupboard and headed for the bookstore, where I could bury myself in as much or as little work as I wanted. As I needed. Alone.

* * *

By the time I wrapped up my day at the bookstore, I had finished shelving the new fiction books, labeled the used-fiction and nonfiction shelves, and tested the inventory system I had purchased. Portia, who had offered to help me every day until she left for school the following week, hadn't shown up. I figured she'd either been warned by Carl to leave me alone or was being irresponsible again. Either way, I didn't care—I did need to be alone.

The drive home was uncomfortable. Between not having eaten anything but a breakfast bar all day and dreadful anticipation of what was waiting for me at home, the fluttery, empty feeling in my stomach caused havoc for me both physically and emotionally. Not helping matters, Carl hadn't called me all day, and I hadn't called him.

Seeing Carl's car in the driveway facing out to the street made me think of someone planning a fast getaway. When I walked into the kitchen and found all three of them—Carl, Portia, and Katherine—sitting at the kitchen table, a disturbing hush fell on their conversation.

"You don't have to stop talking on my account," I said good-naturedly. When no one responded, that hurt. I shook my head in disbelief, poured myself a Scotch, and retreated to my office.

A few minutes passed—long enough for them to plan their next move, I figured—before Carl entered the room.

"You could have joined us," he said.

"You could have invited me to," I responded without turning around from my computer screen.

"Sorry. I didn't know you needed an invitation."

"You don't have to be such a smart-ass."

"Tell me how to act around you, Mags, and I'll do it. I just don't know anymore."

I turned to face him. "Be honest with me. That's all I ask."

"If you're talking about last night, I *was* being honest with you. But apparently, that wasn't good enough."

"Can you shut the door?" I asked in a calm voice.

He did as requested and sat on the chaise lounge. I felt my shoulders tighten up, the way they invariably did when I sensed an impending uncomfortable situation.

"Did you listen to anything I had to say last night?"

"It was hard not to," he replied.

"I know you *heard* me, but did you *listen* to any of it? Did you think about what I said, how I felt about things, what was bothering me?"

"Sure, I did, but to be honest—"

"All that 'but' means is, 'Forget what I just said. Here's what I really mean.'"

"I'm sorry." He shook his head. "Whatever it is that I did or didn't do, said or didn't say, I'm sorry. What's it going to take to get us back to normal, Mags?"

"Normal?"

"You know what I mean."

"No, I don't. Tell me."

"Back to the way things were. Before…"

"Before what?"

"Before they got so screwed up."

"Do you know why they got so screwed up?" I asked, wanting to see if he'd admit to anything I'd accused him of the previous night.

"No."

"That answers my question about your listening." I took a strong sip of Scotch and turned back to my PC.

"Do you have to work on that goddamn thing while we talk?"

"I figured we were done," I said without looking up.

Carl got up and walked toward the door. "The three of us are going out on Lance's boat tonight. You're welcome to join us. Unless you need a written invitation, that is," he added before leaving.

I gave him a minute to create a safe distance between us before I shut the door and cried—long, silent sobs—until my chest ached from trying to hold them in.

* * *

By the time Carl, Katherine, and Portia returned home from their evening with the Richardsons, I had cried enough to be worn out. Loneliness, frustration, and regret had left me feeling completely defeated.

Carl entered our bedroom minutes after I heard them come home.

"So…do you want to talk or be left alone?" he asked me.

I turned around to face him from my reclined position on the bed. "Talk." I told myself that this time I would not lose my composure—no matter what he said, no matter how he made me feel.

He sat on the edge of the bed. "I don't know what to do anymore, Mags. Everything I say and do is wrong. Then you get upset and say things to hurt me. And I do the same. And we end up like this. I've given a lot of thought about this lately, and I'm thinking…"

His voice trailed off, and I was afraid to keep looking at his face, afraid of what he was thinking.

"I'm thinking a separation might be the best thing for us," he said.

His words triggered a tingling in my chest. "Separation?" I barely got the word out.

"I could go back to Chicago, and you could stay here and manage the store. To see how we feel about being apart."

"Separation?"

He nodded.

"How long?"

"Let's try it for a month, then see where we are."

I tried hard not to show how helpless, disabled, and defenseless I felt.

"Okay," I said in a voice so low I could barely hear it myself. "What about Katherine?"

"She can come with me. I'll hire someone to be with her. We have the room in Chicago."

"Sounds like this plan has been in the works for some time."

"You're right. It has."

"What are we going to tell Portia?"

"The truth, of course."

"And when are you leaving?"

"I thought I'd stay through your grand opening…dare I say, in case you need help with that."

"That's three weeks away."

"I know. I'll be around as much or as little as you want during that time."

"I'm okay with your leaving right away. If I need help for the grand opening, I'll hire someone. In fact, I know of a couple of girls who would love to earn some extra money working that weekend." I surprised myself with my calmness.

"You sure?"

"I'm positive." If we were separating, I wanted it to happen right then.

"I haven't discussed this with Mother yet. I'll do that right now."

"And then we'll have to tell Portia."

After Carl shut the door, an unexpected release of the tension that had built up in my body caused me to feel lightheaded. I fell back on the bed, shut my eyes, and concentrated on my breathing—slowly in, slowly out—while what had started out as shock, then strength, then disbelief, slowly turned into fear. I tried to think about other things until sleep was imminent.

* * *

I awoke to the sounds of people arguing. I glanced at the nightstand clock—nine-thirty—I hadn't been asleep for very long. I couldn't make out what they were saying, only the participants—Carl and his mother.

The sound of a sharp knock on the bedroom door made me jump.

"Come in."

Carl came in, closed the door, and stood with his hands on his hips.

"Mother wants to stay here…with you."

A hasty laugh escaped my mouth before I had the wherewithal to hold it back.

Carl stared at me for several seconds before a curl of a smile formed on his lips, and then he laughed too, maybe out of nervousness.

"Why on earth does she want to stay here with me?" I asked.

"She won't say why. Just that she's not moving from here."

"So it's just that she doesn't want to have to move again."

"She told me you weren't that bad."

He couldn't say it with a straight face, causing us both to laugh again.

"Probably the nicest thing she's ever said about me," I said.

"Probably."

"So what are you going to do?"

"I don't know. I can't force her to go with me."

"You could if she was sedated," I half-jokingly said.

"Mags."

"I had that happen to one of my characters."

"And it worked?"

"Until he woke up," I explained.

"We should probably leave that as a last resort."

"Good idea. Well, what do you want to do?" I asked.

"We could sell the brownstone and buy another home up here."

"No. I love that place. All the work we put into to it, the work I put into decorating it. I don't want to do that."

"Well, we have to figure out a way to—"

"Let me talk to her." I said, not knowing what I could say to make any difference but willing to give it a try.

"Be my guest. She's in her room."

"Not right now. I have to think it through first. What if we planned to go out for breakfast tomorrow? She really likes Blue Bay Restaurant up in Mukwonago. Remember? We took her there right after she got here."

"They had cinnamon pancakes, her favorite."

"Right. At the last minute, you'll have to take an important conference call, and I'll suggest we go on ahead. That will give us a chance to talk in the car, maybe in the restaurant too. What do you think?"

"Works for me. I'll go tell her that's the plan."

"Good luck."

For reasons unknown to me, it was perfectly tolerable working with Carl on this level. Perhaps we made better friends than marriage partners.

Now it was time to tell Portia.

"Portia, your father and I want to talk to you about something."

"Sounds serious. What did I do?"

"Nothing, dear. It's about us. Um… We're going to separate. Just for a while."

"Why?"

I looked at Carl—it was his choice.

"It's complicated, sweetie. You know, relationships aren't easy, and sometimes you need time apart to think things through. We need that time apart."

"When did all this start?" she asked.

"It's been going on for some time," he said.

In your head, not mine.

"How long?" she asked.

"A while. Things like this don't really have a distinct starting point. I—"

"Whose decision was it?"

Don't look at me, Carl. This is your doing.

"I guess I did."

"Why?"

"I'm afraid it's not that easy to explain. You know, two people—"

"Did it start before or after I came home?"

"Honey, it had nothing to do with you," I said. I knew this would be hard and didn't anticipate her direct questions, making it even harder.

"Because you're separating from me too, then, you know. How am I—"

"Your mother just said it had nothing to do with—"

"So, my feelings weren't even taken into consideration. Gee, thanks."

"Of course—"

"What have you done to try to work things out? Have you gone to counseling?"

Two good questions.

"Portia, sometimes this happens in marriages," I explained. "And who knows, maybe we'll be able to work through it and things will go back to the way they used to be." *I could only hope.* "You're an adult—we hoped you'd understand."

She got up from her chair. "Well, I don't, and I think this stinks!"

We waited for her to leave the room.

"Well, that went well," Carl said.

"Yeah. I had hoped she'd be more understanding, but maybe that was unreasonable."

"Should one of us go talk to her alone?" he asked.

"I think we should let her think about it for a while."

"And then what?"

"We can talk to her again…hope for the best. She has to accept it."

Right—like I do.

Chapter 18

I couldn't sleep—Portia's emotional reaction to our separation got me to thinking about how much she'd been through in the last year. Now this. And we hadn't told her about Carl's real father yet—it seemed almost cruel at this point. I also got to thinking about my own mom and whether she'd come to the house again. I thought about that often as this was likely the only way I'd ever see her again.

I worried about Portia. This should have been a fun, gratifying time in her life—instead she was having to deal with several serious adult issues. Carl thought she'd get through it—she's young, smart, and resilient. I wasn't so sure.

I managed to get in a few hours of sleep, and at eight a.m., Katherine and I left for Blue Bay Restaurant, a five-mile drive from our home. Carl told us he'd join us if his call didn't last too long.

"So, Katherine, Carl said he told you about our separation."

"Yes, he did."

"I'm sure we can work things through. We just need some time apart to—"

"I don't blame you."

"Pardon me."

"I said I don't blame you. Carl can be, shall we say, hard to live with?"

At first, I thought I hadn't heard her correctly. What mother would say that about her own son, even if she believed it? Then it occurred to me that maybe this was her way to get out of moving again.

"Why do you say that?" I asked her.

"You know better than anyone else how he is."

"I know, but I wondered what *you* were basing it on."

"Same thing you're basing it on."

I was getting nowhere.

"As far as your staying here while Carl moves into our Chicago home, I'd love to have the company, believe me, but I'll be at the bookstore all day, even on weekends."

"I'd be alone at Carl's too. So what would be the difference?"

"Well, I suppose that—"

"I don't mind being alone. I have Fluffy to keep me company."

"Katherine, I don't think Carl is comfortable with—"

"Me being left alone? Well, let me tell you something about Carl's judgment about people. He married Mary. Need I say more?"

I didn't know what to say. With Katherine's mind failing, I didn't know whether to go along with what she said or correct her.

"I don't know much about that."

"Well, I do. Got an earful when he was in Florida with me."

Really?

"How much farther is this place?" she asked. "I'm starving."

"It's up ahead. I can smell the cinnamon pancakes from here."

"I don't smell a damn thing."

The place was packed, and once seated we were crammed between three other tables, leaving no privacy to talk during breakfast. When we finished and were on our way home, I picked up the conversation where we'd left off.

"So…it looks like you're set on staying here, not moving to Chicago with Carl."

"I knew you'd see it my way. You're a smart girl."

"But Carl isn't going to go along with it."

"You'll convince him. He'll listen to you."

Right.

"He has power of attorney over you, you know."

"I signed that stupid thing in a weak moment. Good God, they were going to send me to an old folks' home or some damn place. I'm not that old! And even if I was, I would never go to a place like that. They're for people who can't take care of themselves. That's not me."

We were less than a mile from home, and I needed more time with her.

"Would you like to see the bookstore? It's a lot further along from the last time you were there."

"Okay," she said through a sigh.

I parked the car behind the store and led her in through the back door.

After I gave her the grand tour, she grabbed my arm. "Come with me."

When we reached the middle of the coffee/wine bar area, she let go of my arm and gestured toward the open space. "Look at all this space. You could set up a small place in the back with a chair and a TV. I wouldn't need much. Place for Fluffy. Your customers would love her. She's so friendly."

The right words did not come to me.

"We'd be an asset."

"Um. So you want to stay *here* while I'm at work?"

"I could help you. Making coffee for people."

"You want to *work* here?"

"What else would I be talking about?"

"But they're long days, Katherine. I plan to be open from ten in the morning to eight at night most weekdays. And if there's a book-signing or a reading, then it could be later."

"They're long days at home too."

I couldn't come up with an argument against her suggestion, as far as the space went. But how could I trust her with making specialty coffees and handling money, credit cards, and rude customers? No way.

"Do you know what's involved in being behind a coffee counter, Katherine?"

"How hard can it be?"

"I was going to take a barista class."

"What's that?"

"A barista is someone who knows how to prepare specialty coffees, like espressos and lattes. I'm going to have fifteen different coffees on the menu. See that machine over there? That's a complicated machine that can make all those things. You'd have to know how to operate it."

"Doesn't look that complicated."

You almost burned our house down when you attempted to make dinner for yourself, Katherine.

"Maybe we can talk to Carl about it," I said. "See what he thinks."

She grabbed my arm and steered me toward the back door. "Maybe we should just *tell* him the plan. It's your store, after all."

* * *

"I could see her as an interesting fixture in the store, her and Fluffy," I said to Carl. "It could even be good for business—add a little character to the place. But I can't trust her in charge of the coffee bar, or anything else of any importance."

"I agree. But now what? She's all set to go to work. She's excited about it."

I didn't know what to say.

"No brilliant thoughts?" he asked.

Smart ass.

"I can tell her 'no deal' and say she has to come with me," he said.

"That will have a terrible outcome."

"Worse than her attempting to make a triple, half-sweet, non-fat caramel macchiato?"

"Good point. On another subject, tell me just how it came about that Darlene wanted to help out in the bookstore. That doesn't seem like something she'd offer to do out of the blue."

"What brought that up?"

"Humor me, Carl. Why Darlene?"

"I don't know. It just came up one day."

"And Lance? Why on earth would he want to work in a bookstore at this juncture of his life?"

He shrugged. "It was just to help you get started. That's all."

"Mm-hm. How are those two getting along by the way?"

"I don't know."

"Yes, you do."

"Mags, he's my best friend."

"And I'm your wife."

"Let's not get involved in someone else's affairs."

"He's having an affair?"

"I didn't say that!"

"Yes, you did."

"I did not!"

"You guys always protect each other, no matter what."

"I'm not protecting him."

"I'm going to talk to Darlene."

"About what?"

"About…things." Things that just didn't add up.

* * *

I called Darlene after dinner and asked her if she wanted to take a ride with me to the bookstore. She hesitated, until I told her that I wanted to talk to her about something and thought it better if Lance didn't overhear.

"So, what's this all about?" she asked me in the car.

"I'm just curious, Darlene, what made you want to help out in the bookstore?"

"What do you mean?"

"I mean…I guess I never pictured you working in retail. And you seem to be busy with other things—the yacht club, your women's clubs, all that. Why the bookstore?"

"Um, because Carl said you needed help."

"He did, huh."

"Didn't you?"

"I never asked for it."

"I know, but you said yourself there were times—"

"There's no other reason?"

"Of course not. What other reason would I have, other than to help a friend?"

I pulled the car into the bookstore parking lot.

"Oh, and to keep an eye on Lance," she said.

"What?"

"He offered to help first."

"Why would you have to keep an eye on him? Because of his health?"

"No. Because I think he might be having an affair."

* * *

"What did Dar have to say?" Carl asked when I got home.

"Oh, nothing much. I showed her around. She had a few suggestions."

"Well, I'm glad you worked it out with her. Now, what about Mother?"

"Why don't you pour us a glass of something, and I'll meet you on the patio," I told him. When he arrived, I told him my plan to build out some space for her in the store.

"I don't know, Mags. Is that really what you want to do?"

"I'll manage."

"Okay, so you'll know what Mom is up to when you're in the store. But what about when you're home and want to leave the house for something? We both know it doesn't take long for her to get into trouble on her own."

"It's for one month. Remember?"

"Which month are we talking about? Starting now, like we talked about earlier, or after the grand opening?"

"Now that your mother is going to stay with me, I would prefer it to start after the grand opening. I can't worry about her while I'm trying to get the store ready for business."

"So where does that leave me?" he asked.

"What do you mean?"

"Where will I stay?"

"Here. Just like what we've been doing. Until September eighth, the day after Labor Day." I extended my hand to him, and we shook on it.

"It's a deal, then," he said.

* * *

"I'm going to miss you, sweetie," I said to Portia as I hugged her. "I'm going to be busy trying to get this business going, but never too busy to talk to you, so call whenever you can."

"I'm sorry I wasn't more help in the store," she said, still in the embrace.

"That's okay. I survived."

"I did it with Eddie again."

I pushed her away from me. "What?"

"Don't tell Daddy. Bye! Love you!"

"Where is she?" Carl asked as he walked into the room.

"Probably in the car by now."

"I'll be home tomorrow night. Are you sure you'll be all right until I get back?"

I shooed him away. "I'll be fine. Just go. Have a safe trip."

"Okay, but are you—"

"Just go!" I said laughing.

Katherine appeared. "Are they gone?" she asked.

"They're gone."

"Geesh. I thought they'd never leave. Is there coffee made?"

"Fresh pot in the kitchen." I had no idea what she was up to.

"Two days of freedom," Katherine said. "I feel like I'm seventy again!"

She approached me with two coffee cups in her hands, a bounce in her step, and her face beaming with a strong color and sheen I'd never seen before.

"Is everything alright, Katherine?"

"Of course, everything is alright," she said with her eyes wide and glowing. "Why wouldn't it be?"

"Oh, I don't know. Like you seem awfully chipper this morning. What's this about freedom? Freedom from what?"

"From whom. Carl. He treats me like *he's* the parent. Can't do anything without his approval. He thinks I'm incapable of doing anything for myself. Well, I'm not an invalid, you know."

"Oh, I don't think he thinks that. He's only—"

She held up her hand to my face. "Don't even say it. He only wants to help, make things easier for me. Well, the hell with that! I still have a few good years left in me." She paused to sip her coffee. "Now, let's start planning that grand opening. You need to get a move on, girl—it's less than three weeks off!"

My skin tingled as she spoke. Who was this woman, and what had she done with my mother-in-law?

"Before we get started, I want you to know that I am very aware of the changes going on in my brain these days. But I'm not losing it entirely… not yet anyway. I get frustrated when I can't do something, remember something, and I get confused, but it always comes back. I know the doctors think I have dementia, but I think that's too strong a word. I didn't score *that* bad on the memory tests they gave me. Anyway, the reason I'm bringing this up is that I want you to know that I know, and it's okay to tell me when I don't get something or do something wrong. Now that that's out of the way, can we get started?"

We spent the rest of the day planning the grand opening—establishing a budget; creating a press release and newspaper and social media ads;

designing discount coupons, special event bags, bookmarks, and sandwich-board signs; planning the menu; and scheduling the local authors who had agreed to do book-signings. We planned a drawing for a $100 gift card to the store and sign-up sheets for the monthly newsletter and to join The Indie Book Nook book club.

By seven p.m., we were exhausted and in need of a dinner that I didn't have to cook, so I ordered pizza.

"This was fun," Katherine said.

"It was, wasn't it," I replied. "We got a lot accomplished, more than I would have on my own. Thank you, Katherine."

"What's on for tomorrow?" she asked.

"Well, as we were working, I created a to-do list. How about if we divvy up the tasks while we eat?"

"Who all is helping with the grand opening?"

"Everyone—Carl, Lance, Darlene." I smiled. "You."

"Darlene isn't going to help out."

"She's not?"

"She doesn't want anything to do with it."

"Where did you hear that?"

"Last night on the boat. They must think I'm hard of hearing or something."

We worked for the next two hours, devouring a large loaded pizza in the process, and when we finished, we each had a list of things to do. Katherine and I were on our second glass of wine and wrapping up the day when a knock on the front door interrupted our conversation.

No one ever came knocking on doors in our neighborhood, especially this time of night. Only one possibility came to my mind. I peeked through the peephole.

Even though I hadn't laid eyes on her in over forty years, there was no mistaking that the woman standing on the front porch was my mother.

Chapter 19

Waves of tremors vibrated through my body as I stared through the peephole at the woman on the other side of the door, the cold prickly feeling of goosebumps forming on my arms the only distraction from involuntary shaking. Of all things, what ran through my mind were the many possible explanations about why she had left us that I had conjured up over the years. That she had a terminal illness. That she did something terrible and was on the run. That Dad did something to her and she fled for her own safety. There was a year and a half when I didn't even talk to my dad because I was sure he had done something so terrible to her that she felt she had to leave. Regardless of the reason she had left, I never got over feeling abandoned, unloved, unwanted, and unworthy. To this day. To this second.

For a fleeting moment, I thought about not opening the door.

"Margie?" she said through the door.

Her call to me pulled me back to the task at hand. I opened the door and nodded, afraid that if I tried to speak, no words would come out—none that were coherent.

She looked at me as though wondering what I would do—not sure whether I would throw my arms around her or slam the door in her face. I did neither. Instead, I stared at her until she gave a slight shrug that could have meant just about anything.

"May I come in?" she asked.

Again, I nodded, then opened the door wider so she could step inside.

She glanced around the front room. "Nice place," she said.

She had been twenty-eight when she left. Quick mental math told me that made her close to seventy, and she looked every bit of it. Her clothes didn't help—too-short tan slacks and a wrinkled brown short-sleeved blouse—clean but frumpy. It was hard to imagine she and my father as a couple. Though she was several inches shorter than my five-foot-eight-inch frame and much heavier, a stranger would still have been able to tell we were related—same shaped face, nose, and hazel eyes. And something in her voice was eerily familiar to me, like listening to a tape recording of myself.

"Would you like to sit down?" I managed to ask her.

She glanced over my shoulder. "You have company."

"My mother-in-law. We were finishing up a— Would you like to meet her?"

"Sure."

"Wait here. I'll get her."

Somehow my legs succeeded in transporting me to the sunroom. I held on to the back of one of the club chairs to steady myself. "Um…that was my mother at the door."

Katherine, who now understood my estranged relationship with her, gasped.

"Would you like to meet her?"

She peeked through the archway into the front room. "I think I already have."

"I'll need time alone with her, so—"

"I'll just go to my room. Are you okay?"

"I don't know. Ask me when she leaves."

I sat down on the opposite end of the sofa and faced the woman I knew only by instinct to be my mother.

"Would you like something to drink?"

"No, I'm fine."

"Well, if you don't mind, I would."

I poured myself another glass of wine and returned to the sofa.

"I'm a recovering alcoholic," she said in a monotone voice.

"I'm sorry. I can put this—"

"No, don't. I'm fine being around it. Part of the recovery process." She stifled a smile. "You've turned into a beautiful woman, and this is going to sound a bit like self-praise, but except for the hair, you remind me of me at your age." Her hair, a mix of brown and gray, had been tied back in a ponytail of sorts.

"I'm forty-eight."

"Yes, I know. March eleventh."

"You remember my birthday."

It was hard not to be drawn in by her steady eye contact.

"We have so much to talk about," she said.

Fluffy ran into the front room, followed by Katherine, moving faster than I'd ever seen her move before. "Fluffy! Come back here!" The dog jumped up on the sofa.

"I'm so sorry," Katherine said. "I opened the bedroom door, and she flew out."

Katherine headed toward Fluffy, who had now made herself comfortable on my lap.

I patted the dog's head. "No problem. She can stay here if she wants."

Katherine picked up the dog and shook a finger at her. "You're a naughty girl, Fluffers," she said as she walked away. "Those two need their privacy," she whispered.

"Your mother-in-law lives here?" she asked when the two of them had left the room.

"Mm-hm. A little over a month."

"I was here once before, you know. She told me no one named Margie lived here."

"I know. My husband calls me Mags, never Margie. And she gets confused."

"Where's your husband?"

"Driving our daughter to college. She's a junior at Ohio State."

"My granddaughter."

"Would you like to see a picture?"

"Yes. I would."

From the mantle, I picked up a photo that Lance had recently taken of the three of us on his boat. I handed it to her.

She leaned back deeper into the sofa, tears welling up in her eyes. "I've missed so much, haven't I?"

"Yes. You have."

"And Frank. How is he?" she asked about my father.

"He died in 1986."

She stared down at her lap. "I didn't know that. I'm sorry for your loss. He was still young."

"Massive heart attack."

"That left you alone."

"I was nineteen. Old enough to fend for myself."

She surveyed the room. "It looks like you've done okay."

"Mm-hm."

"How much do you know about me?" Her gaze wandered over my shoulder after asking the question.

"Not very much. Can we start with why you came here?"

She stared at me speechless for several seconds, her body slumped over like a rag doll. "Guilt. Remorse. Curiosity. You name it. I rehearsed what I wanted to say to you a million times, but do you think I can remember any of it now?"

"How about if we start at the beginning." I focused on her eyes, expecting to see something redeemable. Instead, I was distracted by the fine lines that fanned out from their corners. I couldn't stop staring at them, even though nothing could have mattered less. "Like, why did you leave?" I asked, surprised at the steadiness in my voice.

She asked for a glass of water. When I returned, I found her sitting up a little straighter, running the palms of her hands over her pants to smooth out the wrinkles, perhaps at the same time smoothing out her thoughts before she spoke them.

"I don't know if you know this or not, but I was an actress when I met your father. Nothing significant, but I thought I was on my way to something big at the time. We met in a bar. Had too much to drink. Went back to his place. I'll spare you all the details. Anyway, as soon as I found out I was pregnant, with you, I called him, and then we got married."

So, I was the result of a one-night stand. Lovely.

"I didn't know most of that," I told her. "The actress part I knew because I found some old articles about you after he died. So you barely knew him when you got married."

"I'm not proud of that, but it is what it is." She paused to sip her water. "Anyway, Frank didn't like what I did for a living, didn't support me on it at all. He actually forbade me to go back into acting after you were born. Said he'd pay for any schooling, any training I needed in order to go into some other kind of work." She snickered. "I have no idea why I picked nursing.

Maybe he suggested it. I don't remember." She paused. "Look, I don't want to sit here and put your father down. God knows I'm in no position to put anyone down, but he was so…I don't even know the word for it. He had me believing I wasn't capable of doing anything on my own. That I needed him to help me through life, make decisions for me, map things out for me so I wouldn't get lost."

That sounded uncomfortably familiar—I had to concentrate on her words so I wouldn't get distracted by my own experience with him.

"So I went to school to become an LPN and took a job at Forester Hospital. I hated it. Hated school. Hated wearing that godawful uniform every day. Hated the work. And eventually hated Frank for ruining my life."

"Did you hate me too?" I said trying to maintain my composure.

Her sigh, mournful and palpable, touched me. I could tell she was fighting to remain calm. "I didn't realize what I was doing at the time, but I know now that I didn't want to get close to you. I think I knew long before I left that I would someday, and if I had become attached to you, maybe I wouldn't have done it." She took time to sip her water and clear her throat. "Now…that doesn't sound fair, does it? Sounds like a terrible thing to do to a child. Well, it was. But I'm 'fessing up to it."

"Do you have any idea what I've been through because of your irresponsible actions?"

She shook her head.

"Would you like to hear about it?"

"Yes, of course."

"I didn't know why you left. No one explained that to me. Throughout the years, I was forced to make up stuff in my head. Dad kept saying that you left us for something better, but I never thought of you running toward something. No, in my little six-year-old head, you were running away from something—and that something was me. And what did that say about me? Was I that unlovable? Unworthy of your love somehow? Did I let you down in some way? How do you think that made me feel?" The words were out before I realized them in my mind—the emotions I had spent so many years suppressing rose to the surface.

She shook her head. "You must have felt—"

"Don't even attempt to tell me how I must have felt. How the hell would you know?"

"I'm sorry. I— I'm sorry you had to go through that."

"Sorry doesn't quite cut it, I'm afraid. Do you understand that?"

"Look, nothing I can say will come close to telling you how I regret having made that decision…now. But I must admit, it took me a long time to get to this point."

"After Dad died, I tried to find you."

"You did?"

"I didn't try very hard," I said. At that moment, I wanted to hurt her. "Do you want to know why?" I didn't wait for an answer. "Because I was afraid of knowing the truth, which in my mind was that you had moved on… probably to another family…never having looked back. I had pictures in my head of you living in some beautiful house with a big backyard for your new kids, the ones you cared about. I was jealous of an imagined family unit. How pathetic was that? But even realizing how stupid that was, for years I couldn't get that idea out of my head. I even considered hypnotherapy to permanently erase that image from my brain. That's how hurt I felt."

I took a moment to exhale a breath I didn't know I'd been holding before I continued.

"Did you know how we were doing? Did you care? No, don't answer that. Let me finish. When I had my daughter, the love I had for her was overwhelming. It still is. Even when she does something wrong, ridiculously wrong, I still love that child and would do anything for her. That's the normal bond a parent has with their child."

I stopped talking, ran out of words, then sipped the last of my wine while listening to the ringing silence that followed. As painful as the memories were, I found comfort in bringing them to the surface for her to hear. Most of my life I had tried not to think about how her leaving had made me feel—I thought it better to keep everything inside where I didn't have to deal with it or allow it to affect my life, which it had anyway. Letting it all out felt good. I hoped I still felt the same way the next day.

"You didn't even say goodbye," I said through choked-back tears. "I'm done," I said, flapping my hands in the air.

The disconcerted look on her face she'd been wearing was gone, replaced by an expression I couldn't identify.

"Done talking or done with me in general?"

I had to think about it before responding. "Talking for now. I haven't heard the whole side of your story yet."

Chapter 20

"I was twenty-eight, frustrated, and unhappy," my mother told me. "I knew I'd made a mistake marrying Frank, but I didn't know what to do about it. Looking back, I think I was probably clinically depressed."

"Did divorce ever cross your mind?" I asked.

"Of course, but Frank was raised a devout Catholic, was an altar boy and everything, and he was close to his mother. He never would have agreed to a divorce and jeopardize the relationship he had with his mother."

That was odd—my father had never talked about his mother that I recalled.

"Do you know if she's still alive?"

"She died shortly before I left. Tore your father up."

"I don't remember that."

"I'm not surprised. Frank was good at hiding his emotions."

The similarities between my father and Carl had not gone unnoticed.

"So you two never divorced?"

She shook her head.

"I'll tell you my breaking point. I came home after working a double shift at the hospital one day. I was dog-tired, and all I could think of on my way home was taking a long, hot bath and going to bed.

"When I got home, you were upset about a movie the babysitter had taken you to see, when I was upset about spending the last sixteen hours caring for a bunch of ornery sick people, one of whom had died on my watch. I almost made it to the bathtub when your father came in and wanted to know what was for dinner. I put on a robe, whipped up something for the two of you, and returned to my bath, which was now cold. I remember sitting in it anyway, shivering, not at all relaxed like I had envisioned. I sat in that tub for a long time, thinking about how unhappy I was.

"It was the middle of the night. I couldn't sleep, and I knew if I didn't leave then, I'd be miserable for the rest of my life." She stopped briefly and sighed. "This is going to sound selfish and so small-minded, but it's the truth. I didn't think about anyone but myself. I didn't think about any of the consequences of my leaving. I just left."

"Where'd you go?"

"I got in my car and drove. West. And when I stopped for gas—I drove a white '66 Fiat back then—I picked up a road map and headed for southern California."

"To pursue an acting career?"

"Yes."

"Do you remember the last words you said to me?"

"No."

"I had said to you that one day I was going to make a movie that everyone would like. You don't remember what you said to me?"

She shook her head.

"You said that was a fool's dream. The last thing you said to me before you abandoned me was that I was a fool." The tears I'd been fighting came precariously close to the surface. "That was a horrible thing to say to a child, don't you think?"

"I was the fool."

I got up from the sofa and walked away from her. "I'll be back in a few minutes."

While in the bathroom, I let the tears flow, not realizing how affected I still had been by her parting words on that fateful day. Midnight. We'd been talking for hours, and fatigue had gotten the better of me.

The longer I stayed in the bathroom, the more I feared I wouldn't find her there when I returned, and the more I feared that perhaps it would be better if that were the case.

A knock on my door broke my thought process.

"Mags?"

"Yes."

"Are you okay?" Katherine asked.

"I'm okay. I'll be out in a minute."

"Just checking."

I couldn't help but smile. "Thank you, Katherine. I appreciate that."

I found my mother standing in the front room when I returned. I held in one hand the pocket watch, and in the other, the note she had left behind on the day she departed. I showed her the watch.

"Your Grandfather's," she said.

"Your father?"

She nodded.

"I don't remember him."

"I probably didn't talk about him."

"Why?"

"I don't know. Like I said before, looking back on things, I probably didn't want to get too close to you."

"It would have been nice to know him."

"He died before you were born. I was still in high school. That watch was all I ever had of his to remember him by."

"Why didn't you take it with you?"

"I must have overlooked it…in my haste I guess. I always hoped you had ended up with it."

"Do you know anything about the inscription?"

"Time is a gift?"

"Yes. Is there a story behind it?"

She reached into her purse and pulled out a book.

The book was beat-up. I read the title—*The Phantom Tollbooth.* "Oh my God! I remember this story—it was my favorite book. Milo, Tock the watchdog. I haven't thought about this book in years. What does this have to do with your father?"

"He knew he was dying, and he gave it to me. It's obviously a children's book, so I was puzzled as to why he thought I'd be interested in it. Then he gave me the watch, with the inscription. I didn't get the connection until I read the book."

"I'm afraid I still don't get it."

"If you remember, Milo and Tock went on this fantastical journey to a place called Dictionopolis."

"Where all words come from."

"Right. And on their way, they stop at places like The Land of Numbers and—"

"The Island of Confusion. It's coming back to me."

"They learn that nothing is possible without time. Time is our most valuable possession, and it's given to us. A gift."

"You took the book with you."

"That I did."

"Why?"

"Looking back, maybe deep down that lesson was important to me. It is today, that's for sure."

I thought about the truth in what she'd said.

"What's that?" she asked about the folded piece of paper in my hand.

The timing didn't seem right to hand it to her, but I did anyway.

"Do you remember this?" I asked.

After reading it, she said, "It's been a long day. I don't know about you, but I'm really tired. I want to finish telling you my story, but not tonight." She handed the note back to me.

I wasn't sure if I wanted to hear anymore, whether I could take anymore. I stood there staring at her. When I realized my nails were digging into my crossed arms, I unclenched them and tried to relax.

"You can come back tomorrow afternoon. I need the morning to do things to get ready for the grand opening, which is in less than three weeks."

"Grand opening?"

"I'm opening up a bookstore in Lake Geneva."

"How nice."

"Where are you staying?"

"Whitewater. I have a room there."

"Not too far from here. You'll take Route 20 then?"

"Yes."

We parted without another word, without touching each other. As I closed the door, I wondered if I'd ever see her again.

* * *

Still rattled the next morning after the abrupt visit from my mother, I joined Katherine in the kitchen where the sweet-smelling essence of Earl Grey lingered.

"How'd it go?" she asked as she poured a cup of tea for me. "I heard her leave pretty late."

"We talked…and talked and talked. She told me about her mindset when she left. I told her what effect it had on me at the time and even now after all these years. That was mostly it. She's supposed to come back this afternoon."

"Did you tell her anything about Carl and Portia?"

"Just who they were. Not much more. It was like two strangers meeting, really. I don't know how I feel about her yet."

"Give it time."

"For all I know, she was just checking me out, see what all I had."

"Why do you think that?"

"I don't know. She seemed to scrutinize every corner of the room." Perhaps I'd written too many cozy mysteries—my mind shouldn't have gone there.

Katherine and I talked about what each of us wanted to accomplish that day.

"Can we work from the bookstore today?"

"I guess so. Why?"

"I can think better if I'm actually in the space."

The phone interrupted our conversation.

"I couldn't help but notice a strange car pull out of your driveway late last night. Is everything okay?" Darlene asked.

I was in no mood for her nosiness but didn't want to leave anything to her imagination either.

"Everything is okay. It was my mother." I gave her a brief rundown on our visit.

"Wow."

"I'm surprised you saw her leave. The tall bushes and all."

"I was waiting for Lance to come home."

"Oh?"

"I'm convinced more than ever he's cheating on me."

"How can you be sure?"

"I went through his wallet this morning looking for clues."

"Did you find anything?"

"I found a number I didn't recognize and called it."

"And?"

"It was the detective who was working on his case when he had his accident."

We both laughed.

"I still can't see him cheating on you."

"I don't know. But I did find out from the detective that they recently arrested someone who confessed to mugging several people over in Whitewater by hitting them on the back of the head. The guy admitted to doing the same thing in other towns but couldn't remember which ones, so we're thinking that's what might have happened. Lance got mugged, wandered aimlessly into the woods, and passed out."

"He was lucky someone found him."

"Mm-hm."

* * *

Before my mother arrived, I considered the timing of her return. What if she had come six months earlier, when Portia was home from college and we were eating Thanksgiving dinner. Or six years earlier before we had purchased the lake home and Portia was still in high school. How would it have turned out then? How different would her homecoming have been?

My mother arrived at one p.m. with a photo album under her arm. We sat at the kitchen table with a pitcher of raspberry iced tea I had made for the occasion. Her appearance was better today—she was not as tired looking and wore nicer clothing. In the light of day, I could see where she could have been in the entertainment industry—beneath the wrinkles and dark circles under her eyes, she was still quite beautiful, something I'd not realized the day before.

"I would like to hear about your life, if that's an okay place to start," she said.

I glanced at the album. "All our photos are on CDs. I can show them to you later."

"I'd like that. I'd like that very much."

"Where to start," I said. I relayed to her the saga of my life—grade school, high school, my first love, Dad's death, college, how I met Carl, Portia, our careers, and Portia's growing up. I left out any reference to our current rocky marriage. By three o'clock, she knew more about me and my family than anyone else besides Carl.

She had let me talk, didn't interrupt or ask many questions. When I finished, we went into my office where I showed her photos taken throughout my life.

"You missed every milestone," I told her.

She attempted to comment but had too hard of a time getting the words out.

When I had finished, we retreated to the kitchen table where she opened her photo album.

"It's easier to remember things with the photos in front of me." She pointed to the first one—my birth photo. I peered down the rest of the page and onto the next page—each filled with images of me as a child.

"This explains why I don't have any photos of me for those years," I said.

"I took them with me when I left, in a shoebox that I had duct-taped closed, and they stayed in that box, unopened, until…well, I'll get to that later."

"May I scan these?"

"Of course."

When she turned the page, my eyes immediately went to an obvious publicity still of her in a very flattering pose, wearing a bathing suit, sitting on a large rock with clear blue water in the background, her knees bent and her arms reaching around them—absolutely stunning.

"Before we get to that," she said, "this is that '66 Fiat I drove to California, and this is a photo of the flat I shared with three other actress-wannabes I met when I arrived there. Sharona, Magdalene, and Fred."

"Fred?"

"Cross-dresser and a very good dancer. Here they are in this photo."

"Which one is Fred?"

She pointed to one of the individuals—he blended in well.

"This PR shot was the first one I had taken when I arrived." She glanced up at me. "Not too bad, huh?"

"You were gorgeous."

"A good photographer has a lot to do with it. I was lucky." She made a face. "No, I wasn't. I promised myself I'd be truthful with you. I slept with him in exchange for a few photos. Everybody did it back then. Maybe they still do. Even Fred did. Not that that made it right, but that's what we did when we had low-paying jobs and no money for a few headshots."

"What did you do? For work I mean."

"Waitressing and then…I'll get to that."

She flipped past a few more PR photos before pointing to a newspaper article with an accompanying photo. "My first part—*One Flew Over the Cuckoo's Nest*, 1975."

"You were in *Cuckoo's Nest!?*"

She laughed. "I was one of the cuckoos," she said. "Big movie. Small part."

"Wow."

"Then *Bugsy Malone*."

"You're kidding."

"1976. Another small part—one of the floozies. Rock Hudson was *so* handsome. We all had a crush on him, and then we thought he and Jeannette Nolan had something going on behind closed doors, but of course, we now know that probably wasn't true. Then in *Sophie's Choice* I was one of the extras, one of the Jews being led to the gas chamber. I never even watched that film—too disturbing."

"You were in *The Breakfast Club*?" I asked when I noticed a small poster with Emilio Estevez on it.

"I played a sexy teacher. You never saw my face. Only my rear end." She paused to take a sip of tea. "I had a pretty nice ass back in the day."

When she turned the page, her expression changed. "This film was the beginning of the end for me. *Cry-Baby*, 1990. Can we stop for a minute? I need to take a potty break."

"Sure. It's around the corner."

The beginning of the end, she'd said. 1990. Fifteen years ago. So far, our conversation had been relatively temperate, but I sensed that was about to change.

When she returned, I could tell she'd been crying.

"You okay?" I asked.

"Yeah. I had to get something out of my system before I get to the next part. When do you expect your husband?"

I checked my phone to see if Carl had left any messages. He had. "He says if traffic is good, he'll be home by seven."

"I can be gone by then."

"You don't have to be if you don't want to. You could join us for dinner," I said without thinking.

"No. Not today. But maybe some other time?" She had better sense than did I.

"Okay."

"Let me back up some. I've been giving you just the highlights of my career as an actress. There are ten times as many lowlights—long periods of time with next to no money, bad relationships, lots of drinking and carousing. Being an actress is not a glamorous life. I don't care what anyone tells you."

"Were you happy with what you were doing?" *Happy to be away from us?*

"I thought so at the time, but looking back…no, I don't think so. That's why it was so easy to—. Let me continue with what happened during *Cry-Baby*. I met Brent Dawson III during that film. Hooking up with him was a huge mistake. He was an extra, like me. We hit it off and began hanging out. By then, I was drinking heavily and smoking a lot of pot. He introduced me to heroin and other stuff, including…prostitution. Let's just say I had a few really bad years."

I hadn't been prepared for such a disturbing account of this part of her life.

"How did you get out?" I asked.

"He died. Was murdered, actually, in a drug deal gone wrong. Left me homeless, hooked on drugs, and alone. I had one garbage bag of belongings to my name, and inside was that taped-up shoebox of photos. I dragged that bag to a free rehab center, and that's where I stayed for sixty days."

"What happened to all your friends?" I asked.

"So-called friends."

"Had you opened the box yet?"

"No. I wasn't ready yet."

"Where did you go from there?"

"Santa Monica." She paused. "Good place to be homeless."

"Why is that?"

"It's relatively safe. Access to public bathrooms and showers, especially on the beach. Lots of soup kitchens, but I used to go to the farmers markets where they'd give out samples. I slept under the pier, in people's backyards, and sometimes just under the stars. Nobody ever bothered you there."

"That's sad."

"I'll tell you what's sad. I don't know how many homeless people there are in Santa Monica, but it's a lot, and a percentage of them are vets, and it's not a small percentage."

"Really?"

"Vets and kids. That's what bothered me the most. And that's what led me to opening the box."

"Vets or kids?"

"Kids. One kid. I was organizing my belongings one morning on the beach when this dirty little kid wearing nothing but a raggedy pair of underpants came up to me. He couldn't have been any more than four or five years old. 'What's in the box, lady?' he asked me. He was referring to the shoebox with your photos in it. I told him, 'Nothing.' He asked me why it was all taped up. I looked around for a parent or someone, and, finding no one, I politely told him to leave. When he didn't, I went back to my sorting.

"Well, that little bas— child grabbed the box and ran off with it. So I scooped up all my stuff, shoved it back in the bag, and went after him. But he was gone. Vanished. Didn't see him anywhere." She paused. "I was devastated. I walked that beach the entire day looking for that kid, then into the night. I checked the shelters, food kitchens, doorways, all the other places I knew I'd find homeless people. But I never found him."

I stared at the album, which she had closed when she'd gotten to the part about meeting Brent Dawson. "So where did these photos come from?"

"I'm getting to that part. I walked all over Santa Monica that night, determined to find the kid. Never went to sleep. And then, right at the break of dawn, I walked by a dumpster next to this diner I knew where instead of throwing away yesterday's food they would set it out nicely next to the dumpster so people like me wouldn't have to go rummaging through the real garbage. Anyway, there it was. The box. Ripped open and lying half under the dumpster, like it had been flung there.

"I scrambled around on my hands and knees—among the dirt and grime and putrid smell of rotting food—collecting all the photos, forcing myself not to look at any of them for too long. Then it dawned on me that if these pictures were important enough to me that I would wallow around in such filth to retrieve them, then I needed to do something about it."

I stared at her face—a roadmap of hard times—the mixed feelings I had worsening my ability to hold back tears. What she had told me touched me in so many ways. Yet I couldn't ignore the fact that the woman sitting across from me had abandoned me for a better life when I was only six.

"I spent the next several hours sitting by a drinking fountain near the boardwalk, cleaning each photo with napkins I took from an outdoor café.

One by one, I wiped them clean, and of course I couldn't help but look at them then. The longer it took me, the more I realized what a selfish, stupid thing it was to leave you." She looked up at me warily. "You may be wondering why I'm not crying over this. Well, I can honestly say that I think I'm all cried out."

"You said that was what, fifteen years ago? What did you do between then and now?"

"Got sober for one thing. I was off drugs, but still drank. I couldn't come back here a drunk, so I got treatment for that too. What else did I do? Whatever I could to pull myself together enough to be able to come find you and hope for the best. I moved from one shelter to another, worked odd jobs until I had enough money to buy a car, lived in that for a while until I could afford a small apartment. And then I saved up for this trip."

"When did you get here?"

"I got to Chicago in March."

"You've been out here since March?"

"It took me a while to find you."

"Where are you staying in Whitewater?"

"Bethel House. It's a homeless shelter. A nice one."

A nice homeless shelter. How sad was that?

"Where do you want to go from here?" I asked her. I hesitated at the end of my question, thinking I should address her by some name, but what? Mother? Marilyn? Neither seemed to fit.

She studied my face. "I don't know. I don't know how to read you," she said.

"It's been a bit overwhelming—I'm not sure *what* I'm feeling, to be honest."

"That's fair. How about if we leave it there, and I'll wait for you to get back in touch with me."

"How would I do that?"

She wrote down a phone number. "You can leave a message for me at this number. They'll make sure I get it."

"I hope you're not disappointed that—"

She smiled. "I was just going to say the same thing to you."

<h1 style="text-align:center">Chapter 21</h1>

"How did the trip go?" I asked Carl when he returned home from taking Portia to school.

"Fine, but I was worried about you."

"Why?"

"You didn't answer half of my texts or return my voice-mail messages."

"Sorry. I've been so busy…"

"Is everything okay?"

"Mm-hm. Have you eaten dinner?"

"I grabbed something on the road. Did you and Mom eat?"

"No. I'll go ask her what she's in the mood for."

"No, don't. I'll take care of her. You sure you're all right?"

"I'm fine. Go see your mother."

I didn't tell Carl about my mother's visit—I wasn't sure why. When he returned, he said his mother asked for Chinese food for dinner.

"Do you want something?" he asked.

"No. Not really."

As soon as he left, Katherine came out from her room.

"You didn't tell him about your mother, did you?" she asked.

I shook my head.

"I won't say anything either," she said before shuffling back into her room.

I made a quick sandwich and buried myself in things that still needed to be done for the bookstore. My mother's timing couldn't have been worse.

Looking back over the past two day's conversations, I questioned how I'd made it through them. A part of me felt sorry for her. Maybe that was it.

I struggled to put our conversation in the back of my mind, but then I kept taking it out again to examine every word separately, and when I did, it didn't take long for my sympathetic resolve for her to turn into rage. How dare she try to come back into my life now, after all these years? And why should I welcome her back with open arms or believe anything she has to say? After what she had done to me? Was still doing to me? Why? Because some kid made her feel guilty about it?

She said it took strength for her to get up the nerve to knock on my door. I'll bet it did. Forty-two years. That's how long it took her to decide that maybe I was an important aspect of her life.

She was probably looking for a handout. Tired of living like a damn vagrant. Well, screw you, Mother. You can't shut me out of your life for that long and expect much in return.

I knew that reuniting with my mother was going to change my life— just how was what worried me.

* * *

It took until two a.m. to finish my work for the day. It would have taken less time if I had been able to rid my mind of the intractable thoughts about my mother, but the more I pushed them away, the more persistent they became.

Carl had left me alone, for whatever reason. After peeking into the front room where he had taken to sleeping lately, I headed for our bedroom. Exhausted, both physically and mentally, I went to bed without showering or even brushing my teeth.

* * *

"Fire!"

It took me several seconds to gather my wits about me after his shouting jerked me awake. I jumped out of bed at the sound of more than one smoke detector blaring and ran into the kitchen where I found Carl slapping wet towels on the stove top amidst thick smoke and an overpowering stench.

"Do you have it under control?" I yelled at him. "Should I call 9-1-1?"

"I got it," he said as he plopped down into one of the kitchen chairs.

I opened windows and doors to get rid of some of the smoke.

Carl held up what was left of a burnt dish towel.

"Your mother?"

"Either her, or we have a covert arsonist living with us who likes to cook."

"Carl, she's going to burn the house down one of these days…with us in it."

"I know. I know. I thought she'd be okay until…this."

I joined him at the table. "What are we going to do?"

He shook his head. "I don't know," he said without making eye contact. "She's good one day, and the next day she pulls something like this." He put his head in his hands and muttered something that sounded like, "Just shoot me."

"And leave it in my hands? Thanks a lot."

He raised his head, forced a smile, and uttered a sigh.

"She needs supervision in a controlled environment," I said.

"That pretty much sums it up, doesn't it?"

"What if we went ahead with the master-suite plans for upstairs?" I asked. It had been something I'd been thinking about since the last fire she had almost started. "That would free up a bedroom on the first floor for a live-in caregiver."

"And then whose bedroom would it be upstairs?" he asked.

"Ours, if we make it through the separation." I immediately regretted the comment, the sharp tone I'd used, and having created an opening to a discussion about our marriage. One catastrophe at a time.

"At least one of us is trying," he said.

"What's that supposed to mean?"

"What have you done lately to try save this marriage?"

"What do you mean, what have I done?" I asked. "What have *you* done? Can we go outside and talk? I can't stand the smell in here."

"You might want to put on some clothes first," he snapped.

I glanced down at my skimpy nightgown.

A few minutes later, we were sitting on the patio with cups of hot tea.

"Is she okay? Did you check on her?" I asked.

"Of course, I checked on her. She's sleeping. Like nothing happened."

"Can we forgo the marriage conversation for another time?" I didn't wait for a response. "Look, even if we went ahead with the upstairs remodel, we need a short-term solution."

"I know."

"Her bedroom is right next to my office. I could give that up, hire a live-in caregiver, and we could start construction upstairs. I can set up my computer and other stuff in the sunroom temporarily."

"I suppose that would work," he said.

"And when my store is up and running, she can spend her days there if she wants, or she can be here with the caregiver."

"Maybe we could find someone who could be both caregiver and a help in the bookstore," he suggested.

"Maybe. That would be nice. But, Carl, I have way too much on my plate right now to deal with this. I have a grand opening in two weeks and two days, my mother—" I cut myself off. I wasn't ready to tell him.

"I wondered when you were going to tell me about her."

"You know?"

He nodded.

"Let me guess—Darlene?"

"You didn't tell her it was a secret."

I ignored his remark and filled him in on the two visits.

"So when are you going to call her?"

"I'm not sure."

* * *

The days flew by, and after the third time Darlene asked me how she could help, I accepted her offer. Her motivation wasn't to help me—I knew that— she just wanted to pick my brain for what I could find out from Carl about Lance's comings and goings. I didn't care—help was help.

Katherine helped too. Unfortunately, sometimes the extra work she caused because of her help negated any benefit we had with her being there. Even so, having her and Fluffy in the store personalized the surroundings in a way that I thought could pay off in the long run. And I didn't really mind having her around. In fact, I rather liked having her around.

Carl forged ahead with the remodeling plans for the second floor, telling me I could be as much or as little involved as I wanted, which I interpreted as his way of trying to find out whether I wanted to be in the marriage for the long haul. For the time being, we decided to live separately in our lake home—not easy given its size. Carl carved out a small section of the second floor for himself—an inexpensive desk from IKEA, a blow-up mattress, and a dorm-sized fridge temporarily satisfied his needs. I had too many other things on my mind to worry about what he was doing behind my back, if anything, or what he was going to do once the space was under construction.

I found the live-in caregiver Carl hired to watch over Katherine more than a little troubling—too young and too cute. In all fairness, he had given me the opportunity to interview the candidates, but I didn't have the time to spare. Blond and blue-eyed with a shape most women—myself included—would die for, she was too tempting for a middle-aged man technically separated from his wife. And to make matters worse, her name was Candie. Candie Caines—the perfect stripper name. I pictured her and Carl going at it on the blow-up mattress in his second-floor hideaway when I wasn't home.

But Candie Caines didn't occupy my mind much given all the work involved in getting the store ready during those long days that stretched well into the evenings.

Two days before the grand opening, it all came together. I set things up so that when customers would walk in the front door, they could turn right to head toward the coffee bar, turn left to browse the new paperbacks, or walk straight ahead to the used paperback section. All the books—all three thousand of them—had been previously vetted and given to me on consignment, and based on the response I'd received when I'd solicited books from indie authors all over the world, I hoped to be on to something.

A ten-by-ten-foot pen in the center of the room could accommodate two cashiers, if needed. Several racks of reading-related items were scattered throughout the store. The few pieces of artwork on consignment from the art dealer down the street didn't fill the walls, so with my limited budget I managed to fit in a few framed posters. My favorite was a reprint of a 1946 print ad encouraging travel with the Airlines of the United States—it featured a picture of a man reading to a boy and girl sitting on his lap, with the caption, "I'm getting to know my children again."

The area directly behind the coffee bar's back wall housed four computer terminals where people could order the Kindle or Nook version of most of the books I shelved, giving people the opportunity to browse books in paperback form and then order the less expensive electronic version. I would receive a small commission on the e-book sales as well. And customers who belonged to book clubs also had the opportunity to hook up directly with authors to invite them to participate in their discussion about their book either in person or via Skype, something traditional bookstores didn't offer.

Behind the wall that closed off the computer terminals, I had set up a semi-private area for Katherine—a place where she could read, watch TV, or nap. With her help in designing it, we included an easy chair, side table, console for a small TV, and a decorative privacy screen. We found a poster of *Pride and Prejudice*—her all-time favorite book—to hang above the easy chair.

Exactly what Katherine would do each day had yet to be determined. She talked about walking around and helping customers and stopping by tables in the coffee shop to see how they were doing—being a good-will ambassador of sorts. It remained to be seen how that would go.

Much to my delight and surprise, Portia texted me that she'd be home for the long holiday weekend and would help with the grand opening as much as I needed her—hopefully, not just another example of good intentions. In addition, Katherine's caregiver would be there, plus Darlene, Lance, Carl, and Frances, the twenty-year-old daughter of the art dealer down the street, someone who already knew how to make gourmet coffees.

Portia made it home the day prior to the first day of the four-day event, at which time I told her about the visit from my mother.

"No shit. That must have been weird," she said.

"I guess you could say that."

"So, did she apologize to you for running away on you?"

"I think she's remorseful."

"She better be."

"She's been through a lot herself. I'll fill you in on those details later. Right now, we need to meet everyone at the store for a pre-opening last-minute discussion."

When Portia and I met the others at the store, we sat at what would be the special events table.

"Okay, gang. Everyone have their checklist?"

The collective weak murmur from my crew was not exactly reassuring.

"Carl, what are you going to do?"

"Stand outside and flag people in with my irresistible charm."

He could be charming…when he wanted to be.

"Fine. Lance?"

"I'll back up Carl, because he isn't really all that charming."

"Really?" I was in no mood for humor.

"Sorry. I was trying to be funny. I'll be wandering around like a customer when business is slow and asking the rest of you if you need anything in between."

"Check. Darlene?"

"I'm in the checkout pit."

"We should really come up with a better name for that. Portia?"

"I'm going back and forth between the computer terminal area in case customers are having any trouble and the coffee bar to meet and greet customers, offer them free sweets, and encourage them over to the bookstore side."

"Excellent. Candie?"

"I'm helping out in the coffee bar. Can there be a tip jar for Frances and I?"

Candie had worked in a Starbucks during college. I was hoping her coffee-service skills were better than her grammar skills.

"Sure. I'll put that on my list to provide both of you with a tip jar. Katherine?"

"Yes?"

"What are you going to do during the grand opening?"

"What do you want me to do?"

"Do you see your name on the sheet in front of you?"

She lowered her head. "I forgot my reading glasses at home."

I handed her my readers. "Here, try these."

"It says I'm to be my friendly self with the customers and help out where needed."

"Can you do that?"

"Do you think I'm inept or something? Of course I can do that." She dropped her gaze to the sheet again. "What if I don't like them?"

"Who?"

"The customers."

"We're always nice to customers, Katherine. Even if we don't especially like them. But remember, they're getting free coffee and sweets, so they'll probably be in a pretty good mood."

"I'll try," she mumbled.

"And Frances?"

"Barista."

"Any questions?" I asked.

"Yeah, what are *you* going to be doing?" Katherine asked.

I ignored the collective chuckle.

"I'm going to be walking around, greeting customers, introducing myself as the owner, making sure you all have what you need. Backing up Darlene at the cash register. Stuff like that."

"Can I bring Fluffy? She's going to be lonely at home with no one else there."

"I don't think that's such a good idea, Mom," Carl said. "Not during the grand opening. What if someone opens the door and she runs out? Then what?"

"I'd watch her. She won't do that."

"You can't watch her every second, especially if you're helping a customer with something."

"Hell with the customers. Fluffy is more important."

Carl turned toward me. I'm not sure why. An awkward silence followed.

"How about this? What if we picked up a crate to put in your private area in the back, Katherine? That way she'll have a place to nap throughout the day. And when she's not napping, could you keep her on a leash?"

"You're a lot smarter than Carl's first wife."

Good grief.

Portia shot Carl a puzzled look. He mouthed to her that he'd explain later.

"So that will work?" I asked her.

"Of course it will work."

"Okay, that's a wrap, folks. Get lots of sleep tonight because we're open from ten tomorrow morning until eight at night."

"When does the wine come out?" Candie asked.

"I thought six would be a good time to change from coffee and sweets to wine and munchies."

"Got it."

"Candie, can you stay after we're through here? I want to talk to you about something in private."

Her eyes widened, and then she shrugged.

"See you guys bright and early tomorrow. I'll be in the store by eight."

I sat across from Candie while the others vacated the store.

"Did I say something wrong, Mrs. Manning?"

"No, not at all. Why do you ask?"

"Because I feel like a kid being held after school for something I did wrong."

"I'm sorry. I didn't mean to—"

"Sometimes it's not what you say. It's how you say it."

Even though she may have had a point, she had no right saying that to me. Disrespectful little—

"My mother is like that too," she added.

I sucked in a breath and continued.

"All I wanted to say is that while you have dual roles when you're in the bookstore, your primary responsibility is with Katherine. I'm relying on you to know where she is at all times, what she's doing, and how she's doing it. Is that— Does that sound doable? There's 1,500 square feet of space and a few walls, so I know that won't be easy, but you know how she is and—"

"I know how to do my job, Mrs. Manning. I've received very good training."

"I don't doubt that, I just—"

"I won't disappoint you." She rose from her chair. "Is there anything else?"

"No. That was all—"

"Then I'll see you tomorrow morning. I'll come in with Katherine and Carl."

"See you later, Candie."

I did not like that girl.

Chapter 22

As soon as I awoke on the morning of the grand opening, the tightly wound knot in the pit of my stomach told me I had forgotten to do something important. Or two things. Or three. But at least one. Despite many checklists, I knew there had to be something I'd overlooked.

I wolfed down a hard-boiled egg and piece of toast before driving to The Indie Book Nook. On the way, I racked my brain for things I might have let fall through the cracks.

As soon as I arrived, I toured the store imagining myself a customer—an astute, critical customer. I couldn't find any defects in the layout, signage, or aesthetic appeal, but that didn't mean I wouldn't fret over it all day anyway. I tested the cash register and computer terminals to make sure they were working properly. Then I used the microwave to make myself a cup of tea. That's when the overhead lights went out.

I had no idea where the circuit-breaker panel was located, so I began my hunt to find it. After crawling around on my hands and knees behind the coffee bar, I found it tucked up under a lower cabinet. After cussing out the electrician for putting it in such a hideous place, I snapped the spring breaker back into place, and the lights went on.

When I raised myself up off the floor, grunting and groaning in the process, Carl, Katherine, and Candie stood before me. Katherine had Fluffy on a leash.

"What are you doing down there?" Carl asked.

I could have come up with many different smart-ass responses, but instead I contained myself. "The microwave blew a circuit, I think. I guess the electrician thought this would be a good place to hide the circuit-breaker panel. The lights are back on. I hope that takes care of it."

"The lights went out?"

"Yeah. When I tried to use the microwave."

"Try it again," Carl said.

I pushed the START button, and again the lights went out.

"Shit!"

"Calm down," Carl said. "I'll take care of it."

Mad at myself for getting worked up about something so minor, I was about to get back to the business at hand when I did a double-take upon looking at Katherine. On her face was a rather generous amount of makeup—thick blue eye shadow, heavy eyebrow pencil, and gaudy red lipstick. The conspicuous foundation line of demarcation she'd formed along her jawline topped off the look. I shot a glance at Candie who shrugged and walked away.

"Well, let's get started everyone. Candie and Frances, would you please make a few sample drinks to make sure everything is working properly? Portia, can you check out the computer terminals? And you know what—snatch a scratch pad and pencil to put by each of them in case someone needs to jot something down when they're making a purchase."

"Aye-aye, captain," Portia said, saluting.

"Very funny."

"Darlene, would you walk the floor like you were a customer and see if you see anything wrong?"

"Got it."

"What can I do?" Katherine asked.

I had a hard time looking at her with all that makeup smeared on her face. "How about if you walk around the store with Fluffy so she can sniff stuff and get used to the space. I think dogs need to do that."

"And me?" Lance asked.

"If Carl isn't finished with the electrical problem, can you cover for him?"

"So that means *I* have to be charming?"

"Give it your best shot," Darlene shouted from across the room.

"The sandwich-board signs are in the storeroom," I told him.

I found Carl in the computer terminal area on the phone with the electrician when Katherine walked up to us. "Can I borrow your readers?" she asked me. "I left mine at home."

"For a minute, but I need them too."

"I'll bring them right back."

"I wouldn't have done that," Carl said in a low voice. "And what does she have all over her face?"

"Her idea of glamming it up with a little makeup, I guess."

"How many gallons did she use?"

"That's the least of my worries right now. As for my glasses, I got a call from the eye doctor down the street that my new ones are in. I'm going to run over there before we open. I'll be back in ten minutes."

When I returned, Lance and Carl were putting the sandwich boards out on the sidewalk and tying the balloons to them.

The sign over the door looked great. In big black letters on a green background it said, THE INDIE BOOK NOOK. Below it, in smaller letters were the words QUALITY BOOKS BY INDEPENDENT AUTHORS.

"Looks good, guys." I checked my watch. "Fifteen minutes to opening!"

"Nervous?"

"Yep."

"You'll do great, hon," Carl said after kissing me on the forehead.

I took several seconds to savor the effect his words had on me. I needed to hear them, especially today.

As soon as the three of us reentered the store, people began to gather outside the door. When I turned around the OPEN sign, at least fifteen people, mostly women, entered the store. Some went straight to the coffee bar for the free coffee and what we called the "sweet of the day," which I'd purchased from the bakery down the street. Some browsed the bookshelves. Others gathered around the special events table where I had placed flyers, promotions, and information on upcoming events.

By noon, twenty-five people had already signed the guest book and had included their e-mail addresses so they could receive announcements. That pleased me. My goal of one hundred e-mail addresses accumulated during the four-day event looked promising. Another thing I found especially satisfying was seeing so much traffic in the children's section, where I had gone to extra lengths finding the right children's books authors and developing fun incentives for children to read more books. The large colorful rug and bean bag chairs helped to draw in the children.

Next came the book-signing. When author Vineta Atkins walked through the door with a rolling case that I suspected held copies of her newest book, I set her up at a table visible from the front windows. As we were chatting, two people from the local newspaper walked in—a photographer and a reporter. The reporter interviewed me while the photographer roamed around the store snapping pictures—all a bit overwhelming, even though I knew in advance that they were coming.

When the photographer asked me to sign a consent form, I put on my new glasses to read it. Suddenly, out of the corner of my eye I noticed something coming at me. I jerked my head back involuntarily. It happened so fast, I couldn't be sure what it was—all I saw, for just a second, was a faceless woman in a long, flowing black robe.

"Are you okay?" the reporter asked.

I whipped off my glasses, and the image disappeared. Then, I wasn't sure I'd even seen it.

"Yes, I'm okay. Just a little something weird with my glasses." I put them back on my face, but this time way down on my nose while I read and signed his form. I couldn't wait to take them off again.

"Nice turnout," the reporter said. "I'll go see how Mike is doing. Can we get a group shot of you and your staff while we're here?"

"Sure."

I gathered everyone in front of the coffee bar so the photographer could get the shot. Afterward, I went to check on Vineta.

By six o'clock, at least a hundred people had come through the store, and I think I must have talked to every single one of them as I was pulled in one direction and then another with questions, comments, and suggestions.

"Nice store, but why don't you carry any *New York Times* bestsellers?"

"Can I sit at the coffee bar if I don't intend to buy any books?"

"My sister self-published a book. I'm going to tell her about your store."

I grabbed a power bar from my purse and went back to Katherine's area, where I hoped I could grab a short break from all the activity. Glad to see that neither Katherine nor Fluffy was there, I sprawled into the easy chair and closed my eyes for a minute.

"She peed on some books."

I opened my eyes to find Katherine standing before me, holding Fluffy, the eye shadow on her left eye smeared halfway down her face.

"What?"

"I didn't get her outside fast enough, and she peed on some books."

Great.

"Show me where, and I'll take care of it. No, wait. Would you please tell Carl to take care of it?"

Katherine didn't move.

"Is Carl around?"

Katherine shook her head.

"Do you know where he is?"

She shook her head, but I didn't believe her.

"Katherine, where is Carl?"

Portia came around the screen. "No one is at the cash register, Mom."

"Where's Darlene?" I asked.

"I don't know."

I didn't like her tone. "Portia, can you go with Katherine and take care of whatever mess Fluffy made. I'll go to the cash register."

Muddled thoughts ran through my mind while I rushed to the checkout pit—like where Carl and Darlene had gone without checking in with me. As I took care of the last customer in line, Darlene and Carl walked in the front door.

"Where's Portia?" Darlene asked.

"With Katherine. Apparently Fluffy had an accident and—"

"Calm down, Dar," Carl said.

"What's going on?" I asked.

"I'll tell you what's going on," Darlene snapped. "Your daughter is sleeping—"

"Dar, not here," Carl said as he took her arm and led her toward the back of the store.

It didn't take much to figure out what had just happened—Darlene had become aware that Portia had slept with her son. But why now—at my grand opening?

Lance came by and asked about Darlene's whereabouts.

I shrugged.

Suddenly, Darlene stomped through the store toward the front door. "I'm done here!" she shouted before exiting. Their mouths agape, customers who were within hearing distance—just about everyone in the store— stopped what they were doing. Within a minute, their lips were moving, and I suspected the topic of their conversation wasn't books.

Carl came over to me as soon as I had no more customers in line.

"How'd she find out?" I whispered.

"You knew?"

"Yes."

"You didn't tell me?" he said in a low, wrathful voice.

"It was between Portia and me at the time."

"Bad decision, sweetheart."

"So how did *you* find out?" I asked him, trying to ignore his implied threat.

"Dar confronted me about it…just now."

"How did she find out about it?"

"Apparently, Eddie called Portia's cell while she was here. Portia's cell went berserk this morning, and she couldn't make or receive any calls, so when Eddie couldn't get through, he called his mom looking for her. She casually asked him why he wanted to talk to her, and he avoided the question. When she mentioned it to Portia, she got defensive. Dar got suspicious. And somehow it came out. I'm not sure exactly what was said."

I wanted to know more, but a customer had come to the counter asking why we didn't have James Patterson's latest book and informed me she was heading off to Barnes and Noble to buy it. I tried in vain to explain the nature of independently published books while Lawrence Rossie, my second book-signing author of the afternoon, packed up to leave.

"I can't believe that's all you have here," the customer snapped. "Self-published books are crap!"

Nice thing to say within earshot of Lawrence, who had written four award-winning sci-fi books. He continued to pack up his remaining books, smiling but not saying anything to add to the conversation.

"Much of what is self-published isn't very good, I'll admit," I told her. "But every book on my shelves has been professionally edited, the same way traditional books are edited. I don't accept 'crap.'"

My explanation was pointless. The woman wanted James Patterson.

As she was leaving, Portia raced through the store and asked me if she could borrow my phone. I didn't ask questions and gave it to her. She grabbed it out of my hand and disappeared out the back door.

I hadn't pictured the first day of the grand opening going quite like this—had not counted on being stuck behind the cash register knowing that somewhere in the store sat a bank of books that had been peed on. I looked at my watch. An hour and a half to go.

I put my glasses on to scan the cash-register history for the day and then quickly swooped them off my face when I saw fast-moving images out of the corner of my eye. I resolved to bring the glasses back to the place where I'd purchased them. I had plenty of readers at home I could use until these were fixed.

Eight o'clock didn't come soon enough. I let the others go home, and after turning the sign on the door to CLOSED, I picked up the last finger sandwich and piece of hazelnut torte and fell into Katherine's easy chair in the back, allowing the balm of being surrounded by books in complete silence to comfort me.

A half hour later—after savoring the last bite of the intense sweetness of the torte's layers—crushed hazelnuts and grainy dates that had been soaked in liquor and smeared with honeyed cheese—I turned out the lights, took one last look at the sign-in sheet, and headed toward the back door. As soon as I opened it, a large gray-striped cat with an unusually short tail dashed by me and into the store.

"Hey! Come back here you!"

The scruffy-looking cat jumped up on the checkout pit counter and stared at me as if to challenge me to get him off. As I got closer, I noticed that he had only one eye—the other one was completely shut.

I cautiously approached the animal and examined it. No tags. No collar. Inflamed ears I could see from a distance probably meant it had mites from being outside. When I got close to him, the cat hummed a deep-sounding purr and rubbed up against me. I lifted its tail—a girl.

I'd always intended to have a cat in my bookstore, but now was not the right time, and a one-eyed cat with ear mites and a severely cropped tail was not exactly what I'd had in mind anyway.

I stared at her. She stared at me. It was all over. I walked down the block to the drugstore, picked up some cat food and basic supplies, and welcomed Borgne to her new home.

Chapter 23

I entered my house with trepidation, not knowing who would be there or what the topic of conversation would be. Carl, Katherine, Darlene, Lance, and Portia were all seated with drinks on the patio. I poured myself two fingers of Scotch and joined them.

Darlene stood up to greet me. "Before you say anything, I have apologized to everyone here for my behavior today, and I want to apologize to you as well." She gave me a quick, awkward hug. "If I embarrassed you or offended you or anyone in the store in any way, I'm sorry."

"Okay. Apology accepted. So, everyone here is okay with everyone else?" I asked.

Nods from everyone.

I couldn't imagine how things could have changed so quickly, and I didn't dare question it.

"So, I have a full crew tomorrow?" I asked with a smile.

Nods from everyone again.

"I hope you don't think I'm being rude, but I have a lot of work still to do tonight, so I'll be at my computer. Good night everyone. See you in the morning."

I spent the rest of the evening pouring over sales figures, entering new subscriber information into the database, and reading e-mails. Eleven e-mails were from grand opening guests, all of them complimentary except one that said, "The old lady with the Halloween face and obnoxious dog ruined it for me." I know from being an author, you can't please everyone, so I didn't worry over that one comment. Three others included favorable comments on Katherine and Fluffy, which furthered it being a non-issue.

The day's sales figures exceeded my expectations and goals, and I couldn't wait to tell one of my authors that all her books had sold out. My own books, which I had prominently displayed near the cash register, did well too.

I went to bed weary but feeling good about the day.

* * *

Before opening the store the next day, I walked to the optometrist's office to complain about the glasses.

"They're defective," I told the young woman behind the counter.

"How is that, Mrs. Manning?"

"I keep seeing images reflected on the lenses."

"Can you point to where you see these images?"

I ran my finger around the section of rim where I kept seeing things.

"Do you mind if I put them on to see for myself?" she asked.

"Be my guest."

She swiped the glasses with a wet wipe, put them on, and rolled her eyes up, down, and all around before taking them off.

"I'm afraid I don't see what you're seeing, but wait here, and I'll get someone else to try them."

She returned a minute later with an optometrist.

"May I?" he asked, picking up my glasses.

After wiping them off, he put the glasses on and did the same thing the young woman had done.

"I don't see any images. I can see reflection of the overhead lights, but that's it. We do have a sixty-day guaranty on the glasses, if you're unhappy with them."

"I'll try them a little while longer and see what happens, but I may be bringing them back."

I left their office utterly perplexed, disappointed, and a little embarrassed. Just my luck the glasses worked fine while they examined them. Sometimes they worked okay for me too.

When I reached the bookstore, Candie and Katherine were waiting outside. Katherine's makeup had been toned down. A wink from Candie told me she may have had something to do with it.

"Sorry, gals," I said as I unlocked the door. "Had to run a quick errand."

"We came early in case you needed help before the store opened," Candie said.

"I sure do. I was so tired last night that I left without getting the place ready for business today—something I promised myself I'd never do."

They took the coffee bar side of the store, and I took the rest. By ten o'clock when we opened, everything was in order.

Except for when Fluffy discovered the cat and chased her all around the store, day two ran more smoothly than day one. Afterward, Portia approached me to see what the commotion was all about.

"Fluffy discovered Borgne," I told her.

"Huh?"

"I brought in a stray cat last night after you all left, and Fluffy found her."

"Born? What kind of name is that?"

"It's French. B-o-r-g-n-e. It means one-eyed."

"The cat has only one eye?" she asked me while we searched.

"And a severely cropped tail."

"Some cat."

"She's really very sweet. Come help me set things up for the first book-signing."

After Portia and I set up the special events table, I relieved Darlene at the cash register so she could take a break. When the next customer came to check out several books, I put my glasses on to conduct the transaction. This time, I made sure I peered out of them in a perfectly straight line—instead of moving my eyes to the left or right, up or down, I moved my head. That seemed to work.

The rest of the day went without incident. As I turned the CLOSED sign around at six o'clock, I couldn't help but wonder how I would feel at this time a week from then, a month from then, or even longer. I hoped things would be calmer, easier, and less exhausting.

When I headed to the now-deserted coffee bar to start putting things in order, Portia followed me and offered to help straighten things up for the next day.

"So, do you want to tell me how it all came down with Darlene yesterday?" I asked.

"Okay. So I was helping a woman at one of the computer terminals with her order when Dar came over to me saying, 'My son wants to talk to you.' She took me by surprise, and I dropped my coffee cup on the desk in front of the customer, luckily it was empty, but it caused the woman to jump out of her seat and walk away."

"Good God. Did it hit her or anything?"

"No, but it startled her for sure."

"I wish I knew who it was so I could apologize."

"I tried to find her later, but she'd left the store."

"Great. So, what was said between you and Darlene?"

"I had no intention of telling her anything, but she kind of goaded me into it. You know how she can get."

"You told her you slept with Eddie?"

"Not exactly, but she could kind of read between the lines. She called me a home-wrecker."

"Well?"

"Mother!"

"Portia, you slept with a married man—twice!"

"That doesn't make me a home-wrecker."

"And then you said…"

"I told her she needed to have this discussion with her son, not me."

"Then what happened?"

"She left. Lance followed her, and I think you know the rest. When Dad and I got home, we had a drink on the patio. Not much later, Dar and Lance came over and asked if they could join us. And then the first thing she said was that she had talked to Eddie, and he told her that it was true, that we'd been together, and that he'd admitted it to Melodi, and they're going to go to counseling. And that's why he was trying to get in touch with me. To tell me that."

"Wow. And Darlene was suddenly okay with you?"

"She said when she first suspected something, all she could think of was 'How could you do that to my son?' Then, when he admitted it, it became more like, well, people make mistakes."

"That's true, of course, but some mistakes are bigger than others."

"Maybe."

"Maybe?"

"Am I going to get lectured again?"

"No. You know the difference between right and wrong."

"Maybe not."

"Portia. Yes, you do."

"We kind of had another go at it late last night."

"What?"

"You're so gullible, Mom."

I put my arm around her. "C'mon. Let's go home…smart ass."

"Mother!"

* * *

The third day of the grand opening weekend went well—no embarrassing incidents. Even the pets behaved. Borgne had found her special hangouts—the cozy-mystery section being one of them. The customers loved her, and she and Fluffy quickly became friends. Most noteworthy, sales and subscribers went beyond my initial conservative goals.

At the end of the day, Carl asked if we could talk alone after everyone else had left. He initiated the conversation while we prepared the store for the next day.

"Now that your grand opening is almost over, I suppose I could move back to Chicago," he said.

"Mm-hm."

"But I was thinking that would leave you with overseeing the rest of the attic reno."

Carl had hired a general contractor to coordinate the project, but that didn't eliminate owner involvement altogether.

"I can't be involved with that, Carl. I have my hands full here. When will they be done?"

"He's saying four more weeks."

"Why is it taking so long? They do a whole house in a week on TV."

"Apparently, business is good, and his plumbers and electricians and others have other jobs lined up. I don't think the work is actually going to take that long."

"So, what do you want to do?" I asked.

"I don't know. How do you feel about me staying up here until it's done?"

"You're the one who wanted the separation, remember?"

"Are you saying you don't?"

"That's not what I said."

"Well, I don't know how long I can hang out where the work is going on."

"You can hang out anywhere you want in the house when I'm here."

"What about the sleeping arrangements?" he asked.

"Why can't you keep sleeping upstairs? They're not going to work nights, are they?"

"Of course not, but—"

"I don't see a problem then."

"Fine." He threw down the cloth he'd been using to wipe down the counter and stormed out of the store.

What did he expect me to say—"Okay, darling, in that case you can sleep with me"? Was he having second thoughts about the separation? Great—just when I was getting used to the idea.

I gave him a minute before I glanced out the window to see where he went—I was his ride home. Not seeing him, I finished cleaning and straightening up, fed the cat, and drove home.

Chapter 24

On Labor Day—the last day of the grand opening—I expected a respectable turnout given the decent weather and the end of the tourist season. By noon, twenty-one more people had signed the guest/subscriber book, and revenue was already higher than the previous day's full take. People who had come in on previous days were reappearing, sometimes introducing me to a friend or neighbor. Lily stopped in, which didn't surprise me as she said she would, giving me a sense of comfort that I sorely needed. But a visit from fish-hat guy—who I still thought about now and again—took me by surprise.

I was relieving Darlene on the cash register for a lunch break when I spotted him—same hat, same stance, same guy. He eyed me briefly, flashed a guileless smile, and then browsed the shelves for a while, disappearing behind the used book section, reappearing now and again, sneaking a peek my way. I wondered if he recognized me and if he did, whether he'd approach me. He still struck me as handsome, in a rough-around-the-edges sort of way. And he obviously had an interest in books—nice trait.

A group of teenagers stood in line with a variety of romance novels waiting to be checked out. When I finished with them, I didn't see fish-hat guy anywhere in the store, although his presence still lingered. I wiped my clammy palms off on my pants and went back to what I had been doing. It felt good to see him again.

At the end of the day, after the last customer had left, everyone hung around to partake of the champagne and hors d'oeuvres that I had ordered from the restaurant down the street. Carl walked in as I shared preliminary sales results with the others and thanked them for all their hard work.

Darlene stayed behind after the others had left.

"Can I talk to you about something?"

"Sure. What is it?"

"I'd like to keep working here, if you could use me, that is."

Had I heard right? She'd been a big help during the last four days, had picked up on things quickly and didn't need to be told what to do.

"Are you sure? What would make you want to do that?"

"Except for that unfortunate little incident, it's been fun. Got me out of the house for something other than yacht-club schmoozing. What do you say? Could you use me? Not full-time or anything. Maybe a couple days a week?"

"I'd be paying you minimum wage, just like anyone else."

"I don't care about the money. And this may or may not surprise you, but it would be the first paycheck I've ever received."

"You've never worked a day in your life?"

"Not one."

"You do realize that if you were a stranger applying for a job, I wouldn't hire you."

"Why?"

"You have no experience…with anything!"

We both laughed.

"I am trainable though," she said.

"Sure, let's give it a try. You do have a Social Security number, right?"

"I think so. I'll dig it out."

* * *

In the days following the grand opening, I experimented with my new glasses to figure out exactly when they played tricks on my eyes and when they didn't. The images I saw, while maybe not as frequent, were lasting longer and becoming more distinct. Like the day I clearly saw in my peripheral vision someone—a woman in a long dress—lunge at me. Fortunately, I was in the back of the store straightening out the fantasy section of used books when it happened, and no one observed me almost lose my balance when I tried to avoid being struck by her. I wanted so much to relay these images to the optometrist, but how could I do that without her thinking that I probably needed a head doctor more than an eye doctor?

I decided to keep the glasses but go back to wearing readers.

* * *

Within the promised timeframe, the contractor finished the second-story master suite—an awesome room that took up the entire U-shaped floor. The king-size bed we'd purchased had been anchored in the middle of the U, directly in front of a cathedral-shaped window overlooking Lake Beulah—the expansive breadth of the lake from the higher vantage point was remarkable.

On the north leg of the U were a large walk-in closet and master bath. On the south, a seating area. Carl surprised me by having a wet bar installed in the corner. We hadn't talked about that, and it wouldn't have been my choice, but then I had given him full rein to do it the way he wanted, so I couldn't complain. The teal and gray color scheme added a romantic feel to the space.

With the master suite completed, Carl was free to move to Chicago full-time as planned. We talked about it one evening after Katherine and Candie had gone to their respective rooms for the night.

"So, when are you going back to Chicago?" I asked him, trying to act as nonchalant as he did on many occasions.

"Hmm. Not sure."

"Not sure *when* or not sure *if?*"

He stared at me for a long moment without saying anything.

"Tell me what you're thinking," I said.

"Is this going to turn into an argument?"

"It doesn't have to."

"Well, I feel that's where it's going."

"Carl, it's important for me to know what you're thinking. Are you going to go back to Chicago? Separate from me? Is that what you want? Just tell me, so I know."

"I don't know what to think."

"What's confusing you?"

"You."

"What do you mean?"

"I don't know. One minute, we seem to be getting along like we used to, like working together in the bookstore. And then you say or do something that conflicts with that."

"So it's me?" I asked. "I'm the one causing our marriage to not work?"

"That's not what I said."

"That's what you implied."

"Like that."

"Like what?"

"Like I'm trying to have a civil conversation with you, and you sabotage it right away, make it into an argument. You never used to do that."

"*I* sabotaged it. You accuse me of being the one responsible for ruining our marriage, and you're telling me I sabotaged the conversation?"

"You're twisting it around. What I said was—"

"I'm well aware of what you said. There's nothing wrong with my hearing."

He got up, glared down at me and, with an inscrutable absence of expression, said, "This is why— You know, I don't want to be in a relationship with someone who makes me feel pressured to do something all the time." He paused for an uncomfortable moment. "I'll be gone by the time you get home from work tomorrow. If there are any issues with Mother, bring them to Candie's attention. She'll involve me if necessary."

I poured myself a healthy serving of Glenlivet on the rocks and retreated to the patio where, while not doing a very good job at fighting back tears, I watched the reflection of a low-hung moon slow-dance rhythmically on the still water, the luminous blue-gray sky both comforting and depressing.

As I sat there, the night air hung still, in deep contrast to the tension that had built up in my body. I rolled my shoulders several times to relieve some of it and closed my eyes while I pictured the world rushing past me. When I opened them, the mesmerizing quiescence of the water caused me to pause and reflect on what had just taken place with Carl. He was right. I had shunned him when he was trying to make amends, and that confused me.

* * *

The day after Labor Day—the day that each year for the past six years Carl and I would head back to our Chicago brownstone for the next eight months—began with a thunderstorm so loud that I awoke with a jolt. I jumped out of bed to peer outside at the lightning display, and then knowing I wouldn't be able to get back to sleep, went to the kitchen to make myself a cup of tea. Katherine, whose hearing we thought to be deteriorating, joined me shortly thereafter, followed by Fluffy and then Candie.

"I guess Carl is the only one sleeping through this," I said to no one in particular.

"He's gone," Katherine said. "You didn't know he was going back to Chicago?"

"He told me he was going to leave sometime today, while I was at the bookstore."

"He came in to say good-bye to me sometime in the middle of the night," Katherine said. "I didn't look at the clock. The next thing I knew it felt like we were having an earthquake. Did you feel the house shake?"

I raised the cup of tea to my face and allowed the warmth of the steam to greet and then comfort me. I took a sip and let the hot liquid soothe my throat.

Candie, still in her pajamas, nodded a greeting. "Some storm," she said.

A loud crack of thunder immediately followed a series of lightning strikes that lit up the charcoal sky, the wind appearing to scream at us as it ripped by the large sliding-glass doors, bringing with it a collage of tree branches and other debris.

"I don't like this," Katherine said.

"I haven't seen anything like this since the flood of 2010," Candie said.

"What flood was that?" I asked.

"Northwest Pakistan."

"You were in Pakistan?"

"Army Medical Corps."

"You were in the Army?"

"Not actually the Army, but when we were sent somewhere, it was always to an Army base. I guess that's how it got its name."

"What did you do for them?"

"I'm a registered nurse."

"And you went to Pakistan?"

"Afghanistan. We were there to help some of the 20 million or so Pakistanis affected by the flood."

I couldn't imagine Candie in such an environment.

"How long were you there?"

"Six months in Afghanistan, three years in the Corps—long enough to never want to see another wounded soldier or civilian again."

"So you have a college degree in nursing."

"Johns Hopkins."

"Impressive."

A smile played at the corners of her mouth. "Mom and Dad are proud."

"Where are they?"

"Maryland."

"What brought you here?"

"A guy, what else."

"Are you still with him?"

"Nope." She rolled her eyes. "Long story."

"But you stayed here."

"I like it here. I'm still friends with his parents."

We gazed out the window at the darkness—darker than normal for daybreak.

"All my life's a circle, sunrise and sundown. The moon rolls through the nighttime 'til the daybreak comes around," she said.

"Harry Chapin."

"I love that song," she said through a sigh.

It was one of my favorites as well. My first true love, Wayne, had given me the album, and I would listen to it all the time. "That came out long before you were even born," I remarked.

"Not that long before. I'm thirty-five."

She looked twenty-five.

By eight o'clock, the rain had let up, and after Candie and I went out to assess the damage, I made breakfast for the three of us and then went upstairs to get dressed for work.

As I walked around the new master bedroom suite, I pictured Carl and me hanging out up there—a huge space with plenty of room for two people to do whatever they needed to do without bumping into each other. I had carved out a place for my PC in the sitting area where I had a full view of the lake. A writing sanctuary one floor higher and away from everyone else more than adequately suited my needs.

While rearranging a few things in and around my desk, I came across the Limoges Eiffel Tower box in a drawer where I'd never kept it. My first emotion was anger, as I assumed Carl had had something to do with it—

one last hurrah before he left. Curious to see if anything was missing, I scrambled for my key and opened the drawer that I always kept locked.

A second Limoges Eiffel Tower box stared back at me. How could that be? So, Carl hadn't stolen the original box and hadn't sold it to the pawn store? Or did he find another one and plant it in my desk? I decided to put my money on the latter. Something was rattling around inside the box. I opened it. There was the pearl-drop earring, the one that had been in the missing box. Suddenly, everything seemed distant and surreal.

A wave of dizziness mushroomed inside my head, causing me to sit down on the bed. Lightheaded, disoriented, and a little nauseous, I stayed there for several seconds. When the fingers on my left hand went numb and then started to tingle, I got scared. And when an image resembling my mother wearing a jeweled crown on her head drifted toward the bathroom, I became petrified. Within seconds, the tingling stopped, and the image had vanished.

I closed my eyes and told myself it was nothing—it had lasted such a short time—but deep down I didn't believe it.

Candie must have sensed something bothering me as we drove to the bookstore. She asked me if everything was okay.

"Of course," I told her. "You know that section of romance novels by the front door? If you have time today, would you tighten that up for me? Maybe Katherine can help. I'm getting more books in but not until next week, and they've been selling so well, there are large gaps on the shelves. And make sure the books are lined up with the front of the shelves, not pushed back."

Throughout the day, I avoided talking to people as much as I could. Fatigued—perhaps more mentally than physically—and grateful for the alone time I had coming after Darlene, Katherine, and Candie left for the day, I prepared the store for the following morning.

Alone with my thoughts and no customers to worry about, I thought about the first time I'd seen images out of the corner of my eye. They'd coincided with when I'd started wearing the new glasses. But now I still visualized them even though I'd stopped wearing the glasses, so I believed the glasses had initially caused them, and now they were in my head. I knew that sounded absurd, but without any other explanation, what else could I think?

I took my time tidying up the store, and when I finished, thinking it was the right time to contact my mother, I left a message at the number she had given me, telling her to feel free to stop by the bookstore the following week. Contacting her more out of a sense of duty than anything else, I still didn't know what to expect from the relationship, if anything.

When I arrived home, Candie and Katherine had already eaten dinner and were watching the sunset from the patio. I grabbed a leftover half-sandwich from the fridge and retreated to the office area of the new master bedroom.

The incredible autumnal sunset with its blazing crimson and gold streamers lingering like a dream above the shoreline left a reflection on the water that appeared to live on even after the sun had finished its descent. I pictured Darlene and Lance enjoying it together next door—a pang of jealousy tugging at my heart.

I hadn't thought about Carl much lately. I didn't miss him. At least, I didn't think I did. His being in Chicago kept him from playing tricks on me. Like shortly before the grand opening when I found out from my attorney that the screenwriter contract had been a complete farce. My attorney was concerned about it enough to investigate the source of the e-mail, so if Carl was behind it, he could get exposed.

With him in another city, no more of that nonsense.

<h1 style="text-align:center">Chapter 25</h1>

It happened at the end of the second full week of the bookstore opening when I was behind the coffee bar getting it ready for the two-hour wine-bar time slot. Darlene was taking care of a customer in the checkout pit.

At first, it felt like a spasm in my left leg—a bad one. I couldn't shake it off. Then my leg completely froze up on me—no matter how hard I tried, I couldn't move it. I waited until Darlene finished with the customer and called for her.

"What's the matter?" she asked.

"I can't move my leg."

"You can't move your leg," she said, her furrowed face rigidly focused on mine.

"I can't move it. It's frozen or something."

"What do you want me to do?"

"I don't know," I managed to say, my chest so tight, it was hard to get the words out.

"Should I call 9-1-1?" she asked.

I felt that if I tried to talk, I would cry, so I nodded. I didn't know what else to do. The numbness, the inability to move, had travelled to the other side of my body. Feeling like a statue from the waist down, I supported myself with my hands and arms on the counter.

Darlene told the few patrons in the store that we were going to close the store due to a small emergency. She kept her eye on me as she ushered them out the door. Within minutes, the paramedics arrived. Before I could finish explaining what happened, I lost the ability to stand on my own.

* * *

I awoke to the stark smell of cleaning products.

After several seconds, I desperately tried to lift my head but couldn't. Slowly, I took in my surroundings until I realized where I was—a hospital room.

The room—pristine, clean, and cheerless—contained the typical hospital bed, guest chair, and beeping monitors. The depressing pale-blue walls and gray linens on the bed rounded out the scene.

I couldn't remember how I got there or why until I tried to move my legs and couldn't. Then it came back to me—I had frozen in mid-step somewhere. I searched for the button to call a nurse or someone but didn't find one.

Every segment of my body—the ones I could feel—were weak, my brain like mush. I tried to move my legs again, but either they had been strapped down or I didn't have the strength to move them. I couldn't remember my name, the day of the week, or where I lived. All I could remember was standing somewhere and not being able to move. My thoughts scrambled to the point where I couldn't follow them. Not wanting to face whatever it was I was about to face, I closed my eyes and willed myself back to sleep.

* * *

When I heard people talking, I kept my eyes closed until I recognized one of the voices.

"She's awake," Carl said.

"Where am I?" I asked.

"You're in the hospital, Mags," he said.

"Why?"

"You had an episode."

"What kind of episode?" I asked as I tried to sit up. I propped myself up on my elbows as far as I could go. Tubing ran from both my forearms to somewhere above my head.

"They're not sure. They're running tests. In the meantime, you need to rest. You should probably lie back down."

Carl appeared to me to be surrounded by haze, so I couldn't see who all was in the room.

"Who else is here?" I asked.

"It's me, Mags. Darlene."

"Hey, Darlene."

"Who else?"

"Just us."

"I want to go home."

"You'll have to talk to the doctor about that. He'll be in shortly," Carl said.

"Are they telling you when I can be discharged?"

"Best to ask them yourself."

I didn't like the way that sounded—vague and avoidant. And why was he here with *her?*

"Who's minding the store?" I asked.

"We closed the bookstore until further notice."

"Really."

"Well, you've been in here and—"

"How long have I been here?"

"Four days."

"What?"

"It's Tuesday, Mags. You were brought here on Friday."

"I have to get to the store!" I sat up straight, not caring what tubes attached to me I jostled loose.

"Settle down, you're—"

"I'm fine. Get me out of here!" I tried to swing my legs over the side of the bed, but something under the covers held them in place. I whipped off the blanket and sheet to reveal ankle restraints.

"What the hell is this for?" I shouted.

A nurse came in and gently pushed me back down to a reclined position.

"Here, take this," she said as she handed me a small paper cup containing two pills.

"What's this?"

"Something to calm you down," she said. She held out a glass of water with her other hand.

I knocked the glass out of her hand.

"Let me out of here! I don't belong here!"

The nurse adjusted something above my head, and within seconds my brain fogged up. I tried to speak, but sleep pulled me in another direction.

* * *

"Wake up, Mags." I recognized Carl's voice. "Open your eyes, if you can."

"I've been drugged," I said without opening my eyes. "Where am I?"

"You're still in the hospital."

"Why?"

"You're not well."

I managed to open my eyes, but keeping them open proved too difficult.

"I feel fine. They can't keep me here."

"The more you cooperate, the sooner you'll be released," he said in a low voice.

"What day is it?"

"Wednesday. You've been here five days."

A dark-skinned man in a bright white lab coat walked into the room.

"Margaret?"

"Yes."

"I'm Dr. Kumar. How are you feeling today?"

"When can I go home?"

He laughed. "Can we talk about your health first?"

"Shoot."

He gestured toward Carl. "Would you like him present while we talk?"

"Sure. Can you take these ankle cuffs off of me first?"

"Do you promise not to bolt?"

"Of course not."

"We didn't want you to hurt yourself. You're quite the athlete."

His remark puzzled me.

"Margaret, we've done a myriad of tests on you, and frankly, we're a little puzzled. Your blood work is normal. We've run an EKG, EEG, MRI, and CT scans. Nothing appears out of the ordinary. Your glucose level is normal, and so is your protein level. And a complete metabolic panel was unremarkable. We've screened for autoimmune disorders, and we've ruled out a number of viruses." He raised his sites from the folder he held. "You are somewhat of an enigma to me, Mrs. Manning."

"Then let me go."

"I can't do that."

"Why?"

"Because based on your physical behavior since you've been here, I believe you are a danger to yourself and possibly others."

"That's bullshit."

The doctor stared at me for a long moment. "Nurses, orderlies, and cleaning staff have all reported instances of extreme agitation, so much so that they were afraid to come near you."

"That's not true. Why would they say such things?"

"Do you remember much of what has transpired these last five days?"

"Yes, I remember everything," I lied.

"Tell me about your confrontation with the day nurse this morning."

"I had no confrontation with anyone this morning."

The doctor peered down at the file. "It says here you threw a full pitcher of water at her."

"I did no such thing!"

"Yesterday, you called the orderly who was checking your monitors the *n*-word."

"I've never used that word in my life!"

"Mrs. Manning, your memory is severely impaired."

"It is not."

"Do you remember my name?"

"You can't expect me to remember everyone's name."

"What is your name?"

"Mrs. Manning. You just said it."

"What is your first name?"

I almost said "Mary" but didn't want to be wrong.

He turned toward Carl. "The thing is that this is not the right facility for your wife to be in—they don't have the appropriate staff, and the environment isn't conducive to her needs."

"What do you recommend?" Carl asked.

"Hey, remember me? The patient."

The doctor turned back toward me. "What you need for a proper diagnosis is an inpatient psychiatric facility. They have—"

"Get him out of here!" I shouted. "I don't need a psychiatrist!"

A nurse entered the room. I pulled out the tubes from both of my arms before she could stop me. Another nurse came in, and the two of them held me down while the doctor injected something into my arm.

* * *

I didn't know how much time had lapsed when they transported me to the "behavioral health hospital"—a politically correct term for nuthouse—by ambulance. Then they rolled me through the back door by wheelchair— the whole thing utterly ridiculous. I was not crazy and shouldn't have been there. At that moment, I hated the doctors, my husband, the Richardsons, everyone for making me think I needed to be there. And Aunt Rosie if it was she who had passed on her crazy genes to me. They could all go to hell…except for Aunt Rosie, who might already have been there since she was dead.

I recalled something Carl had said to me while in the regular hospital. "The more you cooperate, the sooner you'll be released." I suspected he was right and vowed to maintain a calm demeanor no matter how difficult.

Without reading them, I signed some forms before they wheeled me into an exam room where several different staff members wearing scrubs checked my vitals, height, and weight. The last one took a couple of vials of blood before sending me to the bathroom for a urine sample.

My rights were explained to me, twice. They made it clear that if I didn't agree to be there voluntarily, someone could petition for me to stay there for an evaluation. Thinking again of Carl's words of wisdom, I chose the voluntary route.

They gave me a pair of baggy blue scrubs to wear before being taken on a tour of the facility. Day room with a TV, cafeteria, activity room, nurse's station, and lots of patient rooms. When they showed me to room 109-A where I'd be sleeping—a ten-by-ten-foot-square room with two beds, two nightstands, a desk, chair, and a bathroom—I cringed. No window. No decorations. Just dingy-gray walls and a tile floor.

"Who's the other bed for?" I asked.

"We're not full, so you get your own room…for now."

Thank God for small favors. That's the last thing I wanted—having to share a room with some crazy person.

It didn't take me long to get into the unwavering routine. Six a.m. wake-up call followed by breakfast, a semi-physical, and meds. After an hour of group therapy, you could have visitors for an hour before an 11:30

lunch break. More meds after lunch as needed and then a second group-therapy session. An hour of free time preceded an individual visit with a psychiatrist, which was followed by an hour and a half of activities—fun for some, I supposed, but dreadful for me. Dinner was served at 5:00 p.m. followed by meds if needed and then one more group-therapy session. From 8:00 to 10:00, we could watch TV if we wanted or sit around in the common areas if we didn't. We had to be in our rooms by 10:30 each night but not before a final round of meds…as needed.

I felt like I knew what it was like to be in prison—stripped of your clothes, your freedom, and your rights. You had only what they gave you. You were told what to do, and you did what you were told. Nothing was within your control. But one thing there gave me immense satisfaction— they called me Margaret. Not Mags, or Maggie, or Marge, or Madge— Margaret. The other patients, the staff, even the cleaning lady who dust-mopped the floors and cleaned the bathroom in my room respected my name and took the extra nanosecond required to say it in full.

The only part of the day I found to be worthwhile were the one-hour sessions with the resident psychiatrist Dr. Ram—short for a much longer name I couldn't remember or pronounce. He listened to me, attentively. He recorded his notes using a laptop and referred to them in each session.

During one of these visits, I told Dr. Ram about the images I periodically envisioned out of the corner of my eye. He asked me several questions about these visions—their frequency, timing, and what the images appeared to be. When we were done, I got the impression that what I had told him held some importance.

Carl visited me every other day. On his first visit, I asked him about Portia.

"What have you told her?"

"The truth—that you're being evaluated for a little bit of a puzzling illness."

"What did she say?"

"Not too much. She understands."

"How's it going in the bookstore?"

"Right now, Dar, Lance, Candie, and Katherine are there…and so is your mother."

"My mother? How did she get involved?"

"She showed up one day when you were in the hospital, said you'd invited her a while ago."

"I don't remember doing that."

"Well, she came an hour before closing time, and we talked with her afterward for a while."

"So Portia met her?"

"Yes. We all had a nice conversation, in fact. She asked if there was anything she could do to help while you were in the hospital, and we took her up on it. She's been a big help. In fact, without her, I don't know how we could have pulled it off."

"She's been there every day?"

"Yep."

"Has she asked about me?"

"Every day. She wants to see you, but she doesn't know if you'd want her to come here, so I told her I'd ask you."

I shook my head. "Not like this. But would you thank her for helping out…for me?"

"Of course."

"And I don't want anyone but you seeing me here, like this. No one. Is that clear?"

"Not even Portia?"

"Not even Portia."

"Whatever you say."

Before he left, he kissed me on top of my head and said he'd be there for me. I wasn't sure how to take that as I wasn't convinced he couldn't have prevented me from being there in the first place.

* * *

Life in the psychiatric facility would have been boring had it not been for the other residents. I considered myself the only sane person there, but then maybe that was what everyone else thought about themselves too.

Mia was the "yes" person. No matter what anyone said—whether to her or someone else—she agreed to it. One time, another resident said to her that Mia's parents were from another planet where spiders ruled and it was against the law to kill flies. She agreed that was true.

Jackson didn't talk unless the subject was baseball, and then you couldn't shut him up.

Mr. Know-It-All, aka Luke, claimed to have a PhD in biology from some obscure school and to be an expert on all subjects, including what it took to be a successful author. I had to admit, he talked a good game.

Aubrey apparently considered her role to be to stir things up—always jabbering about something negative about another resident or staff member.

One resident stood out from the others—Nora. She didn't say much, and she steered away from other residents most of the time, but every so often, she would join in on a conversation, begin in English, and then switch to another language. I understood enough French and Spanish to know she was fluent in them. She also spoke German, Italian, and other languages I couldn't identify. She would conclude her dissertation (or whatever it was she was saying) in English, so we always got the beginning of what she wanted to say and her conclusion, just not the middle part.

After exactly a week, I was so thoroughly fed up with being in a place where I clearly didn't belong that I walked out. Just like that. I saw a delivery person head through a door I hadn't noticed before, and I tailgated him before the door had a chance to close all the way—through a hallway and out a back door. The parking lot was fenced, with a gatekeeper booth on one end. I watched as the delivery person got into his car, drove to the gate, and when the gate went up, drove off. I walked toward the gate, but before I made it halfway there, someone grabbed me from behind and escorted me back inside.

That attempt earned me a one-to-one guard for twenty-four hours and a warning that if it happened again, I would be transferred to another place that I would probably like less than this one.

* * *

The next day, Dr. Ram said he had a possible diagnosis for me—anti-NMDA receptor encephalitis. "I can't be sure, Margaret," he told me. "Not until I run a few more tests, but I think we may be on to something."

The ominous-sounding name of the condition frightened me. "What is it?"

"It's an immune-system disease in which the antibodies you produce attack protein in your brain that is critical for you to perform certain functions."

"Like what functions?" I asked.

"Unfortunately, there can be a whole host of functions. In your case, judgment, memory, perception of reality. It's often associated with tumors, generally benign, that exacerbate the situation, so I want to screen you for that straight away. You've mentioned being confused at times, unable to find the right words and grasp simple information, hallucinations, and of course the movement disorder you experienced right before you were admitted to the hospital. Your charts also mention low-grade fever, frequent episodes of agitation, headaches, and erratic blood pressure. These are also often associated with the disease. Tell me, how long have you been having the hallucinations?"

I was inclined to say it was when I got my new glasses, but then I remembered having them earlier than that—far less real and far less frequent. I explained this to him.

"Can we talk a little more about perception of reality," I asked. "What does that mean?"

"You said to me in one of our sessions that you suspected your husband was misbehaving in ways similar to characters in your books. I remember an incident involving a Limoges box."

"How do you know that didn't happen?"

"I don't. That one incident may have happened. But when you consider all the other incidents, ones you mentioned to me, there appears to be a pattern of dubious behaviors of your family and friends that lead me to believe your perception of reality may be distorted."

I didn't buy it but went along with it for the time being. Anything to get out of this place. "What's the cure?"

"It's not a well-understood disease, fairly rare, but there are medications we can try. Some have been quite successful."

"So I'm not crazy?"

"I never thought you were crazy, Margaret."

"I had a crazy Aunt Rosie, you know."

He laughed. "Many of us have an Aunt Rosie in our families."

"Will medication work for me?"

"We'll have to see. It's a matter of trial and error, I'm afraid."

"What's the next step?"

"Scans. It could be many. I'm on a mission to find tumors and remove them. That will increase your chances of being successfully treated."

"And if you find none?"

"We'll keep looking—sometimes they are too small to detect, and we have to wait for them to grow."

"Let's get on with it then, because I want out of here...bad."

Chapter 26

I didn't understand why it took so long for them to take a few scans for tumors and then analyze them, nor did I understand why they couldn't go by the tests already taken at the other hospital. But I kept going back to Carl's advice about cooperating, so I could get the hell out of this place.

Some answers came from Dr. Ram two weeks following his diagnosis.

"We have found no tumors," he said. "That doesn't mean they're not there—they could be too small to detect, as I mentioned before."

"Now what?" I asked.

"I have a treatment plan in mind, but I want to consult with another doctor who has more knowledge about this disease than I."

"Where is he?"

"Johns Hopkins in Maryland. He's written several articles on the disease. I have a call in to him."

"What kind of treatment plan?"

"A regimen of pills and IVIg infusions for a while."

"IVIg?"

"Intravenous immunoglobulin. It assists your body to make strong antibodies."

"What else?"

"We'll see about speech therapy too."

"Why?"

"You may not be aware of this, but you often mispronounce your words."

That was news to me. But it made sense, since people there, as well as Carl, often asked me to repeat things.

I gave Carl the update when he came to visit that afternoon.

"Do you know when you're coming home?" he asked.

"We didn't get that far. My guess is that they're going to want to observe me for a while after I start taking this medication. I don't know."

He seemed confused.

"What's the matter?"

"What about the living arrangements?"

"What about them?"

"Well, I've been sleeping in the upstairs bedroom."

I assumed by the way he said it that our sleeping in the same bed was out of the question.

"There's plenty of room for a second bed up there."

He avoided making eye contact with me.

"Carl?"

"I've moved on, Mags," he said in a low voice.

"What does *that* mean?"

"I'm seeing someone else," he said, scraping his hand through his hair and staring at the wall. His words sounded hollow in my ears, like they weren't real.

"You're what?"

"Look, we said we'd give it a month. We had that discussion in the middle of August. It's now the middle of October."

"We're still married, Carl."

"Things happen."

"So someone is sleeping in my bed?"

"Our bed."

"So someone is sleeping in *our* bed?"

"Metaphorically."

"How could you? I'm in the hospital with some rare disease that has affected my brain and you're out screwing someone else?"

"But you said you're getting treatment and—"

"We're still married, remember?"

"We're separated, remember? I can't deal with this anymore," he said.

"*You* can't deal with it! How about me?"

"Look, I was going to wait until you got home to tell you, but—"

"Your timing is reprehensible."

"You're right, and I'm not going to get into how hard this has all been on me, because I know full well it's been harder on you, but it is what it is, and I can't take it anymore."

"I will get better you know."

"And I hope you do. But…"

"But what?"

"I've been in treatment myself, and my doctor—"

"You've been seeing a psychiatrist?"

"A therapist. Anyway, you and I haven't been close in a long time and you've become so…unpredictable. I feel like there's no hope for us. The bookstore partnership, yes, but not the marriage. Does that make sense?"

"So much for 'for better or for worse.'"

"I'm sorry."

"My condition is treatable."

"Can you be honest with me about something?" he asked.

"I've always been honest with you."

"Were you ever in love with me?"

Stunned by the question, I stared at him in silence while I thought of an answer.

"Don't bother answering—your hesitation confirms what I've thought for a long time."

"You didn't give me a chance to—"

He stood up. "There's no future for us, Maggie, and I'm beginning to question our past."

Go to hell.

I felt blameless, the victim of yet another abandonment in my life.

Wasn't I?

* * *

I wanted out. I wanted out of this institution so bad. I wanted to get hold of my life—start over if I had to—and settle into a normal routine again. Normalcy was all I wanted. It was all Carl's fault. And my mother's. And Portia's and Darlene's. A conspiracy was what it was. A conspiracy to make me think I was crazy. I had been informed on various occasions that each of them had requested a visit with me. I'd said "no" to everyone except Carl.

I was angry with them, didn't trust them, and didn't want them to see me like this.

I desperately wanted to call Lily, to whom I hadn't spoken since I'd been hospitalized, but phone calls weren't allowed, at least not long ones. She seemed to be my only hope—the only person who listened to me, accepted me for who I was, believed in me. Damn nuthouse.

Two-thirty came and went—no Dr. Ram. I stormed the nurse's station to see why he didn't show.

"Dr. Ram wasn't able to come in today, Margaret. His wife died. We expect him back on Monday."

"Monday!" I shouted. "You can't be serious." I grasped the edge of the counter so tightly my whole body shook.

"Margaret, please calm down. Monday is only a few days away, and his wife died. Let's give him some time to grieve."

I didn't like Nurse Kim—she reminded me of this Asian drug dealer I had seen on a *48 Hours* segment—permanent smirk, never looking directly at you.

"So bring in another doctor! What's wrong with you people?"

"If you don't calm down, I'm going to have to call security, Margaret."

I pounded the counter with my fist. "I don't give a rat's ass about his dead wife. Bring in another fucking doctor!"

Before I got the last word completely out, two vice-like hands grabbed my upper arms from behind and held me in place for several seconds.

"Let go of me," I screeched, trying to free myself from the person's grip.

When the Queen of the Nuthouse Miss Bagley appeared, she gave me a stone-faced glare.

"And on top of it, Miss Bagley, she made a racial slur," Nurse Kim said.

"I did not!"

"She referred to me as 'you people.' I think we all know what she meant."

"That's bullshit!" I screamed.

The grip tightened.

Without warning, a staff nurse walked over to me and poked a needle in my arm. "Bring her to Room C," Miss Bagley said.

* * *

I awoke with a splitting headache, my head and all four limbs strapped to a gurney in a ten-by-ten room, empty but for me. A small eye-level window in the door allowed staff to periodically peek in to check on whoever had acted so crazily that they deserved to be in the dreaded Room C. After spending five minutes lying on the table, unable to move anything but my fingertips, toes, and eyeballs, I prayed to God—who I was pretty sure didn't know who I was—that I'd never have to see the inside of this room again.

I reflected on the chain of events that had gotten me there. I remembered arguing about something with the nurse behind the counter and acting like a crazy person, but not much else. I knew it had to have been bad for me to have ended up in Room C.

I lay there—not able to do anything else—thinking about my recent behavior. Maybe I did need to be there.

A few minutes or maybe hours later, an orderly came into the room.

"Are you okay, Margaret?"

I liked Randy—he was my favorite. A couple of times, when he thought I was having a bad day, he'd brought me Oreo cookies from the staff vending machine.

"I'm fine. When can I get out of here?"

"I'll go get a doctor. They're the only ones who can release you." He smiled. "I'm sorry if I held you too tight out there. You were ready to jump over the counter at Nurse Kim."

"I was?"

He nodded and then winked. "Tell the doctor you remember the incident, but you'd rather not talk about it. That usually works."

Five minutes later, a nurse and a doctor I'd never seen before entered the room.

"How are you feeling, Margaret?"

"Fine. And you?"

"I'm fine," the doctor said with a somber face.

The nurse untied my arms, released the band that held down my head, and helped me sit up.

"Do you want to talk about what happened out there yesterday?"

"Yesterday? What day is it? What time is it?"

"It's Thursday. Eight a.m.," he said.

"Those are some knock-out drugs you have," I said.

"Headache?" he asked.

"Yep. A killer one."

"We'll give you something for that."

The doctor signaled to the nurse to untie my ankles. I swung my stiff legs over the side of the gurney.

"Can I go now?"

"I want to talk about what happened yesterday," he said.

"I'd rather not talk about it right now. Is that okay?"

"Please make sure she gets some breakfast," he told the nurse as he walked toward the door.

"I'll be a good girl until Dr. Ram comes back on Monday. I promise," I told him.

"I'm going to hold you to that, Margaret," he said.

* * *

Dr. Ram pulled me out of group therapy to apologize for missing our last several appointments.

By this time, I was me again and felt terrible about what I had done. "Please don't apologize," I told him. "I'm the one who needs to do that. My behavior was unacceptable. And I'm so very sorry for your loss—this must be a very difficult time for you."

"You're right. It is. Twenty-two years we were married. She meant everything to me. But let's talk about you. I've reviewed your chart, and the lab results look good. But I do want to add a mild mood-stabilizing agent to control your impulsive aggression. It's a fast-working drug. We should see results, and you should feel the results, rather quickly."

"And then can I go home?"

"I am prepared to release you on Friday, if everything goes well."

"Not 'til then?"

"I want you here for three full days into this medicine regimen. Believe me, if these meds conflict with each other, you'd rather be here than out and about somewhere."

* * *

Ultimately grateful for the three days I had before being released, I contemplated what I would do once I got out. I used the phone in the nurse's station to call Carl, but only after bringing Nurse Kim a chocolate bar from the vending machine and apologizing for my improper behavior days earlier.

"Believe me, I've been through much worse than that," she said with smirk. "And rarely do I ever get an apology, so thank you for that. And for the candy bar."

I then asked for and received permission to use her phone to call Carl, who agreed to come by to talk.

The following day, Carl and I sat in one of the visitation rooms to discuss living arrangements. Nurse Kim lent me one of her sweaters to wear over my scrubs so I looked less like a patient and more like a normal person. Nurse Kim didn't seem all that bad to me anymore.

"Look, I get your decision to call our marriage quits," I told him. "I'm not saying I agree or disagree with it, but if one person wants out, there's really not much else the other person can do. I also get that."

Carl's face remained unreadable, nodding at appropriate times, but saying nothing.

"Do you plan to stay here or move into the Chicago home?" I asked him.

"Here, for the time being."

"Where does that leave me? Look, your decision to quit the marriage changes my life, not to mention the ordeal I've been through with this illness *and* having my mother back in my life. I need time to regroup. We have two homes—if you don't want to live under the same roof with me, and given I have a business to run here, why can't you go live in Chicago? You've said all along that you can work from anywhere."

His stare outlasted my ability to wait for a response.

"So?"

"I lost my job last week."

"What? What happened?"

"Cutbacks, layoffs. On a national basis, a quarter of the staff is gone. I've known about it for some time."

"You knew you were going to lose your job?"

"No, that came as a surprise. I knew about the layoffs—I did the analyses for Ted."

"That stinks."

"Tell me about it."

"What will they do without a CFO?"

"Ted's nephew."

Ted, Garfeld Group's CEO, had always been fair to Carl, so I knew it had to be something unusual that led him to let Carl go.

"Let me guess. Right out of college and in need of a job."

"Right out of Harvard's MBA program and in need of a job."

"Well, at least it's someone with a good education."

"Mm-hm."

"But you're good at what you do. You'll find something else."

"CFO jobs aren't that plentiful."

"I know, but what does that have to do with our living arrangements? You can't live in Chicago while you look for another job and I get my act together here?"

"I suppose I could, but…"

"Let me guess. Your new girlfriend is here."

"She was never a girlfriend. And she is no more."

"What was she then?"

He shrugged, giving me that I-don't-want-to-talk-about-it look.

"Why are you so hesitant to talk about this?"

"I had a bit of bad news from Dr. Oliphant last week."

"What was it?"

"They found precancerous cells during a colonoscopy."

"Precancerous. So that means no cancer."

"That means it may be coming. I'll need periodic screening."

"And you want to stay up here because you want to stay with Dr. Oliphant. Is that it?"

"That's part of it."

"What's the other part?"

"Mother won't move."

"So, let me see if I have this right. You want to stay in the lake house because it's more convenient for you and your mother, and I have to find somewhere else to live."

"You're making me feel like a real heel."

"If the shoe fits."

"Nice pun."

"Well, I'm getting released on Friday, and my plan is to pick up where I left off at the bookstore, so I am going home, to our lake home, whether you're there or not." I got up. "Too bad I can't just disappear, like in one of my novels. That would solve all your problems, wouldn't it?" I said before shutting the door behind me.

* * *

The next day, I asked for a private session with one of the group therapists I particularly liked. I told her about my predicament with Carl, the bookstore, and the two homes we owned together.

"What would be your preference?" she asked me.

"That I could go home, here in East Troy, and he'd go live in Chicago until we decide how we're going to split things up for the divorce."

"And you think he wants you to just go away and not be his problem anymore."

"Right."

"And you know this because that's what he told you."

"Well, not in so many words."

"What were his words?"

"I don't remember exactly," I told her. "But that's what he meant."

"Is it possible that what he really wants is to be with you, to give it another go, but that he just isn't coming right out and saying it?"

"No, I'm sure of it."

"How about you? You were very quick to say your preference would be for him to live in Chicago and you here, until the divorce. Is that your preference because you think he doesn't want to be with you or because that's what you really want?"

I couldn't answer her question without thinking it through.

"I can't trust him, and that's a big issue."

"What's the worst thing he did that makes you feel this mistrust?"

"He didn't tell me about his real father."

"Do you know why he held that from you?"

"He said because he was ashamed of him. But what that says is that he didn't trust me enough."

"Trust is important—relationships need to be anchored in it to survive."

"Exactly."

"After you leave here, I want you to think about what you really want and what you think he really wants too. Remember, sometimes pride gets in the way of people showing their true emotions, and, in fact, sometimes it makes them act in a way that reflects the opposite of their true feelings. Think back to his exact words to determine if you can unequivocally rule out the possibility of him wanting to give your marriage another chance. And talk to him about the trust issue, about why he didn't tell you about his father. Then, let's talk again. Sound fair?"

"Sounds fair."

I skipped activity time and sat facing a window in a far corner of the main living room to think things through, starting with what I honestly wanted.

I had always found it difficult to be honest with myself when it came to relationships when I didn't know what the other person wanted. The more I thought about that, the more dishonest I knew it to be. Still, it seemed like a waste of time contemplating staying with Carl if he wanted out—it took two to make it work. I went back and forth on it until I asked myself the most important question: Did I love him? And if so, was my marriage worth fighting for? Would I ever be able to trust him again?

I had loved Wayne, of that I was sure. I'd never gotten over him. Did I love Carl? I'd lived with him for twenty-one years, but did I love him? How could I be so sure I'd loved Wayne but not so sure about Carl?

Carl and I had had our share of disagreements during our marriage, but nothing serious...until this past year. Up until then, we had agreed to disagree on matters that weren't that important, and I believed that helped to keep our marriage intact. He had been a good source of support over the years for whatever I wanted to do, like leaving my high-paying career to write novels. We supported each other that way. Was the love ever there? I didn't know.

Our relationship had been built on a solid foundation of friendship... and trust. Now I wondered if that friendship had ever morphed into an intimate relationship. We'd been having sex all along, of course. Friends with benefits? Is that all we were?

I tried to recall when things started going downhill. Maybe when his mother fell and needed his help. Maybe before that. When Portia disappeared? I couldn't remember. Maybe that was when we'd stopped respecting each other's space and needs. Maybe that was when *I* had stopped respecting *his* space and needs. Or when I'd begun having reality-perception issues, if Dr. Ram was right.

I borrowed the nurses-station phone to call Carl to ask him if we could talk again on Friday after my release. We agreed that he would pick me up and we would talk at home while the others were at the bookstore. As eager as I was to get back to the bookstore, I was even more eager to talk to Carl about our future.

Chapter 27

The new medications made me feel much better, but on the downside, they caused diarrhea, dizziness, and fatigue, something I didn't admit to anyone at the psychiatric facility for fear of them not releasing me.

Even though we had occasionally been allowed to go outdoors—most often as a group—it didn't compare to walking out the front door as a free person. I waited for Carl outside in the chilly October air on the bench in front of the facility, all the while trying to shed recurring thoughts about Aunt Rosie. My brain understood my disease, which wasn't a form of mental illness. But some of my behaviors mimicked hers—the delusionary thoughts, hallucinations, confused thinking, paranoia. An image of her little ramshackle home flashed before me, and I pictured myself sitting in a rocking chair on its front porch. I wondered what had happened to that house after she died.

When Carl drove up in my car and asked me if I wanted to drive home, I was pleased, hoping he had offered that because he still cared about me. When we got home, I asked him if we could continue the conversation we'd started a few days earlier. I began with a sentence I had rehearsed over and over in my mind throughout the day.

"I want to talk…about us…but I want for us to promise that we'll be completely honest with each other, and with ourselves. No holding back. No vagueness. Just blatant honesty. Can you agree to that?"

Still stone-faced, he nodded.

"I've thought a lot about us these past several weeks—had plenty of time to do that—and I've decided that I'm not so willing to throw away what we've had all these years. When I think about all that we've done together, where we've gone, how we've dealt with things, everything, well, it was good, maybe not perfect, but still good.

"But things changed somewhere along the line, and it got to the point where I didn't trust you, and I felt that you were ignoring me half the time. My temper usually came too quickly, and yours did too." I paused to calm down my nerves. "Before we call it quits, I want to figure out what triggered these changes."

When he didn't respond, I continued. "I think my health played a part, and I hope that doesn't sound like an excuse, but the more I understand this disease, the more I think it affected my behavior in so many ways."

I paused, hoping he'd say something…anything.

"Keep talking. I want to understand that more," he said.

I explained the disease to him, as much as I understood about it, the possible symptoms that could surface, my treatment, and my current condition.

"I didn't know that," he said. "Why didn't you tell me this before?"

"Well, obviously I didn't know I even had it, or had anything wrong with me medically, for that matter, until recently. And it's taken me a while to figure out what it all means. I'm still learning. In fact, to learn even more about it, I'm going to sit in on a webinar next week given by an expert on the disease. It's not that well understood, not like I had—" I stopped short of saying cancer.

"Cancer?"

"That was a stupid comparison. I'm sorry."

He finally broke an uncomfortable silence. "I guess you've been going through more than I realized…for however long you've had this thing, and maybe that explains some of your behaviors—blaming me for things I didn't do, picking fights over nothing, being short-tempered, and then the episode you had in the bookstore. I have to say, I didn't know what to think half the time. I even thought that you might have been having an affair."

"I wasn't. You know that, right?" I said.

"I believe you. And while we're on the subject of lying, I never lied to you…about anything."

"Except when it came to your father…your biological father."

"I never lied to you."

"You withheld the truth—same thing."

"He's an embarrassment to me. I want nothing to do with him. I only see him once in a great while to appease him. We have a short not-so-bad conversation, and that's it. I forget about him until the next time he calls."

"Why couldn't you tell me that?"

"I don't know. Maybe I didn't want you to think any less of me or Mom. It was safe. Maybe that's what it was—if I didn't tell you, I wouldn't have to deal with it. But that was it. I've never kept anything else from you or lied to you."

"What about the other woman?"

"Okay, and that."

"I believe you," I said. "Now."

"As far as us, I think my contribution to our problems started with Lance."

"Lance?"

"Lance and I were a lot closer than you might think."

"Oh?"

"We were close, like brothers are close—something neither one of us ever had. When he went missing, I was devastated, and then when he was found in the condition he was in, I was afraid I had lost him… And then Mom's accident and you being upset I was in Florida for that week, and her coming up here. I felt like a hollowed-out version of myself just going through the motions to get by."

"I didn't know Lance's accident and everything else had affected you like that. You never said anything."

"Right or wrong, I kept saying to myself that if you didn't get it, if you didn't understand what I was going through, then you must either be blind or just don't care."

"I can assure you that it wasn't that I didn't care. The blind part, maybe."

The haggard expression on his face told me he was still having a hard time dealing with something, maybe everything.

"What do you want to do, Carl?"

"I don't know."

"Let me ask it differently. Do you want to try to make this work…our marriage?"

He shook his head.

"Does that mean you don't?"

"That means I don't know. I truly don't know. You asked for honesty?" He got up from his chair. "You got it," he said and left the room.

I didn't know what I was supposed to do. Go after him? Leave him alone? Jump in my car and go to the bookstore? Cry?

The meds I had been prescribed might have been working a little too well—I should have been emotionally drained. Instead, I sensed calm, the same kind of feeling you get when standing barefoot on a warm beach with waves gently lapping across your feet—that kind of calm. I made a mental note to ask Dr. Ram about that in my next weekly e-mail update to him.

I left Carl alone and hoped that by nightfall I had a place to sleep other than the sofa. Not knowing where Carl had gone in the house complicated matters. I desperately wanted to take a shower and change into something other than what I'd been wearing when I'd been taken to the hospital six weeks earlier. My clothes were in the upstairs bedroom—at least, that was where they were the last time I saw them.

I checked the garage—Carl's car was gone.

The phone rang. I didn't answer it. After four rings, it went to voice mail.

"Carl, please pick up," Darlene said. "It's Katherine. She fell."

I picked up the phone just as she hung up. I called Carl's cell phone. No answer. After leaving him a message, I called Darlene's cell phone.

"Is she okay?" I asked her.

"Candie is on her way to the hospital with her. I'm here alone, Mags. Are you home now? Can you come in? I can't do this alone."

"Whose car does Candie have?"

"Carl's."

That explained Carl's car being missing. "Let me find Carl, and we'll be right there."

I checked the house for Carl, calling out his name in every section of the house. No response. I called his cell phone and left him a message that I was on my way to the bookstore.

Darlene hadn't told me much about Katherine's condition, but the fact that they hadn't called 9-1-1 and relied on Candie to drive her to the ER told me it couldn't have been life-threatening. The closer I got to the bookstore, the more nervous I became. I didn't know what to expect after having been away for so long.

When I reached the bookstore, I parked the car behind the store, took in a deep breath, and entered through the back door. Fluffy greeted me—a friendly face and wagging tail. That I could handle.

The first thing I noticed was that the display rack just inside the back door was missing. Its placement hadn't been the best, so it didn't bother me too much that someone had moved it. Then I noticed an entire shelving unit filled with pet supplies. Was I in the right store?

I perused the shelves—doggie beds, water and food bowls, chew toys, grooming tools, bags of dogfood. I walked the length of the shelving expecting to see another one of my display racks, but that one was missing as well.

As I neared the checkout pit, I observed Darlene checking out the first customer in a long line of customers, the expression on her face screaming for help.

"I'll be right there," I said to her as I flew past toward the coffee bar where two couples sat at tables and two young women with perturbed looks on their faces stood in front of the counter with no one behind it to wait on them.

"Give me a tall skinny vanilla latte with a drizzle of caramel," the young woman said rolling her eyes.

"Make mine a chai tea latte, skim milk, lite water, no foam, extra hot," the second customer said while chewing a big wad of gum.

I couldn't say what I wanted to say, nor could I make their drinks because I had no clue how to do it.

I dipped down behind the counter for a few seconds and when I stood up again I said, "Well, will you look at that—the espresso machine blew a fuse. I'm afraid we'll be out of business for a while."

The two young women gaped at each other. One of them said under her breath, "I told you we should have gone to Starbucks," and they left the store.

Darlene summoned me.

"You take the pit, and I'll handle the coffee," she said in a tone I'd never heard from her before. A "Hi, how are you?" would have been nice.

"Where's my mother?" I asked as we switched places.

"She called in sick." She scrutinized me up and down. "Isn't that what you were wearing when you—"

"Yes. I haven't had a chance to change."

"Well...welcome back," she mumbled while giving me a quick hug. "Are you okay?"

"I'm—"

Darlene's phone rang.

"Carl, hon, where are you?" she asked. After a short pause, she said, "She's here, with me. I'll pick you up."

Darlene shot me a quick look and said, "Carl says close up the shop. I'm going to run over to the hospital."

"I can—"

"No, I'll go," she said.

I nodded but didn't say anything. This wasn't exactly the homecoming I'd expected. I watched as Darlene told the remaining customers that she was closing the shop due to a family emergency. After putting the CLOSED sign on the front door, she walked past me without saying anything more.

"C'mon, Fluffy," she called out to the dog.

"Where's Borgne?" I asked.

"Who?"

"Borgne, the cat."

"Oh, the cat. She's around here someplace."

I waited for her to leave before I cried. As if on cue, Borgne came from around the corner and peered up at me. After I plopped down on one of the chairs in the coffee bar, she jumped up on my lap and raised her head to be petted. I hugged her, which most cats don't like, but she let me.

After I calmed down some, I toured the store to see what else had been changed, starting with the coffee bar. At first glance, it looked the same, but when I went behind the counter, I noticed the absence of wine glasses and red wine. I opened the countertop fridge to find the absence of white wine as well. The section of menu signage that listed the hours for the wine bar had been covered up with a crudely taped piece of white paper.

As my body temperature rose, I walked toward the back of the store past the computer terminal area. An OUT OF ORDER sign had been taped to each of the four terminals.

A few more steps led me to the storage room. Upon opening the door, I was horrified at the disarray. Gone were the neatly arranged shelves of supplies, excess inventory, and cleaning and bathroom items. Those things were still there but in no particular order—some crushed up against each other, and others hanging half off the shelves. An opened box of Cheerios lay on its side, some of its contents strewn across one of the shelves. Shoved in the corner were the four display racks of book-related items I had so carefully arranged with book lights, pens and pencils, bookmarks, calendars, and other items. Unable to bear the chaos, I closed the door and perused the bookshelves.

I had originally arranged the books first by genre, then by author, then by book title. But that didn't appear to be the case any longer. I found mysteries mixed in with adventure books, romances mixed in with cozy mysteries, and literary fiction among the fantasy books—making the shelf labels utterly meaningless. Some books were standing up and others lying down. Few of them were lined up with the front of the shelf like I'd left them. Large empty spaces on the shelves told me no new inventory had been brought in since I'd left. It looked like the bookshelves you'd find in a dilapidated thrift shop about to go out of business.

Feeling deflated by the blatant disregard for all the hard work I had put into creating a well-organized, respectable place of business, I sat down behind the checkout counter and stared aimlessly out into a store of which I was now too embarrassed to claim ownership. I couldn't imagine what customers must have thought.

I sat there stewing until I thought I'd better call Carl to see how Katherine was doing.

"We're on our way home now," he said. "She has a bruised hip and sprained wrist, nothing worse. Where are you?"

"I'm at the store. I'm going to work some here, and then I'll be home."

I fed Borgne, replaced the crudely written CLOSED sign that had been stuck to the window with duct tape with the sign I had originally purchased for the store. Feeling as depressed and beaten-down as I'd ever felt in my life, I dove into restoring the bookstore back to the way I'd left it.

* * *

After spending hours fixing the bookstore shambles, I was greeted by a dark house when I arrived home. Exhausted, I slipped into bed and immediately fell asleep.

The next morning, I found Carl, Katherine, Candie, and Darlene seated around the kitchen table eating pastries.

"Pull up a chair and join us, Mags," Carl said. "Katherine was just filling us in on more details of what happened to her yesterday."

I retrieved a folding chair from the closet and squeezed it in between

Candie and Katherine. Candie put her hand on my leg and gave me a "welcome back" smile.

"The reason I had Fluffy on her leash," said Katherine, "was because this woman came in with two kids who started teasing her. Spoiled little brats they were. Their mother wasn't paying attention to them at all. Too busy gossiping with another customer. Anyway, after they left, I forgot to take her off her leash and I tripped over it when she walked in front of me."

"You're lucky you didn't break anything," I said.

"Who are you?" Katherine asked.

Chapter 28

Everyone, including myself, stifled reactions to Katherine's question. "I'm Margaret, Carl's wife," I said before thinking. She had probably never heard anyone call me that before. "Maggie? Mags?" When she appeared to become more confused, I wished I had stopped at Margaret.

No one said a word for a long awkward moment. I looked at Carl.

She's your mother—say something.

"How about those Bears?" Lance chimed in.

"What do you mean? They lost their last game to Detroit," Carl said.

"Yeah, but they won the previous two…I think."

"Won five, lost five."

"Just trying to make conversation."

"I still don't know who you are," said Katherine. "Carl married someone named Mary, but she's gone. Right, Carl? Did she die or what? I never did care for the woman."

"I think you're thinking of an old girlfriend of mine, Mom. A long time ago. I never married her."

"Good."

"Mags and I have been married for a long time."

"I know that," Katherine said. Looking directly at me, she asked, "What nationality are you?"

"Mom, it really doesn't matter."

"It does to me."

"I don't mind, Carl. Both my parents were Irish and English, with maybe a little Scottish thrown in."

"I knew a schoolteacher from England once. Cheap as they come. Damn Brits think they know more about being English than we do."

"Really, Mother?"

"Well, it's true."

After the pastries had been devoured, Katherine and Candie disappeared, but not before Katherine turned to me and said, "I hope you're home for good now. We need you here."

Lance and Darlene turned to each other, shook their heads, and departed. That left Carl and me. I got up and started cleaning off the table. Carl walked up behind me. He didn't touch me, but I could feel his heat. "Can we start all over?" he whispered.

That was the last thing I'd expected to hear.

"It's been such a long day. Can we—"

"I'd like to talk, Mags."

I dried off my hands with a paper towel and sat back down at the table. Carl sat down across from me and reached over to cover my hands in his.

"Can we start over?" he repeated.

"You mean the day or the last five months?"

"The last five months."

It took me several seconds to absorb what he'd said.

"What's changed your mind?"

"I haven't been happy for a while," he said. "I think you know that."

"I knew something had changed in you. I wasn't sure what."

"I first noticed it when I realized I felt lonely even when I was around people," he said. "I don't have it all figured out yet."

"At least you're aware of it. That's the most important part. You can't figure out the cause if you don't acknowledge the issue."

"At first, I thought *you* were the cause of it, but I don't think that anymore."

"But I didn't help matters, did I?"

"You didn't. Mom didn't. Portia didn't. I throw my biological dad into that mix as well. Living through one crisis after another, most of which I didn't understand. I felt like I was living in a house of cards—a good wind could make it come tumbling down."

"I had no idea."

"My quick fix was to leave. But then I realized that, at some point, I had to take responsibility for my own well-being. Figure out what I had to do differently to feel better about myself. Stop blaming other people, things, circumstances."

"That's heavy stuff," I said. "And here's the thing. I saw you changing, and I guess I took it personally, and that made me change the way I felt about you."

"And the more you changed, the more I changed."

"I'm getting dizzy."

"You're not the same person you were twenty years ago," he said.

"Neither are you."

"No. But isn't that to be expected? No one stays the same over time. Not entirely."

"And we can't base our relationship, our current relationship, on how we were back then. Not on our past expectations of each other. Maybe that's where we went wrong. Can I tell you something without you getting mad at me?" I asked.

"That depends."

"Well, I'll say it anyway. The way we're talking right now. That's how we used to be. Or at least how I remember it. Talking about our feelings."

"I'm still not comfortable with it, but…"

We talked well into the night—it felt so incredibly good to have the old Carl back. His casual, caring demeanor. His laugh. His frown. The sincerity in his eyes. The whole package.

He filled me in on everything that had gone on at home and at the bookstore while I was gone, and I told him about some of the funny and not-so-funny things that went on at the psychiatric facility.

When I asked him about the changes I'd discovered at the bookstore, he became defensive and explained that it was all they could do to keep it afloat.

"What about the dog stuff on the shelves?" I asked.

"Katherine thought that would be a good idea since we ran out of books."

As much as it pained me, I told him how much I appreciated all they'd done for me.

While we slept in the same bed that night, we didn't make love, but I didn't care. At least we were in the same bed.

* * *

Before I left for the bookstore the next day, Carl filled me in on his job search.

"A decent CFO job is going to be hard to find, especially at my level. But consulting work is plentiful." He told me about two consulting jobs he had lined up for the following week. "There's enough work to keep me busy full-time and then some," he said. "That way we won't have to rely on the bookstore at all."

"What are you saying?"

"The bookstore is history, Mags. Let's face it."

"What are you talking about? The first few weeks were successful, better than I'd planned."

"Well, it's not now. We lost money while you were out."

"How much?"

"A lot."

"What's a lot?"

"I told you before what we lost. That's why I brought in Lance and Darlene as investors."

"What?"

"Don't act so surprised. We had this discussion when you were in the hospital."

"I don't remember any such discussion."

"Well, we had it. And you signed off on it."

"Carl—"

"Forget it, Mags. You'll never make it with that bookstore. You may have had a surge of business with the grand opening, but that was short-lived. We all tried to make it work. You're just not getting the customers."

"Did you follow any of my business plan while I was away?"

"We couldn't find it, and even if we did, none of us had time to delve into it. It was all we could do to try to keep the doors open."

"I have a solid plan, one that will work if followed. I know it."

"Give it up. It's a money pit. Sell off the assets and see if you can pay back Lance and Dar. Call it quits."

"No. I won't."

Even though it was two hours before the bookstore opened, I gathered a few things to take there and headed out the door.

"Here," Carl said. "You'll need this." He handed me a bag of candy.

"What's that for?" I asked.

"Halloween. Apparently, kids come to the stores to trick-or-treat."

I had lost track of the days and didn't realize it was the end of October already. I snatched the bag from him and proceeded out the door.

"Good luck," he called out after me.

He could play games with our marriage all he wanted, but he wasn't going to do it with my bookstore.

* * *

As soon as I arrived at the bookstore, I took another look around the entire floor before sinking into Katherine's easy chair. I thought I had made more progress than I actually had in getting the store back to normal. How could Carl and the others do this to me?

How could a person be so understanding, so compassionate one minute and then crush me like a bug the next. I wasn't the one who needed counseling—he did. "Sell off the assets and see if you can pay back Lance and Dar," he'd said. He was more concerned about them than me.

Just when I didn't think I could feel any worse, I remembered a pithy statement made by one of my college professors when we were discussing the consequences of someone telling you that you can't achieve something that's important to you. *You can either cry about it or prove them wrong.* I was out to prove them wrong.

Figuring they were all in cahoots about closing the bookstore, I was surprised when Darlene showed up a few minutes before the store was scheduled to open.

"What are you doing here?" I asked.

Before she could answer, Katherine walked through the front door with Fluffy in her arms. Candie followed her in.

"Okay, what's going on?" I asked.

"Store's going to open soon. You don't want our help?" Katherine said.

"Of course I do, but—"

"Let's get going, then," Katherine said and strutted to the back.

I looked at Darlene. "I figured everyone had given up on me."

"Well, we're here," Darlene said. "Do you want me in the pit?"

Candie headed toward the coffee bar without saying anything.

Too flabbergasted to ask questions, I proceeded to the front door to flip over the OPEN sign. But one person was still absent—my mother. I asked Darlene about her.

"I'm not sure why she's not here, unless she thought we no longer needed her since you're back," Darlene explained. "It was never discussed, to the best of my knowledge."

I made a mental note to call her later.

Toward the end of the day, after dishing out treats to fifty or so ghosts, goblins, and a bevy of princesses, I turned the coffee bar into a wine bar per the original plan. Darlene poured a glass of wine for me and a Dr. Brown's for herself.

"So how did it go today?" she asked me. "I've been so busy that I haven't had time to ask you."

"Fine. It took me a while to get used to some of the changes you guys made while I was gone, but…"

She asked me about my condition. I gave her the short version of what it was.

"And the meds you're on, how are they working for you?"

"They're fine." She didn't sound that interested, more like nosy. "Hey, isn't Melodi due soon?" I asked.

"Three weeks."

"Excited?"

"Yes, of course. I'm sorry you missed her shower. Carl dropped off a gift bag of everything nautical—toys, clothes, books, picture frames. I forget what all was in there. Lance loved it."

"I'm glad he did that. So how was it having my mother here?"

"She's been great."

"What's she like? I mean, what's her personality like?"

"She's nice. Not much of a talker but a good worker. Carl didn't tell you about her?"

"Well, there's been so much other stuff to talk about…"

"Oh?"

"Yes, lots of other stuff. Like how you and Lance pitched in to try to save the store while I was out."

"Think nothing of it. But since you brought it up, what's your plan? You're pretty deep in the red."

"I need to pour over the books. I'm not sure how things went south so quickly. As soon as I figure this out, I'll know exactly how much trouble I'm in, and I'll create a plan to get out of it."

"You seem pretty sure of yourself."

"I am." I really wasn't. "And you'll get your money back. All of it."

Before I left the store that day, I called the number my mother had given me and left her a message. Having her back in my life should have evoked a heartening emotion, but instead I felt numb to it. But I think I would have been numb to just about anything at that time in my life—so many upheavals, unknowns, and surprises—numb was probably a good thing.

Chapter 29

Carl's change of heart for making another go at our marriage, while encouraging, didn't make sense given his complete lack of support for me and the bookstore. Not that his support was ever that strong before, but at least he hadn't tried to put a total kibosh on it. And since it just happened to coincide with other problems in his life—his mother's health, his own health, and his job—I couldn't help but wonder if he changed his mind about us splitting just so he wouldn't have to deal with one more problem. Either that, or he was going through some sort of mid-life crisis. Dr. Ram's notion that I had reality-perception issues fought with these theories, leaving me in a constant state of confusion.

I thought a lot about the change in our relationship during our last five years together. After I left my corporate job, we'd bought the lake house and both began working out of our home. We went from being apart ten to twelve hours a day to spending twenty-four hours a day together almost every day, and that's when our relationship started to go downhill. Maybe we weren't all that compatible after all.

I found it rather baffling and wished I had someone I could talk to about it. Lily and I had talked a few times since I'd been out of the hospital, but in those conversations, she'd seemed a little distant. Darlene and I weren't close enough for me to talk to her on this level, and besides that, I didn't trust her. The last person with whom I would have considered having such a conversation was Katherine, but that was what happened.

Close to closing time at the bookstore one afternoon, Candie's sister called to tell her that they had taken her husband to the hospital after he'd complained of chest pains. She wondered if Candie could watch her girls while she was at the hospital. I told her to take my car and said I would call Carl to come pick up Katherine and me. I was tidying up the coffee bar when Katherine came over—purse in one hand, Fluffy in the other—ready to go home.

"Where's Candie?" she asked.

I explained the situation.

She put her purse and Fluffy down and sat at one of the tables.

"Would you like something to drink?" I asked her. "It might be a while before Carl gets here."

"So, what are the two of you going to do about your marriage?" she blurted out.

A bit dumbstruck by her unexpected question, I continued wiping down the counter while I considered an appropriate response, which she didn't wait for.

"Anyone can see you two are having issues. Can I tell you something about Carl?"

Oh dear. Is this something I want to hear?

I put the CLOSED sign on the door and sat down across the table from her.

"He's not like us," she said.

"Excuse me?"

"His father was the same way. So was my second husband, Peter. We can't expect them to handle more than one thing at a time. Their brains aren't programmed that way."

"Yeah. Well, I suppose Carl has a lot going on right now."

"More than he can handle. Trust me. And I'm not helping matters any."

How do I respond to that?

"So, that puts you in a bad place," she said.

I didn't know how much or how little to say and what she'd relay to Carl, potentially making matters worse.

"I guess we both have a lot on our plates," I told her.

"I'm not worried about you, sweetheart. It's Carl."

"Are you more worried about him if we stay together or separate?" I asked.

"Doesn't matter. He's my son, I'll always worry about him."

"I know what you mean."

"I wish I could be of help, but I'm old, and if you believe my quack doctor, I have dementia. I hate that word. Too close to the word 'demented.' Either way, you can't expect much from me."

I couldn't help but laugh. "I don't know, Katherine. You're making an awful lot of sense right now. I think maybe you're hiding behind this dementia thing."

"You're too damn smart for your own good."

"What would you do, Katherine? What would you do if you were me?"

"The minute Carl's father went to prison, begging me not to leave him, I dumped his ass faster than you could say *fahrvergnügen*."

"Fahverwhaten?"

"My Peter used to use that expression. I have no idea what it means. But you can get the picture just by the sound of it, right?"

I acknowledged with a nod.

"Carl's a good man, but you've got to look out for yourself, what's best for you. Don't ever let someone else make that decision for you." She paused. "And Carl doesn't have to know we had this conversation."

"Not as far as I'm concerned."

"Hell, come morning, I may not even remember it."

* * *

While Carl and the others had left my bookstore in a state of shambles, it came in only second to the condition of the financial books. I had thought that with Carl the CFO involved, they would have been in impeccable shape, but they were far from it. It took me several days to make sense of them, and when I did, while still horrified, at least I knew where the problems lay and how I could fix them. Most of the revenue shortfall stemmed from lack of inventory and marketing efforts. Had they followed my business plan… I had to keep trying not to go there. I had my work cut out for me.

When my mother returned my phone call, I asked her if she could come to the bookstore the following Friday, one week after I'd returned. I didn't know what to expect from her, from myself, or from the relationship we were about to cultivate. I had asked her to come an hour before we opened so we could talk. By the time she arrived, I had downed three cups of chamomile tea trying to calm my nerves.

"Thank you for being here while I was gone," I said to her with great sincerity. "I heard you were a tremendous help."

"I don't know about that. I did what I could while you were…"

I sipped my tea, stalling before I responded. "You can say it. I was in a psychiatric hospital. And I'm glad I was because they diagnosed me with—"

"I know. Anti-NMDA receptor encephalitis."

"You're familiar with it?" I asked.

"I am now. When Carl told us what it was, I Googled it. It's when your own antibodies attack the NMDA receptors in your brain, messing up the electrical impulses your brain needs to…well, to do a lot of things. The brain is a complicated organ, the most complicated one you have."

"Looks like you haven't forgotten what you learned as a nurse."

"Some things came back to me when I was reading up on it. Do you have a good doctor?"

"The doctor at The Center recommended someone to me."

"Dr. Chowdhury?"

"How did you know?"

"I told you, I did some checking. He's the best in the area for this sort of thing. How far is Milwaukee from here?"

"Thirty-five miles or so. Not too far."

"If you ever want me to go with you to an appointment, let me know."

I stared at her until it became uncomfortable. She was acting like, well, a mother. I wondered if she knew how that felt for me—how awkward it was. Even though I had fantasized about having a relationship with her so many times, in so many ways, I still felt like I was trying to establish a familial rapport with a complete stranger.

When I put myself in her place, it came to me that she was likely going through an even more difficult time than I was. I hadn't done anything wrong. It had to have taken a lot of guts for her to come back, own up to her transgressions, and stick around to see what my reaction would be. Now that we both had had a time-out of sorts—time to comb through our feelings and reactions to what the other one had to say—I wondered if there would be a change in how we felt about each other.

"You came here to help out while I was gone. Are you willing to continue? I couldn't pay you much, minimum wage…that and all the espresso you can drink."

Her tired eyes glistened. "I'd like that. I'd like that very much."

"If you work full-time, I could let Frances go—she does more flirting than work." I had had Frances stay on after she'd helped with the grand opening but wasn't thrilled with her work ethic.

"I have nothing on my hands but time."

"Good. It's a deal then." I extended my hand to shake.

She stood up. "Could I have a hug instead?"

What started out as a polite hug turned into a long embrace, and after our arms had been locked around each other for several seconds, our tears came. Neither one of us spoke—there was no need.

* * *

The next evening, I found some time to get back to my writing. I had thought *Stand-Alone Groom* was about three quarters finished, but after spending two hours looking over what I'd written, I wanted to throw the whole manuscript in the trash and start over. The writing was bad, the plot unstructured and weak, and the characters one-dimensional. I realized I must have been in a dreadful frame of mind when I wrote it.

Frustrated, I turned my focus to an e-mail I'd received the day before from a young West African girl looking for someone to critique a book she'd written. She'd stumbled upon my website when looking for writing advice. I responded that I'd be happy to do it, and within the hour I had another e-mail from her with the file attached.

I was in the middle of setting up a book promotion for *Almost Murder* when Darlene called.

"Can you do me a favor?" she asked.

"Sure. What is it?"

"I'm at the club. Can you see if Lance is home?"

"Have you tried calling him?"

"It goes directly to voice mail."

"What do you want me to do? Knock on the door?"

"Yeah."

"And then what?"

"I don't know. Ask to borrow a cup of sugar."

"A cup of sugar."

"Or just make something up. Please?"

"Darlene, what's going on?"

"I'll tell you later. Can you go check for me?"

"I'll call you right back."

I proceeded to walk over to their house trying to think of what I could ask to borrow that wouldn't sound stupid when I ran into Lance pulling out of their garage.

"Hey, what's up?" he asked me.

"I was coming over to check your garage door. Darlene thought she might have left it open."

"Why didn't she just call me?"

"She said she did. Went to voice mail. I see it's closed, so I guess everything is okay." I waved. "See you later, then."

He waved back and drove off, leaving me feeling like a real jerk.

"Okay, Darlene, so now I feel stupid." I told her what happened.

"I don't suppose you could follow him…like in one of your books."

"What's going on? And to answer your question, no, I'm not going to tail him like in one of my books."

"Remember when I thought he was having an affair, but I couldn't prove anything?"

"Yes."

"Well, I still think he is. I called him this morning, and he was acting all funny, like he was hiding something. And when I asked him if he was going to stay home today, he hemmed and hawed like he didn't know what to say."

"Have you considered hiring a private detective?"

"I thought about that, but I don't have my own bank account, and he'd see the payment."

"You don't have your own bank account? Darlene, haven't you learned anything from my books?"

"I know. I know. But he never questions what I spend, so I didn't think it was important to have my own account. I gotta go. Let me know if you see anything suspicious, will you?"

"Okay."

I went back to my desk where I could see part of the Richardsons' driveway if I leaned way into the window. It irked me that Darlene asked me for a favor—she hadn't been treating me much like a friend. Still, if she thought Lance was cheating on her, I supposed it was the least I could do to help her.

Having written so many cozy mysteries, I knew from my characters how to position a mirror in front of me so that I could easily see out the window from different angles without leaning way in. I grabbed a hand mirror from the bathroom, propped it up against the side of the printer so that I could see the Richardson's driveway, and went back to work.

After signing up for a webinar on using social media to promote books, I dug into my defective manuscript. By noon, I had made two failed attempts to fix it and stopped for lunch.

Thoughts of Carl and our marriage flooded my mind while I nibbled away at a chicken leg. Carl's motive for wanting to restore our marriage could have been nothing more than a convenient crutch to help him get him through a tough time in his life. In other words, he was using me. If he was using me, I didn't want to be with him. The phone interrupted my thoughts.

"Have you seen anything more?" Darlene whispered.

"No, and I propped up a mirror on my desk so I can keep an eye on your driveway."

"Hey, good thinking. He hasn't come home yet?"

"I haven't seen him."

"Can I talk to you later…in private?" she asked.

"Sure. Where? When?"

"Carl said something about bringing home pizza for dinner tonight for all of us and watching a Bulls game. How about if I invite you over to our house to show you something while they're engrossed in the game?"

"See you then."

She sounded beaten, defeated. I knew that feeling all too well.

I spent the remainder of the day planning two more book promotions. The disruption to my writing and book marketing caused by the bookstore project had taken its toll on my royalties. And that was not all it had taken a toll on. When you're in the throes of writing a book, you tend to get close to your characters—they're constantly on your mind, you talk to yourself about them. I missed my characters.

Chapter 30

"What's going on?" I asked Darlene when we got to her house. "You didn't say a word during dinner."

Appearing about to cry, she said, "I saw a text on his phone. I know Lance is seeing someone."

"Are you sure? Maybe it just appeared that way."

"The text said, 'luv ya baby.'"

"Oh, dear."

"Not too many ways to interpret that. And he's been acting strange lately. Leaving the house when I'm at the bookstore and being vague about where he's been. I was going to ask you if I could work fewer hours next week."

"Sure," I said, even though I knew that would hamper operations at the store. "What are you going to do?"

"I'm going to see where he goes."

"You're going to tail him?"

"Yep."

"He won't see you?"

"I was going to wear a disguise and borrow your car."

I stared at her without saying anything.

"You had one of your characters do that, and it worked," she said.

"Darlene, I write fiction, remember?"

"Well, how else can I catch him?"

"Hire a PI."

"I would, but like I said, he'll know."

243

"Not if I lend you the money."

"Really?"

"Sure. I have a little emergency stash put away. No one would ever know. You could pay me back…whenever."

"That would be great."

"Keep in mind, though, before you decide to do this, if you're wrong, you run the risk of jeopardizing your marriage."

"How's that?"

"What if he finds out you were checking on him and he wasn't doing anything wrong?"

"How would he find out?"

"There's always a risk. Even the best PIs make mistakes. And then you have to live with the fact that you didn't trust him when there was no reason to not trust him."

"But I want to know the truth."

"And then let's say he is guilty. He isn't going to like being caught, so it could get messy."

"I have to do *something*."

"Have you considered confronting him?"

"No."

"Why not?"

"He could lie."

"You don't trust him."

"Not really."

"If you're bent on hiring a PI, I'll lend you the money. How much do you need?"

"Joan told me she paid a five-thousand-dollar retainer for her guy and then another three thousand to finish it."

"That much?"

"Apparently, the good ones don't come cheap. Would that be a problem?"

"No. I have that much. Just make sure this is what you want to do."

"I'll think about it for a few more days and let you know. I can't wait much longer than that. The not knowing is killing me."

I arrived home with the basketball game in its final quarter. Katherine and Candie had already called it a night. I joined Lance and Carl to watch the end of it. When the Bulls lost to the Timberwolves 102 to 93, Lance got up to leave.

"Good luck, man," Carl said to him.

"Thanks, buddy."

"What was that all about?" I asked him once Lance had left.

"You can't say anything."

"I won't."

"Promise?"

"Promise. What's going on?"

"He's asking Dar for a divorce tonight."

* * *

"I thought maybe they'd work things out," I said to Carl a few days later when the Richardsons' impending divorce was out in the open.

"Lance wants out. I know that. His marriage and our business."

"Meaning what?"

"He wants his money back."

"He actually asked you for it back? All things considered, it wasn't all that much."

"He thinks Dar will take him for all she can get. We need to pay him back."

"Not without liquidating something."

"Whatever," he said.

"What about Darlene?"

"Can you talk to her? If they're both wanting out, it would be better to handle them at the same time."

"Maybe you should talk to her since you made the deal."

"I asked *you* to."

"Fine. I'll talk to her."

The following day, I approached Darlene before the bookstore opened.

"The subject of the investor agreement has come up," I told her.

"I know. Lance wants out," she said. "His girlfriend lives in Florida."

"Florida? Are you sure? How'd they meet?"

"High school sweethearts. They reunited on Facebook."

"Wow. Does he plan to move there?"

"Yep."

"What about you? What do you plan to do?"

"I don't know. I can do anything I want, I guess—I'll get at least half of everything."

"Will you stay here?"

"The house is mine. He gets the boat." She let out a long sigh. "I don't know what I'll do."

"What about the bookstore? Do you want to stay in or get out or don't know yet?"

"Here's the thing. I don't want to share too much with you because if Carl asks you questions, that puts you in a bad spot. I don't mean to be rude or evasive or anything, but… Do you understand that?"

"Yeah, sure." *Not really.* "No matter what, we'll handle the bookstore agreement in a very businesslike manner, I promise. Lance wants his money back, and the agreement has an out clause, so it should be clear-cut."

Shortly after we finished our conversation, Carl dropped off Candie, Katherine, and Fluffy at the bookstore. Darlene took the register, and I went to one of the computer terminals to contact our attorney and work on inventory until my mother arrived.

Seeing my mother walk in the door so nonchalantly, like she had been in my life all this time, struck me. I wondered if other daughters—ones who came from normal homes—realized just what they had. I hoped so.

* * *

Two weeks after Lance asked Darlene for a divorce, we invited him to our house to go over the repayment of his investment. When we were almost finished discussing it, Darlene came over and announced through tears that Melodi had had her baby, a girl. In her next breath, she said that she wanted out of the bookstore too, the sooner the better.

"Darlene, what's wrong?" I said as I followed her through our home to the back door.

"Nothing. Please just let me go."

She bolted out the door before I could say anything more.

I returned to the sunroom where Carl and Lance were staring at each other.

"What's her problem?" Lance asked. "She should be happy."

"I don't know. She wouldn't talk to me. I wonder if something is wrong with the baby."

Lance immediately perked up and pulled out his cell phone. "Eddie?" he said. "Congratulations buddy! How's Melodi and the baby?"

After he hung up, he said, "They're fine. Dar is friggin' wacko these days, so who knows—"

"Shut up, Lance," Carl said, and he got up and left the room.

After I congratulated Lance on his new grandchild, he too got up and left.

I waited until I heard the door close and then hunted for Carl. When I didn't find him in the house, I glanced out the front door to see Lance driving away. I called Carl's cell phone, and when it went to voice mail, I suspected maybe he had gone next door to console Darlene. I called her cell phone, but it went to voice mail as well. I toyed with the idea of going over there to surprise them in the middle of whatever they were doing together but decided against it—nothing good would come of it.

Carl came home an hour later and apologized for both himself and Darlene not taking my calls.

"She was pretty upset," he said.

"What exactly was she upset about?" I asked.

"Everything, I guess."

"The baby was good news."

"Yes, it was."

"The divorce is bothering her?"

He shrugged.

"Thanksgiving coming up. Holidays can be hard. Maybe it's a combination of things."

"Maybe."

"Why does she want her money back right now?" I asked. "Did she say?"

"Uh…not exactly. I'm not really sure."

"She didn't give you *any* indication?"

"I don't know, Mags. She didn't say."

You already said that. I asked if there was any indication. There's a difference.

Frustrated that he avoided answering my questions but not wanting to jeopardize our fragile relationship, I dropped the subject.

"I guess it's back to just you and me, then," I said. "I'll have our attorney—"

"Why don't you hold off for a while," he said.

"Why?"

"Because…she could change her mind. She was emotional at the time."

"You don't think she thought it through before she walked in our door? I do."

"I don't know, Mags. All I'm saying is that she may need time to think it through."

"Did she say she needed time?"

"No!" he snapped.

He took a moment to compose himself.

"I'm sorry. I shouldn't have yelled like that. I'm just saying… Let's give her a little time."

"Whatever."

Carl went upstairs, presumably to bed. I contemplated the evening's chain of events. Carl had seemingly been drawing me in with his attentiveness and kindness over the last few weeks, yet somehow it felt like in reality he was pushing me further away. Tonight especially.

I finally went to bed at midnight, but couldn't fall asleep listening to Carl's peaceful, even breathing—his annoyingly peaceful, even breathing.

Chapter 31

The alarm went off at seven a.m., waking me from a sound sleep. I checked Carl's side of the bed—empty. The plan had been for him to pick up Portia at nine at the Amtrak station in Milwaukee, and she would spend Thanksgiving Day with us. I combed the house searching for him. He was nowhere to be found, and his car was gone too. As it was too early for him to have left for Milwaukee, I figured maybe he'd gone out for breakfast first. He could have left a note. I called his cell phone, which went to voice mail. I left a message for him to call me back about the plans for the day.

Eight o'clock and no call from Carl—even though he had a hands-free phone in his car. Why wouldn't he answer his phone?

I went back to the bedroom to get some work done when movement in the hand mirror still leaning up against my printer caught my attention— Darlene's car advancing into her driveway. I gave her a few minutes and called her. While the phone was ringing, I heard our front door close, indicating that Carl and Portia were home.

Darlene's phone went to voice mail. I didn't leave a message.

I found Katherine, Portia, and Carl in the sunroom. After welcoming Portia home with a hug, I asked Carl what the plans were for the day—they had changed at least three times depending on whether Lance and Dar were talking to each other.

"That's what we were just talking about," he said. "Dar isn't feeling up to going out, so I—"

"You spoke with her today?" I asked, not realizing how dry my throat had become.

"So, I thought we'd keep the reservation at the club and bring her back something."

I kept quiet. I hadn't remembered a discussion about going to the club for Thanksgiving dinner—I had assumed we'd go to a nice restaurant.

"What about Lance?"

"He won't be joining us."

I had invited my mother to join us. She arrived at noon. Instead of leading her into the sunroom with the others, I brought her upstairs to show her our new bedroom suite.

"It's lovely," she said after taking the tour. "You have exquisite taste."

"Thanks. I enjoy decorating. Maybe I was an interior decorator in a former life."

"I like the way you've displayed your books. I've read them all, by the way."

"You have? Which one is your favorite?"

She didn't respond right away. "*Break-In at Buttons and Bows.* Not your best work, but your first. I liked it because it was your first."

"That's sweet. Thank you."

We talked about a few of my other books—the characters, the settings, the plots. She'd obviously read them all. More than I could say for Carl.

"Our reservation is for one o'clock," I said. "I suppose we should go down and join the others."

I'd read somewhere that after the initial "honeymoon" period that typically follows a reconnection with someone with whom you've been estranged, you should try to focus on sharing new experiences with each other rather than dwell on the past. I tried to keep that in mind as we piled into Carl's SUV, with him and Portia in the front and me and the two moms in the back.

The yacht club put on a nice buffet for holidays—turkey, ham, and beef at the carving station and elaborate side dishes, more than anyone could fit on their plate. During dinner, our collective stilted conversation, when there was any, made things awkward. I wanted to ask all of them, except my mother, what the hell was wrong with them, but I didn't. After devouring more food than we normally ate, we went back for dessert while one of the wait staff fixed a plate for Darlene.

When we reached home, I offered to take the plate to Darlene, but Carl said he didn't mind doing it. The rest of us made ourselves comfortable in front of the television.

Portia and Katherine got into a conversation about Donald Trump's run for the White House, while my mother and I talked about the recent suicide bombings in Paris. Carl didn't join us until almost an hour later, and when he did his demeanor hovered somewhere between indifferent and withdrawn. I tried not to wonder too much about what he and Darlene could have possibly talked about for so long, especially since she wasn't feeling well.

By seven o'clock, most of us were hungry again, so I put food out for sandwiches. My mother said she had to get going. I threw on a coat and walked her to her car.

"Thank you for including me today," she said. "I thoroughly enjoyed myself, even when Katherine asked you who the old lady was."

"I was horrified when she said that."

"I wasn't. I've been around people who were, um, let's say not always in their right mind. I thought it was funny."

"I'm glad you came, Mom." That was the first time I'd called her that since she had come back into my life.

She teared up, stepped closer to me, and held out her hands. When I took them into my hands, she said, "That made my day." We hugged, longer than necessary, and after blowing me a kiss, she got in her car and drove away. I stood motionless while I watched her disappear down the street, regretting all the tender moments I'd missed over the years, but looking forward to creating new ones in the future. But I didn't kid myself—I knew that this relationship needed serious nurturing and would take commitment, attention, and hard work to make it grow and eventually mature. And time. It would take time. Precious time. Milo and Tock kind of time.

When I returned inside, Katherine and Carl were gone. Portia sat at the kitchen table.

"Where is everybody?" I asked.

Grandma is in her room, I guess. Dad will be down in a minute. They're both going to drive me to the train station. Wanna come along?"

"No, I'll stay here. I'll go see what's keeping him." While my relationship with Portia hadn't quite reached the feel-good-inside level, it had improved greatly since she'd come home—when I'd see her, I'd smile rather than wince in anticipation of what might transpire between us. For that, I was grateful.

Halfway up the stairs, I heard Carl's whispery voice. "I'll see you tomorrow. Bye."

I quietly backed down the stairs without his knowledge and told Portia he'd be down in a minute.

After they left, I poured myself a glass of merlot and walked outside. A sliver of moonlight—barely enough to spray a shadow on the water—cast a luminous glow in the velvety blackness of the sky. I willed myself not to think about Carl. Instead, I recalled my mother's last words, the way her eyes radiated an inner glow as she said them, the genuineness with which she had said them.

But for her leaving me and my father and then getting mixed up with drugs and alcohol, I thought she was a good person. I allowed my mind to wander between the past and present, trying not to dwell on the past.

"We're closed tomorrow, right?" Carl asked when he returned.

"It's Black Friday."

"You think we'll get much business?"

"I would think we would."

"What if we stay closed and reopen on the weekend. Take a break."

"Fine," I said to avoid an argument.

"And then would you mind taking one of the weekend days for me?" he asked.

"Why?"

"I have an important presentation on Monday, and it would help if I had one more day to prepare."

"Is that what you're doing tomorrow too?"

"Probably."

"Okay." He was up to something. "I think I'll ask Darlene if she wants to do a little Black Friday shopping in Chicago tomorrow."

I purposely watched his face for a sign—any sign—but saw none.

"Sounds like a good idea. She may appreciate the company."

"I'll be upstairs," I said.

Even though driving to Chicago to shop in all that madness was the last thing I wanted to do the next day, I called Darlene to follow through on what I had said to Carl and to get her reaction to my offer.

"No, but thanks for asking," she said.

"Other plans?" I asked.

"No. Just not in the mood, I guess."

"Want to talk?"

"I'm not feeling very well right now, but thanks for asking."

"Okay. If you change your mind, or need anything, holler."

"I will."

* * *

The day after Thanksgiving, feeling the need for change, I plotted a new book—a historical novel—something I hadn't attempted before. Carl checked in with me throughout the day, moving around the house like a caged animal, sometimes working in the sunroom, sometimes at the kitchen table, and other times with his laptop in the living room. At noon, he offered to go to our favorite deli and pick up sandwiches for lunch.

Six hours after I'd begun, I resolved that historical novels were not my thing and I was better off sticking to cozy mysteries. Forgetting about the sandwiches that Carl had gone to retrieve and feeling stupid for wasting a perfectly good day, I opened the *Stand-Alone Groom* file to determine what I could salvage when Carl came in with a somber expression on his face.

"What's wrong?" I asked.

He hesitated before saying anything—an unnatural stillness in his stance—appearing to think carefully about his words before speaking.

He cleared his throat a couple of times before saying anything. "I'm leaving," he said without making eye contact with me, his voice especially low and resonant.

My chest tightened inside, and I found it difficult to breath. I knew he meant he was leaving me.

I searched for the right words—nouns, verbs, expletives, anything—but they had become elusive. "When?" I finally asked.

"Now." A clumsy twist of his mouth told me he was having a hard time speaking.

"Okay."

He turned his back on me. "I have a bag packed in the car. I'll let you know when I'll be back for the rest of my things."

"And your mother?"

"She's at Dar's. I'll pick up her things later as well."

"So, this is it," I said to an empty room.

My body went cold as the tears welled up in my eyes. Once the first tear broke free, the rest followed in an unremitting stream. I bent forward and pressed the palms of my hands tightly against my face trying to hold them in, but to no avail.

When my crying had subsided enough to think clearly, I mentally chewed him out for leaving the way he did. Such a coward. Or maybe I was the coward for letting him go without forcing him to talk things through. Then what little composure I'd been maintaining collapsed.

"Bastard!" I shouted, slamming the side of my fist on the desk and then rubbing it to ease the pain.

So did Portia know?

It certainly appeared as though Darlene did.

And what about Katherine? What had he told her?

Did he tell Candie? Will she show up tomorrow morning?

Am I now the sole owner of the bookstore?

Who gets what?

And what was Katherine doing at Darlene's?

I watched Carl's car back out of the Richardsons' driveway, not knowing whom I hated more—Carl or Darlene. Realizing that hatred would only worsen the heaviness in my chest and numbness in the rest of my body, I decided I wasn't about to give them that satisfaction. I wanted to go downstairs and pour myself a stiff drink but was afraid my legs wouldn't support me. I glanced back at the hand mirror on my desk, reflecting the image of Darlene's empty driveway under the glow of the streetlight. I cleared my mind of that image as I snatched the mirror off my desk and flung it against the wall, regretting doing it even before it hit and smashed onto the floor.

Chapter 32

I awoke to Carl calling my name. At first, I thought it was a continuance of the dream I'd been having. Then I opened my eyes and observed him actually standing before me—this was no dream.

"What are you doing here?" I asked him.

"Can we talk?"

I shifted my position in the chair, rubbed my eyes, and asked him the time.

He pointed to his watch. "Two-thirty."

"In the morning?" I asked, feeling stupid, given the lack of light coming through the shadeless window.

"Yes. In the morning."

"If you've changed your mind again, you can forget it. I'm done with—" I wanted to see his face before I finished my thought, so I flicked on the bedside lamp.

"Mother wants to stay here."

He spat out the words so fast, I didn't think I'd heard him correctly.

"What? Have you been to Chicago…or wherever it was you were going?"

"Yes. And back. When she got there, she wouldn't get out of the car. We had to pull her out." A few beads of sweat had formed on his brow, though it wasn't the least bit warm in the room.

"We?"

"Then when we finally got her inside, she refused to go into her room. She said, 'Take me home.'"

"We?"

"This puts me in a very difficult position," he said without making eye contact.

Under different circumstances, I might have been amused. "Yes, it does. Where is she now?"

"Next door."

"What the hell is going on between you two?"

He looked away, making me even madder.

"I can't very well ask you to take her in," he said. "And I already let Candie go."

"So…what are you going to do?" I asked, enjoying the brief moment of having the upper hand.

"It looks like I'm going to have to move back in here. I'll put you up in a hotel until—"

"Negative!"

"Mags, give me a break. What am I supposed to do?"

"How about being a little less self-serving for starters?"

I received no response—just a blank stare.

"Does she want to stay here with you, or does she just want to stay here?"

"She said she didn't mind staying with *that woman,* which I interpreted to mean you."

"That woman," I repeated.

"Half the time I'm not sure she really knows who I am."

"I've got news for you—she knows a lot more than she lets on."

He shrugged.

"Well, I'm telling you this. I am not being put out of my own home and into some hotel room. You got yourself into this mess, and you can get yourself out of it. And I don't care if your mother moves back in here. But *you're* not. Have you got that straight?"

"Yes, ma'am."

"Why don't you take your pitiful—"

"Go ahead and say it. I probably deserve it."

I picked up my watered-down glass of Scotch and went to the fridge under the bar where I plopped in a few ice cubes.

"I'll bring her over," he said from the hallway.

"Asshole," I mumbled under my breath.

Ten minutes later, Katherine, with Fluffy in her arms, walked through the front door, past me, and into her old room. After the door shut, I turned around, thinking I'd see Carl standing there, but I didn't. I peeked out the front window and watched him walk next door to Darlene's house. I watched for ten minutes, and when I didn't see his car leave her driveway, I went upstairs to bed, reminded of a scene from *The Missing Music Teacher* in which the antagonist was playing footsie with the next-door neighbor's wife—one more book of mine that I suspected he'd read.

* * *

The next morning, I called my mother to ask her if she could come into the bookstore to help. Normally, she didn't come in on the weekends, but I couldn't handle things alone, especially on a Saturday, and especially if I had to watch Katherine all day. She said she would.

At nine o'clock, Katherine came out of her room dressed in an outfit she would normally wear to the bookstore—one worry off my mind.

"Did you sleep okay, Katherine?" I asked her.

"Why wouldn't I?"

"Oh, I don't know. I thought maybe yesterday was a bit rough for you."

"No. Everything's fine."

I fixed a light breakfast, and we left for the store at nine-thirty. On the way, I tried to make small talk, but Katherine had other things on her mind.

"They're sleeping together, you know."

I didn't have to ask about whom she spoke.

"Mm-hm."

"You don't care?"

"Not anymore."

"He's my son, but I can't condone what he's done to you. Still doing. There was no way I was going to live under the same roof with those two."

"She was going to move in with him?"

"Looked like it to me."

"Well, ya know what? I hope they're very happy together."

"I don't."

I held my laughter in, though I so wanted to let it belt out.

"Who's coming in today?" she asked.

"My mom."

"The two of you can't handle everything on a Saturday."

"She's all I've got, at the moment. In the last twenty-four hours, I've lost three workers."

"You've still got me."

"And I'm grateful for that, believe me."

"No, you're not. I'm a burden. Admit it."

"I'll admit no such thing, Katherine."

"Well, I am. What can I do to be helpful? I want to carry my weight. And besides, you need me. It's a good thing I made him bring me back here."

"I agree," I said as I pulled into a parking space behind the store.

"Do you think I could learn to use that fancy-schmancy cash register of yours?"

"We can try."

I let us in the back door and immediately observed Candie standing outside the front window.

"C'mon in, Candie," I said after unlocking the door. "I didn't expect to see you here."

She unbuttoned her coat and removed her scarf. "I don't know what's going on in your family, Mrs. Manning, and I don't need to know, but one thing I do know is that you can't manage this store alone, so I came in to help you for as long as you need me." She glanced at Katherine, who had finished feeding the cat and was putting out a water dish for Fluffy. "I thought she was moving to Chicago," she whispered. "That's what Carl told me."

"That didn't work out. She's back with me," I told her.

"For good?"

I laughed. "I don't know because I too don't know what's going on in my family." I put my arm around her shoulder. "Let's get the coffee bar going. And then I'm going to attempt to teach Katherine how to use the cash register."

She gave me a skeptical look. "I'm available to come back to your house to stay with her, if you need me."

I sighed. "Thank you. You don't know how grateful I am to hear you say that."

As I showed Katherine the basics of ringing up a purchase, my mother walked in the front door.

"Good. The old lady is here," Katherine whispered. "But don't tell her

I called her that. I may be older than she is," she said through a titter. "But I doubt it."

I was walking Katherine through her first sale when Carl called.

"I tried to reach Candie to see if she was available to—"

"Don't bother," I told him. "If I need your help, I'll let you know." I hung up without saying good-bye. He called right back.

"I was going to say that I'll see if she's available to come back to stay at the house temporarily or—"

"And I said, if I need your help—"

He hung up on me.

I knew I'd been rude, but I didn't care. Sleeping with our next-door neighbor was way ruder.

Katherine shot me a big smile when she completed the sale without much help from me. I checked her work. She'd completed the transaction perfectly.

"If you keep that up, I'll have to put you on the payroll," I told her.

"I don't come cheap, you know," she responded, absent a smile.

* * *

In the weeks that followed, Carl and I worked out who got what in the divorce. In addition to the lake home, I got his mother and the first-edition *A Picture of Dorian Gray* that his father had left behind. I had the attorney draw up a partnership agreement with Mom and me as equal partners. Portia, who had several innovative ideas for improving the business, would be added to the partnership as soon as she graduated from Ohio State with her double-major degree in business administration and computer and information science.

Carl got the Chicago brownstone—once a testament to my ability to decorate early-twenty-first century architecture, now degraded to just an asset that had to be appraised and relinquished—and Darlene. Candie moved back into her old room next to Katherine's, Mom moved into our old master bedroom on the first floor, and I enjoyed the expansive master-suite sanctuary on the second floor.

When Eddie, Melodi, and their new baby moved next door into the house Lance and Darlene had vacated, I cringed, thinking I would inevitably run into Carl and Darlene as a couple. Then I cringed again at the realization my daughter had slept with someone who might end up being her stepbrother. And while I wasn't about to be the cause of any disharmony between Carl and his mother, I did lay down the law that he was not to visit her in my home. She would have to go next door if she wanted to see him, which turned out to be not every time she had the opportunity, making me gloat just a little.

In the weeks that followed, I made several trips to my doctor's office until we were able to establish a medicine regimen that didn't have so many side effects. Afterward, I paid a visit to my optometrist to let her know that I had a disease that caused hallucinations that just happened to coincide with my getting new glasses. I thought she believed me. I hoped she did.

I still had some mild hallucinations but now recognized what they were and could even laugh at them. Like the time I was in the bookstore one evening and thought the shadow on the wall that I was making with my own body was a customer stalking me. Most of the time, when I had trouble distinguishing fact from fiction, I wasn't afraid to ask someone who was aware of my condition for their opinion. Like my mother. Most of the time, I didn't even have to ask her though—Mom now knew more about anti-NMDA receptor encephalitis than I did.

My mom—the power of that connection couldn't be easily articulated. She may have done little to nurture and protect me as a child, but she was wholeheartedly trying to make up for it. In subtle ways. In helpful ways. In loving ways. Like when a child scrapes her knee and a mother feels some of the hurt as she cleans the wound and places a Band-Aid on it. That kind of nurturing and protecting.

I wasn't sure if I'd ever be off the meds, but I didn't care about that. What mattered to me was being able to function like a normal human being, in control of my life as much as anyone can be in control of their life. I'd never realized how important feeling normal was until I didn't. Not that I claimed to know the definition of *normal*. I wasn't sure anyone did. But when your feelings, emotions, and behaviors disrupted what you wanted to get out of life, that was outside the realm of normalcy, and that was the state I used to be in.

Between the four of us, we managed to create a work schedule that suited everyone on most days. Candie got the short end of the stick because, while I gave her one day a week off and time off in between if she needed it, she still worked as Katherine's full-time caregiver in addition to bookstore duties. I increased her hourly pay without discussing it with Carl, who still wrote the checks to her. After all, he hadn't run it by me before he'd slept with Darlene.

So much had transpired during that six-month period—most of it unexpected and stressful but with positive outcomes. Kind of like the story line for my next book—a novice author takes on cyber-bullying, a cheating husband, and breast cancer while pursuing her writing ambition. The outline I'd created included a thread about the importance of time—how valuable a gift it was in every aspect of life—something I vowed to never forget.

* * *

Christmas Eve—one of the best I'd ever experienced. We agreed to close the shop at three in the afternoon. After Katherine rung up the last sale of the day, the four of us sat around one of the tables drinking lattes at the coffee bar.

I held my cup high in the air. "To my three best friends," I said.

Katherine, Candie, and Mom raised their mugs in the air.

"We love you, Margaret," my mother said.

"Are we toasting something?" Katherine asked.

"Yes, we are," I said.

"Good. What are we toasting?" she asked.

The three of us smiled.

"I wouldn't be where I am today without you guys," I said through choked-back tears.

"Especially me," said Katherine.

"What do you mean *you*?" Mom asked. "What about me? I gave birth to her."

Katherine cocked her head and said, "You're her mother?"

"Yes, of course, I am, dear."

Katherine stared at her for a long moment. "I knew that," she finally said.

I meant what I had said. Thanks to them, and recognizing all the ramifications of my disease, I didn't need imaginary friends anymore. Lily was a fantasy I had contrived when I needed the perfect someone to talk to, confide in. Fish-hat guy had been the fictional reincarnation of the first and maybe only real love of my life.

I didn't have Carl anymore, and I still had mixed emotions about that. I now knew he had nothing to do with any of the missing items, or the mugging, or anything else I had conjured up in my sick mind. Except for his extramarital affairs, he'd always been truthful with me. And when it came right down to it, what married person would alert their spouse to an upcoming affair?

But I did have Portia, Katherine, Candie, and Mom in my life, and they were the real deal. And while I couldn't recall when it happened or why, they called me Margaret.

I hope you enjoyed reading *They Called Me Margaret* and will consider posting a short review on Amazon and/or Goodreads. Reviews and word-of-mouth referrals play an important role in helping authors promote their books, and your help in this regard is much appreciated.

Do you belong to a book club? If you choose this or any other of my books, I'm happy to participate in your book club discussion. If you're local to northern Illinois or southern Wisconsin, I may be able to participate in person. If you are in some other part of the world, I can tune in by Skype or phone. Just shoot me an e-mail if you're interested—info@florenceosmund.com.

Florence Osmund

Other Books by Florence Osmund

Living with Markus

Forced to choose between cultivating a satisfying life for himself and rescuing his dysfunctional family members from their certain demise causes Marc to question the importance of family. Does he save his relatives from their ill-fated lives, or save himself from entering a life of self-sacrifice and missed opportunities? Painful soul-searching and late-night talks with the captivating tenant downstairs guide him to an unexpected decision and discovery of his true purpose in life.

> *The characters, even the young boys, are complicated and believable, and the plot's complexity allows the reader to see the characters from a myriad of angles.*
> —Windy City Reviews

Regarding Anna

After recovering from the shock of her parents' death, Grace Lindroth discovers clues in their attic that cause her to believe the people she called Mom and Dad her whole life may not have been her real parents. In her search for the truth, Grace encounters people whose actions cause her to be distrustful of everyone and believe that things that happen to you in the past can mold you into someone you're not.

> *For a fun, fascinating, and somewhat unpredictable mystery, look no further than Regarding Anna by Florence Osmund. Written in a friendly and straightforward style, readers will enjoy sleuthing alongside Grace as she seeks the truth about Anna. Don't be surprised if you have a hard time putting this novel down.*
> —San Francisco Book Review

Red Clover
The troubled son of a callous father and socialite mother determines his own meaning of success after learning shocking family secrets that cause him to rethink who he is and where he's going. Lee Winekoop's reinvention of himself is surprising; the roadblocks he confronts are unnerving; and the cast of characters he befriends along the way is both heartwarming and amusing.

Red Clover is a wonderfully written detailed story about a man overcoming his upbringing and becoming his own. The finished product, both the man and his story, are exemplary.
—Ray Paul, Windy City Reviews

The Coach House
1945 Chicago. Marie Marchetti flees from her devoted husband when she realizes he is immersed in local corruption, only to discover it's the identity of her real father that unexpectedly changes her life more than her husband ever could.

This book is not only thought evoking but also a genuine pleasure to read.
—BestChickLit

Daughters (sequel to The Coach House)
Discovering who her father is leads Marie Marchetti to discover who she really is and where she belongs, driving her to seek peace and truth in her life. But unexpectedly, the most life-altering consequence of her reunion grows out of an encounter with a twelve-year-old girl named Rachael.

Civil rights, gender roles, and political postures are carefully, realistically, and sensitively present in this story.
—Pens and Needles

Osmund's books are available on Amazon http://www.amazon.com/author/florenceosmund
Or the author's website http://florenceosmund.com/buy_the_authors_books
Or at book stores who order from distributors Ingram or Baker & Taylor

About the Author

After a long career working for large corporations, Florence Osmund retired to write novels. "I strive to create stories that contain thought-provoking plots and characters with depth and complexity, particularly ones that challenge readers to survey their own values," Osmund states.

Florence continues to write literary fiction from her home on Lake Miltmore in a far north suburb of Chicago, where she lives with her 20-year-old feline friend Miska.

If you are a new or aspiring novelist, visit Florence's website where she offers substantial advice on how to begin the project, writing techniques, building an author platform, book promotion, and much more.

E-mail	info@florenceosmund.com
Website	http://www.florenceosmund.com
Facebook	http://www.facebook.com/florenceosmundbooks
LinkedIn	http://www.linkedin.com/in/florenceosmund
Twitter	@FlorenceOsmund
Goodreads	http://www.goodreads.com/user/show/8800692-florence-osmund
Amazon	http://www.amazon.com/author/florenceosmund